Also by Heather Van Fleet

Reckless Hearts

THE RIGHT KIND OF
RECKLESS

HEATHER VAN FLEET

sourcebooks
casablanca

Published by Sourcebooks Casablanca, an imprint of Sourcebooks, Inc.
P.O. Box 4410, Naperville, Illinois 60567-4410
(630) 961-3900
Fax: (630) 961-2168
sourcebooks.com

Printed and bound in Canada.
MBP 10 9 8 7 6 5 4 3 2 1

*To my mom: the only person out there
who really and truly feels the love
of book boyfriends like I do.*

CHAPTER 1

Lia

PEOPLE SAY CERTAIN EXPERIENCES IN LIFE DEFINE YOU AS a human being, and I have to agree. Because the second my fist collided with my soon-to-be ex's face, I realized something very important about my life: it absolutely sucked.

"Damn, woman. I can't believe you did that." Travis fell to his knees on the sidewalk, his hand over his bloody nose.

"And I'd do it all over again if I had to." Sweat trickled down the side of my neck as I shook out my hand.

Knees shaking from adrenaline, I darted toward the front door of Jimney's—the bar where I worked every Thursday, Friday, and Saturday night—but was stopped short by the outstretched arm of my boss, Patricia.

"Turn right around and get on home, Lia." Her lips twitched as she stared down at my hand, then back at Travis.

"But I've still got two hours left."

"Yeah, I get it, baby girl. But I also don't want the cops all up in my place of business."

"Why would the cops come?" It's not like I'd strung Travis's balls up behind his ears and hung him upside down by his penis from the telephone pole.

Although the thought *had* crossed my mind.

Finding your boyfriend screwing the brains out of your coworker next to a Dumpster outside your place of employment did tend to make a woman feel murderous…

Patricia clicked her tongue against the roof of her mouth and nodded her head at something behind me. "I didn't call, but I'm pretty sure one of *them* did."

I turned back around, finding two girls lingering by the Dumpster. Sure enough, one was on her cell, while the other stood with her arm around Aubrey—*said* coworker—trying to console her as she sobbed. I rolled my eyes as an unmarked cop car pulled into the lot, red lights silently flashing.

"You have got to be kidding me."

Patricia pressed her hand between my shoulder blades. "As much as I feel for you, I'm not going to be sticking around."

A car door slammed. Boots crunched against the pavement, announcing the arrival of two cops. I jerked my head their way just in time for the shorter of the pair—the pudgy one with the 'stache—to ask, "What's the problem here?"

"She fucking broke my nose," Travis whined.

I folded my arms. "He deserved it."

With a sigh, I turned toward Cop Two, whose dark eyes were on me. He lifted his eyebrows, sweeping his flashlight over Travis, Aubrey, and her friends, then back my way. This officer was tall, with broad shoulders, a visible neck tat, and a face full of stubble. He was hot—in a badass biker way.

Nodding once, Cop Two switched off his light and lowered it to his side. "Did he hurt you, miss?"

I blinked, taken back by his concern. "Well, I—"

"Cuff her, Mitch," Cop One grumbled as he wrote something in a little black notebook. "Man's pressing charges, and there're witnesses."

I stiffened. *Oh God*.

"Was he *hurting* you?" Cop Two repeated.

"Not physically, no." I folded my arms.

He scratched at his stubbled jaw, then nodded. "Not much I can do for you, then, I'm afraid."

"Wasn't asking you to, was I?" Like a four-year-old, I dug my toe into a crack, willing a hole to open below me. *Embarrassed* didn't even begin to describe the way I felt.

With an apology on his face, Cop Two motioned for me to turn around. "We're going to have to take you in. I'm sorry."

Doing what he asked—because I didn't want to be charged with resisting arrest—I nodded as the cold metal of handcuffs snaked around my wrists.

"You have the right to remain silent…" he began.

Chin high, I swallowed, pushing down the aching throb in my throat. I refused to cry over something that I'd never regret doing. "I want to talk to my law…yer." *Crap*. I didn't have a *lawyer*. I couldn't very well *afford* one either—not when every bit of my savings had been spent that morning on my final tuition payment.

"Anything you say can and will be used against you

in a court of law," he continued, his voice low, his grip strong around my forearm.

I jerked my eyes to the left, just as Aubrey and crew slipped into her car. The motor of her little Mercedes putted along as she passed. Not once did she look over at me as she pulled out of the parking lot, but I saw her smile, those tears she'd been shedding long gone and likely just done for show.

"You'll get to make a phone call once we arrive at the station." Cop Two nudged me toward his car.

I blew out a slow breath, concentrating on the clipping of my boots against the pavement as I moved. Seriously, who could I even call? My brother wasn't an option. Not only would he kill me, but he'd also call my parents and tell *them*. They'd have to hop on a plane and fly back from Arizona, which meant they'd be unable to finish their winter vacation. That's the last thing I wanted, especially since I'd caused enough heartache in their lives as it was.

What I needed was a miracle.

And, yeah, a lottery win would have been nice too.

I sank into the backseat of the squad car, reality smacking me in the face. There was only one person I could call who wouldn't make me feel like the trash I was.

I just hoped he'd pick up the phone.

CHAPTER

Max

SOMETHING KEPT BUZZING IN MY EAR. MY PHONE MAYBE? I rolled over in bed, my arm grazing a naked pair of tits in the process. The girl didn't stir, thank God. I'd messed up by staying the night as it was.

I wrapped my hand around my cell, squinting an eye open to look at the number. It was local but unrecognizable.

"What?"

"Max?"

At the sound of her voice, I shot up in bed. "Lee-Lee. You good?"

"No. I'm not good. I need a loan." She took a breath. "Bail money."

I pinched the bridge of my nose and sighed. "What happened?"

"Nothing you need to worry about."

Instead of questioning her like I should've, I stood, grabbed my jeans off the floor, and yanked them over my hips. "I'll be there in ten. Hold tight."

I ended the call, but my hand stayed clasped around the phone. I wanted to throw it across the room or stomp on it. If I did that though, I'd wake the sleeping woman behind me.

It was better this way, me sneaking out. This is what I did—how I worked things. I never went in for seconds when it came to the ladies I hooked up with. A woman had only one rule to remember with me, and I always made it known up-front: *don't give what you know you won't get in return.*

Didn't mean it was right.

In the car, I turned on early morning talk radio, forgoing the classic eighties I'd rocked out to the night before. I needed to clear my head, focus on what I was doing, and reason out why I was so damn excited that Lia had called me and not Colly, her brother and my best friend.

Carinthia County Jail was only two blocks away, but the drive felt a hell of a lot longer. By the time I got out of my car, I was a ball of nerves.

After posting bail, I was directed to a holding room. Inside the white walls, I pressed my hands against a counter and stared at the cop seated on the other side. "I'm here for Lia Montgomery."

He squinted at me. "You are...?"

"Max Martinez."

"The boyfriend?" The guy scooted his chair back, one eyebrow raised in question.

I shook my head, not sure why that mattered. "I'm a friend."

He nodded, then started to fill out some paperwork on a clipboard before setting it on the counter. "Bail's been posted already."

No shit, Sherlock. I folded my arms. "What'd she do anyway?"

"Not really my place to say." He reached beneath the counter and brought out a basket, setting it next to the forms he'd just written all over.

Curious, I pulled the edges back with my thumb, taking a quick peek. Lia's purse, along with her boots, sat inside. "Why's she not wearing her boots?"

He yanked the basket back and glared at me. When he opened his mouth to say something, a voice behind me cut him off.

"Because my feet hurt."

At the sound, I turned, eyes narrowing as I took in Lia, or more so her clothes. Black miniskirt and a hot-pink, skintight tank to match her hot-pink hair... She looked like a punk-rock goddess, a style that was all her own and sexy as hell.

"That so?" I quirked a brow.

The sleeve of tats covering her right arm looked bigger than the last time I saw her—three weeks and two days earlier, to be exact. It was an endless stream of black rose petals with interwoven hot-pink vines and thorns. The thing was fucking gorgeous, just like she was. My gaze ran the length of her holey stockings. The woman had legs for miles, and not a day went by that they weren't running through my head.

She pressed her hip against mine, ignoring me as she leaned over the counter. "Thanks for everything, Mitch." She grinned at the cop.

I whipped my head back toward the tatted-up man, finding his eyes flaring as he took her in and nodded. Jealousy stabbed at my gut, but I couldn't blame the guy. I'd always known Lia was the sexiest woman in Carinthia. Now it seemed like I wasn't the only one who thought so.

"Take me home, Soldier Boy." She grabbed the belt loop of my jeans and winked at this *Mitch* dude from over her shoulder before tugging me toward the door. Wordless, I let her, the only woman I'd ever be a slave to.

On the way to her apartment, I didn't bother talking, which wasn't my norm. My head was spinning though. I was dying to know what had happened—what she'd done, why she'd done it, and if I had to kick someone's ass because of it. Out of all the girls I knew, other than my best friend's daughter and my half sister, Charlotte, Lia was my number one priority.

"What's this?" She jerked her finger toward the radio, leaning forward to change the station. "You turning old man on me?" She grinned as her heavy metal blasted through the speakers.

"Jesus, I haven't even had my coffee yet." I winced, shutting it off.

She shoved my shoulder. "You're such a girl."

"Touch me or my radio again, and you'll be sorry." I glared at her from the corner of my eye, my lips twitching at the same time. I couldn't stay mad at her, no matter what kind of trouble she'd gotten herself into.

Ignoring my threat, she rolled down the window and leaned her head partway out. It was raining, but she didn't care. In a lot of ways, she reminded me of, well, me. Free-spirited, didn't give a shit, but packed with a world of secrets she'd never spill.

"I love the morning air, don't you?" Her shoulder-length pink hair blew around her face, sticking to her lips.

"No. I don't like mornings. I like to sleep in, like to drink my coffee in bed, like to—"

"Get early morning blow jobs?"

I shrugged. "If the occasion arises, then yeah, a good-morning cocksucking is fine by me."

She pulled her head back inside and leaned it against the headrest, facing me. "S'pose I messed that one up for you this morning, didn't I?"

Had she? Probably. Did I regret it? Hell no. Again, my best friend's little sister would always come first—good cocksucking or not.

"Yup."

"Sorry." She reached over and squeezed my thigh. Our eyes locked, then held for another second, until she finally drew her hand away. An apology lit up her pretty face along with something else I couldn't identify.

Regret?

Pain?

Fear?

She'd looked away too fast for me to figure it out.

I cracked my neck and focused back on the road, just as the stoplight turned green. Lia was an enigma—had been that way since I'd met her nearly five years back. I shuddered just thinking about that night, wishing I could block the memory, knowing I never could.

––⁊⁊⁊––

It was a couple days before my two best friends and I were to be shipped out for our first tour of duty. Since Gavin and I didn't have anywhere else to go, we decided to stay with Colly in Carinthia.

Instead of hanging out at the bar and watching the

Cubs play like we'd planned, Collin had some sort of ESP moment, thinking his little sister was in trouble. So, the three of us hopped in his car and drove to her college town. Colly claimed he wanted to make sure he wasn't just being paranoid, but I knew the truth. He'd already had a crap night knowing he'd have to leave Amy—his daughter's since-deceased mama—and didn't wanna leave any other stones unturned when we left the States.

Macomb was only an hour away. "We won't be gone long," Colly had said. When we got to Lia's apartment, her roommate said she was out at a party, but she had no idea which one, where it was, or who Lia was with. Collin was terrified and about scared the roomie to death with his inquisition. Said his sister, good girl Leanne Montgomery, *didn't do parties.*

Not knowing where to start, the three of us had split up, going from frat house to frat house in search of her. Neither Gav nor I had ever seen Lia before, other than a few pictures Collin had shown us during boot camp. I'd swiped one and stuck it in my pocket when he wasn't lookin'. I was a sick motherfucker, yeah, but I also couldn't help myself. From that picture alone, I could tell she was pretty—far too innocent for someone like me. Long brown hair, big blue eyes, and a sweet smile that said the world was hers to control if she wanted the job. I didn't know it then, but I do now: Lia had me before I even met her.

We finally located her at the biggest frat on campus. It was a moment that'll stick with me for the rest of my life. I walked inside that house like nothing else mattered, my first—and to this day, most important— mission as a man.

The place was loud, crowded, and smelled like sex, pot, and all things party. Nobody knew the girl in the picture when I showed it around and asked if they'd seen her. Hell, nobody gave me so much as a second glance as I tore through the house on the hunt. But I refused to quit searching, not until I checked every room and every face.

Up the stairs I'd ran, searching rooms, slamming doors, shoving dudes off chicks in beds, just to make sure one wasn't her. The last room I went into was quiet, dark, and exactly where I found her.

Sitting in the closet with the door wide open—passed out asleep, clothing ripped, hand bloody—was the girl who had given me purpose I'd never known before. Purpose I'd never understood until the second I scooped her into my arms and carried her out of that house. From then on, I'd vowed to protect Leanne Montgomery like a sister—especially from me.

—∿∿—

"Java Java opened five minutes ago. Caffeine rush on me this morning?" The crack in Lia's voice broke me from my thoughts. Little pieces of her wild hair still covered her temple, and big, sleepy, haunted-looking eyes blinked at me.

"Nah, I'm good." I cleared my throat.

She might have been seducing me with coffee, but I wasn't gonna be swayed. Something had happened last night to land her in jail, and I needed to know what. Most of all, I needed to know if she was okay.

"You good? Wanna talk about anything?" I pulled into the parking lot of her apartment complex a minute later.

"You're not really going to turn down my mocha, are you, Maxwell?"

"I am." I gritted my teeth, hating how she ignored my question. Once I shoved the car into Park, I turned to face her, still clutching the wheel. "Now tell me: Are. You. Good?

She rolled her eyes. "Jeez. You're really pissed that you lost your morning BJ, aren't you?"

"Damn it, no. I just picked you up from County. Sex is the last thing on my mind right now."

She huffed. "You don't have to be such an ass. Take a joke. I'm fine." A shrug. "Just got into a little trouble is all."

I squeezed my eyes shut, white-knuckling the wheel. "Yeah, sure, a little trouble." I shook my head. "Just... go inside, would you? Sleep off whatever issues you're dealing with."

She snort-laughed. "Whatever. Thanks for the loan. We'll talk repayment later." She reached to open her door, but I locked it, not willing to let her go just yet.

"That came out wrong. I'm sorry," I said.

She focused on the roof. "If you ask me, you've been spending too much time with Collin. I already have one controlling big brother. I don't need another."

"Maybe he's not enough anymore if you're getting yourself locked up. Maybe you need to talk to someone again. I know this doc who—"

"No, damn it." She clamped her eyes shut and groaned. "I don't need another doctor, and I sure as hell don't need an additional brother."

My gut grew tight, my hands wet against the wheel. I dropped them to my jeans and rubbed both back and forth as I tried to gather my words. The last thing I wanted to do was hurt her feelings—hurt *her*. But when you're in love with the one person you know you can't have, you don't put yourself through the pain of being with them when you don't have to be. That's why I said what I did next.

"Fine. But we're not through talking about this."

She didn't move this time. Instead, she turned to study *me*. Sad blue eyes worked over my face as she said, "It's going to be like this for us now, isn't it?"

"Like what?" I asked, though I knew exactly what she meant.

"You pushing me away, me drawing you back in…"

"I don't know how things are with us anymore, Lia." Other than the fact that I wanted her in all the ways I shouldn't.

For the forty-millionth time, I had to remind myself I couldn't go there. This was Collin's little sister, the girl with issues who'd probably never fully dealt with them. I'm guessing that was why she was working in some nasty dive bar, living in a shit-hole apartment at the age of twenty-five, and making decisions that had her losing herself along the way.

Not that I was the king of moral standards.

"All right then, glad we got that settled." She plastered on a fake smile, looking past me, not at me. "Now, if you'll excuse me, I'm going to grab an Uber, get my car from Jimney's, then go to Java Java's for some tea."

She reached for the lock this time, but I clicked it shut again. "No."

"*No?*"

I nodded once, wordless again. I've used sarcasm to make it through life for years. Doing the serious thing wasn't something I had down pat yet.

She rolled her eyes to the heavens, a nasty smirk on her lips. "Jesus, Max, when did you turn into such a bossy—"

"Adult?"

"No, I was going to say *asshole*. *Adult* implies you understand that I want Java Java's and will do and say whatever I want to get it." She flicked open the door lock, but I locked it once more.

God, I was a pussy.

"Unlock the door, Max."

"Not 'til you talk to me." I swallowed. "Tell me what happened to you last night." Then I whispered in a last-ditch effort, "Please, Lee-Lee. You're scarin' me."

She blew out a breath and leaned back against the seat. "I don't want to talk about it."

"*Why?*"

"Because it's none of your business, that's why."

I flinched, the meaning of her words cutting deep.

She didn't want me in her life anymore.

She was cutting me off, just like I'd done with her.

I'd messed up by pushing her away these last few months. But I'd do anything to turn back the clock. To the time before I'd decided that being away from her— and serial screwing a bunch of women—was better than being with her as a friend but wanting no other woman *except* her.

I missed her. I missed *us*. The way we'd once hung out, drunk beers, watched cheesy talk shows, and done a little innocent flirting when we could. It was safe then.

Fun. Nothing like how I felt now. Like I'd die if I didn't get to kiss her lips, hold her hand, make her mine.

The whole *Absence makes the heart grow fonder* bullshit was damn painful—and true.

"I deserve to know, Lia." No, I didn't deserve to know. But I was gonna do or say whatever I could because that's what a *brother* would do. "Especially since I'm the one who just bailed you out."

She laughed, the sound bitter. "Just because I'm indebted to you financially doesn't mean you deserve to know what's going on in my life. You've barely looked my direction the past two months. What gives you the right to go all *family* on me now?"

Fuck. Me.

I deserved that. Every bit of her tongue-lashing. But I couldn't tell her the truth about why I'd put distance between us. Not when it might ruin everything that was good in my life.

When I didn't answer, she sank lower in her seat and kicked her feet on the dash. "Fine. If you really want to know, then here you go. Travis—"

"Is he messing with you?" I stiffened. I'd kill the guy if he was hurting her. Then Collin and Gavin would bring him back to life to do it all over again. "I swear to God, Lia, if he hurt you—"

"No. He didn't *hurt* me." Her gaze flickered toward the window. A sure sign she was lying to me. "At least not physically."

I dug my nails into my palms and growled, "Tell me what he did."

Normally I didn't have a temper. Most of the time I prided myself on staying calm, keeping my head clear, and looking at all sides of things before passing judgment. But when it involved Lia and this rat bastard, everything was fair game.

"Travis and another girl happened, so I got pissed. Slugged him in the nose. He filed charges, end of story."

I cringed. "He's a piece of trash. I'm so sorry he—"

"Don't." Her lips flattened, and she pressed her hand against her throat. Her gaze was like a sliver of ice shooting through the windshield. "I'm fine with it."

I stared at my lap, my jaw clenched. If that punk were here now, there was no doubt I'd shove my fist against his face too. Lia deserved the universe, not dickheads like Travis.

"I should've been there," I whispered, more to myself than to her.

"I handled it fine."

I shook my head. "You call getting arrested *fine*?"

Lia was tough—another thing that drew me to her. She'd taken up boxing for fun, had taken self-defense courses at the gym, and also did yoga on top of that. I'd always known she could protect herself, but I still worried about her. Likely always would.

"What else was I supposed to do?" she asked.

"I don't know… Maybe you could've called me, or Collin even? Hell, Gav would've messed him up for you in a heartbeat. Travis has been on our hit list since the day you hooked up with him." Mine more than anyone else's, but I had my selfish reasons for that. Travis was a punk, piece-of-shit Brit with no job and no direction.

Again, not that I was one to talk life direction or jobs.

I'd worked construction for a good three months right after I got out of the marines. Even worked a few weeks at the Gap during the weekends. 'Course neither of those positions panned out. Hell, I barely kept a job more than two to three months at a time. Nowadays, I jumped from restaurant to restaurant, moving from fill-in chef to waiter to host. It was all mundane work that didn't keep me satisfied.

I wanted more outta life. I just didn't have a clue what that more was. My indecision had a lot to do with the fact that my father had died and dropped a lump sum of money into my bank account fifteen months ago so I didn't *have* to work if I didn't want to. I wasn't lazy, more taking my time until I figured out what I wanted to do.

"Please." She scoffed. "If I did that, then you might as well strap a collar around my neck and call me a dog. I deal with all my own issues. I don't need a man for that."

Unable to help myself, I moved in closer. "Lia…" I tipped her chin up and pulled her face toward mine. She didn't flinch or pull away this time, but my hand tingled where it touched her skin, and I quickly yanked it back. *Limits, Martinez. Set 'em.*

The urges were growing harder to avoid every time I saw her. More than anything, I wanted to keep my fingers on her skin, trail them over her cheek, her neck, across the curves that I'd never allow my fingers to touch…

"I'm so sorry that he fucked you over, Lee-Lee." I cleared my throat. "But at least now you know, right? We've always told you he was no good for you."

Her dark brows furrowed in thought. When she didn't say much else, I asked, "Wanna talk some more?"

Innocence lit her eyes as she looked at me. I swallowed hard, taken aback by the honesty in her usually guarded face.

"No," she finally said, that look slipping away. "But I *am* gonna be a good little girl now and go to sleep like you asked." She leaned over and poked my bicep. "Thinking I might even have some tea inside."

"Forget about an Uber. We'll get your car later, yeah?"

"Sure."

"Then run along inside." I leaned back against my seat again, gripping the steering wheel. "And shower too, because you smell like a liquor store." No, she smelled like roses. Always roses. "And if you listen to what I say, then maybe I'll keep this a secret between us."

"You're kidding, right?" She glared at me.

I winked. "I don't kid."

"You used to." A strange look passed over her face, one I didn't recognize, just before her hand shot toward the door handle again. This time, she got it unlocked and shoved open. She slid out, only to slam the door with the sole of her bare foot.

I watched her go, my jaw tight with regret.

I didn't even get to say goodbye.

CHAPTER

Lia

"YOU'RE DAYDREAMING AGAIN." RUBY PEARL, THE DAUGHTER of Betty, Java Java Hut's owner, poked me with her wooden coffee stirrer.

I stared at the extra-sparkly linoleum top I'd been cleaning for the past five minutes and frowned. My job as a barista on Monday, Wednesday, and Friday mornings wasn't something I could give up, but at the rate I'd been going today, I wouldn't be surprised if I were fired due to straight-up distractibility.

"Sorry." I leaned my hip against the counter. "Just been a long week, is all." And it was only halfway over.

"What's up? I'm all ears." She sat across from me, frowning.

"Not much to talk about." That she wanted to hear about at least.

All those months of saving and busting my butt at Jimney's, and I was still short the last of my tuition—a thousand dollars short, actually. Talk about a crap storm of epic proportions. I thought I had this behind me, that I was finally getting ahead, that I could quit that hellish bartending job and find a worthwhile career. Then just before noon Saturday, I'd gotten the call saying that my last tuition payment wasn't enough, and that they wouldn't send me my diploma until I covered the remaining costs. Add in the hellishness of what had happened the night before, and I'd say I had good reason to be distracted.

"See, that's where I think you're wrong." She tucked her corkscrew curls behind her ears and patted my arm. Not only did she wear the hell out of a curly, femme-fatale mullet, but she consistently matched the style with one of her seven pairs of denim overalls. "It's an M&M situation, isn't it?"

"M&M?" I fumbled through the giant box of tea bags I'd organized an hour ago, needing to keep my hands busy.

"Yeah, *men* and *money*. Those are the two things women worry the most about, ain't they?"

My nose scrunched, yet the need to spill my guts was there on the tip of my tongue. Maybe I *would* feel better if I talked to someone. But did I really want my boss's daughter to be my therapist?

"Not necessarily. Most of the time, the root of all evil lies within yourself, not with the people around you."

Fingernails drummed against the linoleum, and Ruby Pearl hummed to herself for a good ten seconds before she replied. "When my husband, Davey, was still alive, my life was a living, breathing hell. Mainly because Davey had a drinking problem and stole all my money for gambling." She tsked. "Talk about M&M issues."

I puckered my lips, because saying "Sorry for your loss" did not seem appropriate to a situation like Ruby's. Then again, what did I know about marriage, other than the fact that fifty percent of them ended in divorce?

"Anyway, once I got the life insurance check after he passed, my life took a turn for the better…"

"Oh yeah?" I cleared my throat, having even less of a clue how to respond this time. Once the tea bags were settled, I moved down the line.

"…and the only time I was happy with Davey was when he took me to the…"

I turned on the coffee-bean grinder and nodded as she spoke. I really liked Ruby Pearl, but her long-winded stories tended to make absolutely no sense. Still, the man part of her M&M scenario? There *was* some merit to it right now.

Travis was an aching throb in my side that wouldn't quit. He'd been calling nonstop since Sunday afternoon. He'd dropped the assault charges, saying he *understood why I did what I did*. Even after I told him I wanted nothing do with him, he kept calling—three nonstop days of endless voicemails on a loop, all begging for another chance that wouldn't happen.

Apologies only went so far when it came to messing up like he had.

Still, the two of us had been together for nearly five months, and I *did* miss his company. More so the constant of having someone around. Without him, I was alone again, and being alone gave me too much time to think about things I couldn't control.

For instance, Maxwell.

Like someone had flipped a switch, his face was all

I could see. The guy was like an earworm I couldn't shake, no matter how hard I tried a new tune.

Max used to come in and get coffee every morning I worked at Java Java's. He'd flirt with Betty a little too, even offer to take the garbage out so neither of us had to do the dirty work. But he'd made himself scarce since I began dating Travis, something that hadn't gone unnoticed by Ruby and Betty.

In the delusional part of my mind, I wondered if he'd put distance between us because he was jealous of my new relationship. Then all I had to do was remember that he was Max Martinez, the serial dater who wanted nothing to do with me or any woman past a first date. He was also why I'd started dating Travis—as a way to curb the growing feelings he stirred up in me. I'd been crushing on the guy for years, and if anything, the wall he'd put between us had only made my longing for him worse. Plus, he'd always treated me like a little sister, and I hated that most of all.

I switched off the coffee grinder.

"...so what I'm saying is, you should become a lesbian."

I coughed, hiding my shocked laughter. "But then wouldn't it just be W&M instead? Because I'm pretty sure that no matter who you date, there's always going to be hell to get through."

"Oh, sweetie." Ruby moved around the counter, her eyes soft, her face flushed with exertion from just that simple move. "You're better off alone anyway. Trust me."

In the blink of an eye, she wrapped her arms around my waist and held me against her sweaty chest. I cringed. This was so *not* what I needed today.

"I think that's why I was never happy with my marriage, ya know? Nobody ever made me feel that spark." She petted the back of my hair, like a mother to a daughter. The scent of her perfume, with the underlying scent of raw meat, smacked me in the face. I cringed, holding my breath.

Dear, sweet Jesus…

"Wish I was fifteen years younger. Then maybe I would've made better choices. Experienced more. Played the field even."

Patting her shoulder, I managed to slip out of her hold and smile in turn. Or grimace, was more like it. Thankfully, she didn't seem to understand what my facial expression meant and moved toward the back of the shop, humming to herself.

Yeah. That wasn't awkward or anything.

The small bell over the front door jingled, and the late-April wind blew into the café, causing goose bumps to form on my arms. A toddler's squeal of joy sounded from the entrance and I smiled, already knowing who it was. Addie, my brother's girlfriend, along with my adorable niece, Chloe, had come for their Wednesday morning visit.

"Hey!" I waved, tossing a clean towel over my shoulder.

I pushed through the swinging saloon-style doors and approached them with open arms. *Gorgeous* was the one word that could best describe my brother's girlfriend—and hopefully, someday, maybe my sister-in-law. She had thick black hair, dark-brown eyes, and flawless skin that reminded me of the lightest brew of coffee we had in this place.

"Hey back," she said, a little breathless as she tossed

Chloe's diaper bag into the booth. I might have lost Max on Mondays and Fridays, but I'd gained these two on Wednesday—a fair trade, I'd say.

Addie handed my niece over with a grin. I snuggled her to my chest. "Hey, Beaner." The scent of her baby shampoo filled my nose, and I couldn't help but smile.

God, I loved this little thing. Not only was she the glue that held my brother and his friends together, but she held me together too. Her birth last year had pushed me to do what I'd wanted most: to go back to college and finish my last semester, to get my life together once and for all. Then when her mom died, something in me had really clicked. Life wasn't forever, and if you didn't make it your own in the short time you were given, then what was the point of living it at all?

"What shall we get you today, little lady?" I poked her on the nose, and like always, Chloe tugged at my eyebrow ring. She'd learned to be gentler now that she was almost fourteen months old, but the kid had mega strength. She was a Thor toddler in the making—likely due to all the testosterone in her house. Living with a dad and two other macho men probably had that effect on a little girl. I was just thankful Addie was there to set them all straight.

Addie stood beside us at the table, a loving smile on her face. Chloe reached for her, and I swallowed around a lump in my throat, willing my jealousy away. I wasn't jealous that Chloe had another leading lady in her life though. If anything, I was happy. Addie was the perfect fill-in mom, and I couldn't have asked for a better person for my brother. I was jealous because I missed being around Chloe as much as I used to be. But I was busy. Working two jobs and finally finishing school had forced me to give something up for a while. Unfortunately, that something had to be Beaner.

"I'll take a poppy-seed muffin. She can just nibble on mine." Addie nudged Chloe in the belly, making her laugh.

"Coffee too?"

Addie nodded and sat, my niece tucked in her lap where she belonged.

A little while later, I took my fifteen-minute break, hoping above hope that Ruby Pearl didn't scare the customers away with her Davey stories. We still had a good half hour before the midmorning rush came in, so this was the perfect opportunity for a little female chat with my favorite—and only—girlfriend.

"So, how've you been?" I leaned back in my seat, sipping my tea.

"Okay, I guess," Addie answered.

I frowned. "What's up, buttercup? My brother being a douche?"

"Uh, no. Not at all. Just personal family drama is all."

Addie's family was crap. They had ignored her, abandoned her, cut her off... It made me love and miss my overbearing parents even more.

"What is it?" I leaned toward Chloe to take a bite of the muffin offering from her tiny fingers, but at the last minute she giggled and yanked it away.

"My mom's sick. She's at the Mayo Clinic in Rochester. It's cancer of the stomach. Apparently she was diagnosed a few months ago, but I only got the call last week."

I cringed. That didn't sound good. "Are you going to visit her?"

Addie shredded the napkin in her hands. "I want to, but Collin thinks I shouldn't."

"With good reason, I'm sure."

Her lips pursed. "I have a right to say goodbye to my mother, even if she did abandon me. He doesn't just get to—"

"Addie." I put my hand on top of hers, my heart conflicted. She needed to make amends with her parents, yes, but at the same time nobody wanted her to get her heart broken if it didn't work out, especially not my brother. "You know why he doesn't want you to go, right?"

Shoulders sagging, she looked at Chloe. "I do. But he's just so stubborn and…ugh. He's just Collin."

"Well, you're Miss Stubborn too." I took another drink of my tea.

She blew out a slow breath. "I don't want to talk about this anymore."

"Then don't."

"But I *do* want to talk about Max." She peered back at me, a knowing, mischievous look in her brown eyes.

My face grew hot. "What about him?"

"He's moodier than normal."

My eyebrows rose. "And your point is…?"

Her lips trembled like she was fighting a smile. "He's *moody* because he's stopped sleeping around. He told Collin and me that last night. I guess he's thinking about finally finding someone to settle down with."

I swallowed hard, staring at Chloe's hands as she tossed her muffin pieces on the floor. Was it coincidence or happenstance that he'd decided this *after* he found out Travis and I had broken up? Likely the first thought, because there's no way my relationship status would make him rethink his stance on dating. I was delusional to think otherwise.

"He must have been drunk." I scoffed. Either that, or he was having a dry spell. Or maybe he'd run out of options. Carinthia *was* a small town. "I mean, even guys like Max are bound to take a break from sex every once in a while. I can guarantee it won't last."

"Don't be dense, Lia." Addie grinned. "All he's done this week is ask about you. I think it's a sign." Addie sipped her coffee, her eyes narrowing with intent from over the rim.

"I'm not dense." Maybe a little unrealistic at times, but *definitely* not dense.

It was easier to pretend nothing bothered me. That way people didn't constantly ask *How are you feeling? Do you want to talk about it?* Playing the role of the uncaring whack job was exactly the persona I'd built my life around over the past five years. I no longer recognized the shy, sensitive girl who used to live within me. The girl who studied on Fridays and dated only the sweetest of the sweet on Saturdays. No way was I the girl who'd created homecoming floats in high school and written for the college newspaper just to receive extra credit. *That* girl was the dense one. She was also dead.

I knew that because I'd killed her myself.

"Fine, fine. I just wanted you to know in case you decide to—"

"Addie," I groaned. "Max and I? We're never. Going. To happen. It's best if you drop the scenario altogether and focus your matchmaking skills elsewhere."

For now, I had two goals: paying my extra tuition fees and then getting my diploma. And neither of those included Maxwell Martinez.

CHAPTER 4

Max

It was five in the morning on a Thursday, and there I was, changing a diaper. If that didn't say I was a damn good guy, I'm not sure anything could.

"Uncle Max and Uncle Gavin are gonna take you out for breakfast. What do you say, kiddo?" Chloe clapped on cue, like the awesome munchkin she was. In response, I nuzzled my face against her neck and tickled her pajama-covered stomach.

Someday, I wanted this. The house, a wife, a couple of kids…exactly what I'd never had growing up.

I picked up my favorite little kid from the changing table in her room, held her above my head like Superman, and raced us down the hall. Since I'd forgone going out at night for a while, I'd offered to take morning faux-uncle duties. Maybe it'd give the sex maniacs in the room next to mine some uninterrupted time to do what I wasn't feeling the urge to do—*without* waking me from a dead sleep.

"Ready, Freddy?" I plopped us onto the couch in the living room and grabbed her jacket off the armrest. No point in putting actual clothes on her when all she'd do was fight me anyway. Toddlers were hellions when it came to being dressed—even the cute ones like Beaner.

On cue, she flailed, silently begging me to dip her upside down. I finally managed to bribe her into letting me put the thing on her with promises of seeing Gavin.

My other best friend lived in the duplex adjacent to ours and had no idea I was gonna wake his ass up this morning. But I knew he hadn't gone out last night either, so it wasn't like I'd be waking a sleeping monster. Plus, Gav and I had some talking to do. Mainly me needing to complain about things I couldn't bitch to Collin about.

Ten minutes later, I was dressed and the two of us stood outside his door. "You knock, pretty girl." I grinned as she pounded her tiny fist against the glass storm door. Ten seconds later, a sweaty-ass yeti of a man answered, towel around his neck and looking like he hadn't seen a razor—or sleep—for months.

"Get dressed. We're taking Beaner for breakfast." In response, Chloe leaped toward Gav's leg and wrapped her chubby little arms around his calf.

"Sabotage," he grumbled, flipping me off over her head. But, like all three of us would've done, he squatted down to her level and said with a smile, "Good morning, Chloe."

The guy wasn't good with kids. The only time he'd tried to take care of Chloe on his own, he'd wound up covered in her vomit and calling Addie. But that didn't mean he didn't love her. And Chloe, for some reason, thought the sun rose and set with her uncle Gavin. Hell, her first real, recognizable word was *Avvy*, which we all knew stood for Gavvy.

"Sorry. First thing she asked for this morning was your dumb-ass." No, it was candy, but a little white lie never hurt anybody.

His bearded face went soft as he pulled back from kissing her forehead. "I'm all sweaty from my run, Chloe. Can I take a shower first?"

I rolled my eyes as he tried—failed—to barter with the kid. Again, the guy didn't have a fatherly bone in his body.

She grabbed hold of his finger and tugged him out onto the front porch, her decision already made. Gavin shot me the devil eyes from over her shoulder, and I held my hands up in defense. "Kid's hungry."

"Fine, fuck. Put her in her car seat. I'm coming."

"Uck!" Chloe repeated proudly, her eyes wide as she watched Gavin stand.

I laughed so hard my eyes started watering. Gavin, on the other hand, turned pale and pointed a finger at her, then me, then her again, his mouth opening and shutting each time. Chloe giggled like she knew exactly what she'd done. I picked her up, propping her on my hip.

"Chloe, you can't say the bad words Uncle Gavin says, all right?" I laughed again, knowing damn well she wouldn't understand.

Gavin moved forward and tucked some of her curls behind her ear. Then he glared at me, his jaw tight. "Give me five minutes."

Fifteen minutes later, we wound up at Stringers, a newer mom-and-pop-style restaurant near O'Paddy's

Bar. It was commercial and cold, and the food tasted like ass, but it was the only breakfast joint in town where we could just sit—other than a McDonald's and the local waffle house we'd gotten kicked out of last fall, thanks to Colly and his need to fight the world and everyone in it.

Gavin grabbed Chloe out of her car seat and set her on the sidewalk between us. I held one of her hands, Gavin held the other, and as we walked inside, the rising sun at our backs, the few eyes in the restaurant at this hour turned toward us.

"Christ. Everyone's staring," Gavin grumbled under his breath, rubbing his hand over his mouth.

I snorted and grabbed a couple of menus, yanking the two of them behind me. "Come on, sweetheart," I said, louder than necessary. "Our baby girl needs to eat."

Unlike me, Gavin was very *un*cool with situations like these. Not to mention he didn't have a funny bone in his body. He was like Collin's clone in some ways. But Collin had an occasional laid-back side, while Gavin was usually all moody and gruff. Except when it came to Beaner.

In the booth, Chloe sat in a booster seat next to me, kicking the underside of the table. Gavin's gaze was drawn to the menu. He was burying his head behind it when our waitress approached.

"What can I get you two?" She looked at me, then the top of Gavin's head, before she smiled at Chloe.

"Coffee for us, milk for the cutie here." I winked at the waitress whose name tag read Bridget. Her pale cheeks flushed, making the freckles pop off her nose. She poured us both a cup, never losing her grin.

"Max."

I blinked, meeting Gavin's stare from across the table after she left. "What?"

"You all right?" He looked from me to the retreating waitress and back again. "Because she just eyed the hell out of you, and you ignored her."

"I'm fine. Just not interested." I leaned back in my seat to wrap my arm around Beaner, hoping Gavin didn't question me. Unlike with Addie and Collin, I couldn't hide the reason for my sudden abstinence.

"You're always interested."

I was. But not today. Or yesterday—or for the past seven days. I shrugged, not wanting to get into it.

"At least tell me why we're here when you could easily have cooked better food than this at home."

I leaned forward to pour some sugar into my coffee. "It's Lia. I wanna talk about her, and I can't do it at home with Collin around."

"You could've just come over to my place."

I rubbed my foot up and down his shin. "And miss out on a secret rendezvous with my lover?" I winked. He jerked his foot back, cussing under his breath as he nailed his knee against the bottom of the table.

"What about Lia?" He narrowed his eyes.

"I…" Fuck. This was a hell of a lot harder than I'd thought. "Do you know how she's been this week? Addie ain't got a clue, and Collin's been too bent out of shape to care about anything." Aside from picking her up from County, driving her home, and fighting with her along the way, I hadn't seen or spoken to Lia since. Which really wasn't much different than the way things had been, but still.

"Why do you ask?" He smirked, probably already knowing the answer.

"Just answer the question, would ya?"

He ran his fingertip over the rim of his coffee cup. "Far as I know, she's fine." He frowned, always observant. "You gonna tell me why you're suddenly asking me about Lia when you're the one who's been keeping tabs on her for the last five years?"

Again. How could I answer without spilling the whole truth? That I missed what she and I had before she started dating Travis. That every time I closed my eyes at night she was there in my dreams. Oh, and that I was ninety-nine percent sure I was in love with her.

"You can't tell Collin what I'm about to tell you."

"Oh Jesus." Gavin leaned back and ran a hand through his hair, reaching over to grab the fork Chloe had been slamming against the table. I was so lost in my head, I hadn't noticed. "I can't *not* tell Collin. You know the rules."

I bit down on my tongue. *Never keep secrets, no matter how bad they are.* That was the motto the three of us lived by. Yet this was different. At least to me it was. Because the secret I was about to tell was not my own to spill. At least not to Collin.

Gavin kept going. "She pregnant?"

"Pregnant?" I jerked my head back, just as the waitress brought our food to the table. She cleared her throat, but I ignored her, too caught up in Gavin's words. "Who'd get her pregnant?"

"Travis maybe?"

My fingers tightened around my fork at the thought. "No. They broke up." Not that the pregnant thing couldn't have happened before they broke up. But I knew Lia was smarter than that.

"Really?"

I nodded. "Yep."

"Then what's up? Why're you so worried about her?"

I sighed, hating that I had to go behind Lee-Lee's back about this, but if I wanted Gav's opinion, he needed to know what was up. "I bailed her out of jail early last Saturday morning."

"What?" Gavin froze, and the spoon he was holding dropped onto his plate.

"Yup."

"What happened?" he asked.

I cut up Chloe's pancakes, then put her eggs on another plate so the two wouldn't touch. "She found Travis screwing some girl in the alley at Jimney's. Lia punched his nose, he pressed charges, and I had to bail her out." I shoved the plate in front of my niece, picking up a bit of her eggs to entice her with. She curled her nose and turned her head, always the picky eater. "I'm worried he'll keep bugging her is the thing." Or worse.

"What are we gonna do about it?" Gavin leaned back, arms folded.

"Don't you mean what am *I* gonna do about it?" Done with trying to force nasty food down Beaner's throat, I relaxed in the booth with my coffee, scowling as I picked it up.

He shook his head. "Lia's like my sister. Not gonna let some douche bag mess with her. We've got to take care of this together."

I laughed. "You sound like a gangster."

"Funny." He flipped me off.

"Seriously." I set my cup back down on the table, not even hungry for the steaming pile of garbage in front of me. "I can handle this on my own. I plan on stopping by Jimney's. Hoping I can talk to her a little more. Make sure—"

"When?" Gavin shoved his plate away too, then stole a slice of uneaten toast off Chloe's napkin. She'd hardly touched anything, other than the eggs, which were all over the table now.

"When what?" I opened a wet wipe the waitress had left behind.

"When are you going to Jimney's?"

I shrugged. "Tonight, most likely."

"Then I'm there with you. Both of us. If she's got issues and Travis shows, we'll take care of him together."

I wanted to argue, to tell him he didn't need to go out and pick fights. His hot head tended to take over, and with all the issues he'd been having lately—like the fact that he'd been put on leave because he'd punched another EMT—I didn't need him doing time, any more than I needed Lia to. Still, I knew he was lonely, fighting his own demons the best he could. And because I had a hell of a hard time disappointing people, I couldn't tell him no even if I should've.

"Fine. But you gotta promise to keep your head on straight." I pointed a fork at him just in time for something warm to hit my cheek. I blinked, turning toward Chloe. Her hands were filled with leftover eggs, mischievous eyes pointed at me.

"Uh-oh." She giggled, knowing damn well what she'd done.

I couldn't help but grin, just as the flash of a camera

went off. I lifted my head to find Gavin leaning back in his seat with his phone in hand.

"Collateral." He smirked, pocketing the phone a second later.

I shook my head. "Cocksucker."

"Ock, ock, ock."

Both Gav and I jerked our heads toward Chloe. She giggled even louder this time and bounced in place. I groaned. "Collin's gonna beat us bloody."

Gavin choked back a laugh and said, "He's gonna do more than that."

CHAPTER 5

Lia

For a Thursday night, Jimney's was pretty dead. A few of the regular patrons were there, of course, but nothing like usual.

At the end of the bar sat James, a well-dressed business professional who had been coming in for about two months now. He didn't wear a wedding ring, but I spotted a tan line on that left finger. It meant he was either having an affair or *looking* to have one.

I tucked my purse beneath the bar, threw on my apron, and covered my windblown hair with a do-rag before approaching him. "What can I get you tonight, James?"

His grin grew wide as he eyed my halter. The stench of whiskey flowed off him in waves, which meant he'd been at it for a while.

"Whatever you're willing to make me, sweetness." He nodded, his lecherous gaze never straying far from my chest.

Because I was used to disgusting behavior, I ignored him as he took me in. Maybe if he got it out of his system with me, he'd go home to his wife and look at *her* later.

Patricia moved in from my right, stacking the tap glasses into their usual design. "You had a visitor earlier."

"Oh yeah?" I finished pouring James's drink and set it on the napkin in front of him. He nodded his approval, moving on to leer at Patricia's chest next. "Who was it?"

"Who do you think?"

My stomach dropped.

Crap. Travis.

I dried my damp hands on the towel in front of me, then slung it over my shoulder. With a hip against the bar, I tried to act casual as I asked, "What'd he say?"

"Not much." Patricia poured a couple of beers and took the money from a guy with lip piercings before she continued. "Just wanted to know when you were going to be working next." She frowned and looked at me. "I thought you two were done."

"We are." Except that Travis wouldn't take a *no*, a *hell no*, or a *get-the-hell-out-of-my-life no* for an answer.

I moved to serve a group of three older gentlemen, all wearing motorcycle vests. They looked out of place in Jimney's, eyeing everything with dark suspicion.

"That all you gonna say about it?" Patricia asked.

I winced. Of course she'd be looking for more gossip. The woman lived vicariously through her younger employees. I had half a mind to tell her to get a life, but I needed this job—and, even more, that thousand extra bucks.

"Yep." I smiled and grabbed the money from one of the biker dudes. He told me to keep the change to a fifty.

I pocketed the rest after sorting out the bar's cut, thankful for generous tippers.

"Not kidding when I say you need to keep your personal business outta my bar. I'm already in enough hot water with fire code violations. Don't need no more drama in here to shut this place down."

I spun around to face her. "If you want to talk drama, then I suggest you speak with Aubrey, since she's the one who screws her coworkers' boyfriends."

"Hey now. Aubrey may be high maintenance, but she brings in business. This sounds like something you two need to work out, not me."

"Whatever." And with that reply, I went back to work.

I'd be fired by the end of my shift if I had to listen to Patricia rag on me all night. Thankfully, two hours later, the place was hopping, so neither of us had time to talk again.

By the time eleven rolled around, sweat was pouring down my back between my shoulder blades, and by midnight, my halter top had practically turned into a second layer of skin.

"Whatcha having, boys?" I hollered at four guys hunched over the far end of the bar. Each of them was wasted and probably not even legal. Yeah, I'd checked their IDs and they looked legit, but that didn't mean much.

"One of your kind, in the back room, naked." The tallest one, a meaty-looking dude with gray eyes and short brown hair, leaned over the bar and grabbed my halter strap. A football player from Western, was my guess; I knew that type far too well.

An unwelcome shudder powered through me, memories taking me on an unwanted joy ride. But like

I'd learned to do over the past few years, I pushed that disgust down, reminding Old Lia she didn't have a place within me any longer.

I unhooked his fingers from my strap, slammed his hand on the bar, and smirked. "I'm not for sale." He flinched while his friends hooted and hollered in that way only douche college boys did.

I turned to my next customer, ignoring the asshole's "What a bitch" comment from behind. Thankfully, I was no longer sensitive about unjustified word vomit.

Two women asked for screwdrivers, and as I was pouring the vodka in, another arm stretched across the bar and grabbed my wrist. "I'm not gonna tell you again, asshole. Hands. Off." I growled and lifted my chin, only to have two dark eyes meet mine.

"You good?" he asked as he let go.

My chest warmed at Max's words, like a soothing fire had been lit inside me. "What are you doing here?" Regardless of my initial shock, I blew out a breath and smiled. Twice in less than seven days he'd graced my presence—though the first time wasn't necessarily by choice.

I handed the two ladies their drinks but didn't miss their lingering stares as they latched on to my new companion's profile.

Max's eyes were soft, while his normally playful grin was replaced with concern directed toward me. "Someone bothering you tonight? Is it Travis?"

I shook my head once, taken aback by his appearance. "No. Not him." Normally, I didn't take stock of what a man wore. But when it came to Max, I couldn't help myself. Dressed in a sky-blue, V-necked T-shirt that only enhanced the hard muscles hidden underneath, he looked like something straight out of *GQ*. The black hair hanging over his left eyebrow only added to the sexy, yet worried quirk of his brow. "Just some over friendly college boys looking to see if the rumors here are true. Nothing I can't handle."

"*Are* they true?" Max's eyes narrowed in accusation.

A shot of ice pushed through my veins, and all the warmth I'd been feeling fizzled out. God, he was worse than my brother sometimes. Jimney's did not house prostitutes in the back room. Sure, this was a scuzzy bar that *used* to have the occasional hooker entrepreneur when Patricia's husband ran the joint, but that'd been stopped the second she divorced him and took over.

"Go home, Maxwell."

Ignoring whatever answer he had for me, I moved to serve my next customers. Surprisingly, he let me go, which wasn't a Max thing to do. I wasn't sure if that pissed me off or worried me more. Maxwell Martinez never let me have the last word, no matter what direction our conversation went.

I used to be his equal, the one he'd fight and make up with. Now, I felt more like his problem than his friend. I already had enough protection from my brother, so the last thing I wanted was to be treated with kid gloves.

Ten minutes later, the sound of glass shattering on the floor broke me out of my trance. Eyes wide, I glared across the bar, finding Gavin in some guy's face and Max driving his fist into the meaty guy's nose.

"Son of a—" I raced around to the front of the bar.

"I'm calling the police," Patricia hollered at my back.

I turned and yelled over my shoulder, "Don't you dare."

I swirled back around, my eyes focused on the back of Max's head as I contemplated how the hell I'd break this up before Joe Bob, Jimney's only bouncer, came in. For the first time since I started working here, I was thankful Patricia was too cheap to hire more than one security guard.

The red fire extinguisher by the door caught my eye. On a mission, I unlatched it off the wall and stood next to the group. "Knock it off," I yelled, not caring who'd get shot with the spray. I did *not* get paid enough to deal with this kind of crap.

I pulled the trigger, and white foam filled the air. It landed on Max's back first. He stumbled off the beefy jerk from earlier and covered his face.

"Get out of here." I glared at the college boys next, pointing the nozzle their way.

Gavin grabbed Max's wrist. Together, the two of them stood—tall, brooding, foam-covered men whom I both loved and currently despised. Max laughed when he looked down at his clothing, while Gavin narrowed his eyes.

The beefy jerk coughed and spit blood all over the floor. I winced, knowing I'd be the one to clean it up. "Fuck you and this fucking bar." The kid swiped a hand over his forehead and stood, drops of white foam flinging through the air.

Gavin darted forward, but Max held an arm against his friend's chest. "Not worth it, Gav."

I snorted at his supposedly heroic words. If these guys weren't worth it, then why was Max throwing punches? *Hypocrite*.

Joe Bob came forward, parting the crowd of onlookers

with his six-foot-five frame. A beast of a man, he tow-
ered over every idiot—man or woman—in the bar. He
was my hero in a black T-shirt, the one person in this bar
I could relate to and love.

"We got problems, Lia?" He moved in from my right,
calm, yet deadly.

"These guys"—I motioned toward the four college
jocks, glaring at the one with the messed-up face and
nasty attitude—"need to go."

Because Joe Bob didn't question me, he took a step
toward the group and managed to usher them all outside.

Gavin darted my way, his pointed glare like a laser
beam. "If that's the kind of bullshit you deal with on a
daily basis, Lia, then you need to find a new job. Now."

Unconcerned with Gavin's orders, I focused my
attention on Max. Unlike Gav, he was bent over, hands
on his knees, chest heaving from exertion and laughter.

"Maxwell." I snapped my fingers, and his eyes met
mine. "Follow me. Now." I pointed toward the storage
room behind me and hoisted the fire extinguisher onto
my shoulder, not bothering to see if he was following as
I headed toward the door.

CHAPTER 6

Max

"ARE YOU REALLY THAT MUCH OF AN IDIOT?"

Those weren't the words I'd expected to hear after defending a woman's honor. There again, Lia was on a whole other level when it came to women.

She slammed the storage room door shut behind me, flicked on an overhead light, and set down the fire extinguisher. Dust filled the air, and I coughed and swatted it away. The side of my head hurt like a bitch from the one shot the guy got off on me, so I used my other hand to curb the pressure with my palm.

"You're welcome," I said.

She pushed me back against a ceiling-high set of shelves, then settled her hands on either side of my shoulders. A few empty boxes rattled and fell to the floor, but even that didn't distract me when Lia's body went flush with mine. "Don't," she warned.

"Don't what?" I grinned, studying her face, the piercing above her lip specifically. The stud was silver, small, shiny, and sexy as fuck. I'd always wondered what it'd be like to run my tongue around it.

Down, boy.

Her bare stomach rubbed against my jeans, and the scent of her skin filled my nose when I inhaled. Always fresh flowers. Always so fucking perfect. My hands clenched against my sides as I fought the urge to bury my face against her neck to get a bigger whiff.

"Don't play the coy card with me. And don't *ever* come into my place of employment and play superhero again." She took a step back and folded her arms, chin high and mighty.

"Why? *You* start fights at your *place of employment*." I lifted an eyebrow.

Her right eye twitched. "That was different."

"How so?"

"It was…*outside* and on my break."

"He was saying shit about you." My smile fell at the memory. "I didn't like it."

She sighed and took an even bigger step back, her anger fading. "You really think I care? I deal with assholes like him all the time. It's part of the job."

"It doesn't have to be." I stepped toward her. Her breath caught as I touched her hip, but the scowl on her face was back. Needing her to get what I was trying to say, I grabbed her hands and pressed her palms flat against my chest. Then I wrapped my hands around her waist and whispered in her ear, "You're better than this place."

Fire burned in her eyes when I leaned back to look at her. She lifted her chin even higher in that *don't fuck with me* way I loved. "You don't know what's good for me. *Nobody* does."

"Then tell me something," I said, pulling her even closer, my hand splaying against her back. Beneath my palm, her skin was slick with sweat, and because I couldn't help myself, I slid my thumb up and down her spine, a calming gesture that did nothing but make my cock go hard. "If I'm satisfied with the answer you give, I'll let you go and leave."

"What do you want to know?" she mumbled, folding her arms between us, clearly uncomfortable with our close proximity. I knew I should have let her go, but the selfish part inside of me needed this.

"Do you feel safe here?"

She hesitated, and I could tell she was lying when she said, "Yeah. Why wouldn't I feel safe?"

"I'm calling your bullshit."

Eyes narrowed, she shook her head. "I want you to go now, like you promised."

"That's not a good enough answer to make me leave." My stomach knotted even tighter, this time because I was pissed. I hated when she lied to me. Hated it when I couldn't do anything to get her to trust me.

"I'm a big girl, Maxwell. I don't need you and Gavin coming in here and fighting my battles for me. I'm not some idiotic college girl anymore."

I flinched and softened my tone. "I never said you were, Lee-Lee. Never *once* gave you that idea."

"No, but you came here and picked a fight when I already had it handled."

"I saw that asshole put his hands on you at the bar. I was going to let it lie, but…" I ran my hand through my hair and took a step back, pulling at the ends to keep myself in check. Only *Lia* could push my buttons like this. Only *Lia* made me want to explode with every emotion known to man.

"But what?" she asked, her voice going hard.

My thoughts took me back, reminding me what she hadn't heard from that *idiot punk kid*. I closed my eyes, willing the rage away, fighting with what I *wanted* to say versus what I *needed* to say instead.

I didn't want to tell her what that guy said, but because I kept nothing from this girl—because she needed this knowledge to prepare herself in case something happened when I wasn't around—I told her anyway. "Those guys, Lee-Lee… They said shit, planned on coming after you after work. I heard them talking about it."

She froze. "Oh."

"That's what you say when I tell you some guys were planning on doing God only knows what to you?"

I pulled her closer by the shoulders this time, slowly lowering my hands to her upper arms. Goose bumps pebbled her pretty skin as I slid my palms down to her elbows, proof that what I said affected her, regardless of her don't-give-a-shit attitude.

"Just stop, okay?" She lifted her finger and pressed it to my lips, those eyes I dreamed of night after night locked with mine. "Guess it's high time I start paying you back for some of what I owe you. First bail, now…this?"

"What?" I jerked my head back, confused. "What you owe me? You don't owe me sh—"

And that's when she kissed me.

Fingers in my hair, lips parting, tongue dancing…

Holy. Hell.

Lia fucked with her mouth, and it was the hottest thing I'd ever done in my life.

She moaned. I might've too. Wet, sweet, hot…everything I'd ever imagined our kisses could be. I bit down on her lip, her fingers grazing my neck, digging into my skin, then my hair. I lowered my hands to her ass and squeezed, jerking her close, grinding my cock against her stomach.

More, more, more. I need more.

Fingers aching, I tucked my hands into the back of her shorts, finding the string of her thong. I tugged it aside, damn near ripping it with my fingers. Our teeth rammed together, my body wound up, hers pliant.

This was it. Our moment. The one I'd been dying for. The one that showed me she wanted me too—that I wasn't losing my mind after all. This was the moment when everything changed.

That is, until she stopped. *Froze* was more like it.

Then her hands were on my chest, shoving me back. Not hard, but just enough to break our connection.

I panted like a dog, reaching for her, *growling* at her. *Needing* her.

But then she winked. Fucking *winked* at me. "That work for you, Soldier Boy?"

"Uh…" I blinked, confused and in a hell of a lot of pain from my dick pressing hard against my zipper. Unconsciously, I adjusted my cock, forgetting she could see, that she was waiting and watching for my reaction. Maybe even waiting for me to say something charming. Which I couldn't, because Lia had mouth-fucked the words right outta me.

An adorable smirk grew on her face, stealing what little brainpower I had left. Instead of talking though, trying to figure out why she'd done that, I leaned forward, needing more—a spoiled, greedy man with a one-track mind. That's all I'd ever be when it came to her.

Before I could get another good taste, she turned her back to me, reached for the door handle, and said, "Now that's one less favor I owe you." Then she unlocked the door and left me behind like a dumb-ass.

CHAPTER 7

Lia

THE ATMOSPHERE AT JIMNEY'S THE FOLLOWING NIGHT WAS far more relaxed and normal than the previous one. The only real difference? Maxwell sat at the end of the bar, quietly observing everything around him—and watching *me* with those dark, protective eyes at the same time. I suspected he was there to play bodyguard in case those guys came back, but he didn't talk to me, just silently sipped his one beer, closed off and contemplative.

Having him so close was unnerving. Especially since all I could think about doing was pulling him back into that storage room and figuring out more ways I could reimburse him for his bail money or his misguided savior duties. The trouble was, all the scenarios I could come up with had to do with the two of us getting naked. Which I was ninety-nine percent sure he would be okay with—just not for the reason I would have wanted.

Max loved the art of *sex*, not *me*.

"You've got an admirer." Aubrey nudged me in the ribs, probably trying to get back in my good graces.

Over and over, she claimed ignorance about Travis, saying she had *no idea the two of us were together*. That could've been true, since he'd never bothered to come to Jimney's until that night. But my bitterness kept me from forgiving Aubrey. Besides that, I knew her type— the fake, convenient friend who only wanted one thing: to rule the roost and be the queen bee of all things in life, not to mention Jimney's. What she didn't know was that I didn't want this job. I was here to make some tips and pay off some bills, nothing more. And Travis was all hers as far as I was concerned.

"He's a friend." I pursed my lips and poured a few shots.

"A very *hot* friend."

"He doesn't date." *So quick to lay claim there, Lia.* My lip curled. I really hated myself sometimes.

"No way," she gasped, leaning her hip against the counter. "I bet I could get him to."

I laughed hard, not even bothering to cover it up. "You're kidding, right?" I glared at her. Her gaze was piercing as she stared over my shoulder at him.

"What?" She licked her lips. "I'm hot enough."

"Yeaaaah." Disgust washed over my tongue, making my mouth dry.

"And maybe I don't *want* to date either. Maybe it's time I try a new tactic."

I snorted. "Oh, you mean like what you did with Travis? *That* kind of tactic?" I rolled my eyes, filling a cup with ice only to slam it on the bar top. "You've got some nerve—"

Before the rest of my sentence was even out of my mouth, she moved around me, ignoring the four new customers who'd made their way to the bar, and headed straight for Max. A glutton for punishment, I followed her as discreetly as I could with my gaze. No doubt Max would be all-in when it came to Aubrey. She was a perfect specimen of a woman, and likely the one to get him to disown the idea of abstinence.

Really, though, what did I care if the two of them hooked up? Just because I had this ridiculous crush on the guy didn't mean it'd ever turn into anything. I wasn't his type, for one. Then there was the case of my brother beating his ass if he so much as thought about kissing me. There again, he *was* still alive, and we *had* kissed.

I mean, it wasn't even that good of a kiss. Not life altering in any sense, even though it was hot and new and…nice. And the way I kept thinking about how obviously skilled Max was with his tongue and his hands didn't mean squat. If anything, the kiss had been messy and rushed. Too hard, like neither of us could get enough.

Ugh. Who was I trying to kid? I'd loved every single moment of that storage room kiss. I wanted to do it again—over and over and over. In fact, there's no way I'd *ever* be able to go back into that closet without thinking about that kiss. Remembering the way he smelled, the way he tasted. The way he'd bitten down on my lips and grabbed my—

"You gonna get my drink anytime soon, lady?"

I blinked, staring at the keg as beer flowed over my wrist and down the drain.

"Shit, sorry." I yanked the glass back and grabbed a rag to wipe off the sides.

"Yeah, whatever." Rude Man dropped his money on the counter, and because I couldn't help myself, I glanced over at Max and Aubrey again.

My heart skipped at the sight of him laughing over something she said. I wasn't jealous. That achy throb in the base of my throat just meant I was content with what I was seeing. Aubrey leaned over the bar, the top of her shirt gaping wide open. Max grinned at her before glancing down said shirt.

My fingers shook against my side as I moved down the bar to take another drink order. A cute guy in his mid-thirties asked for a rum and Coke. I took his order, smiled, and flirted, pretending that what was happening to my left did not make me want to throw up in my mouth.

"Thanks, sweetie." His hand settled on top of mine. "What do you say you and I spend some time together after your shift?" He licked his lips.

Resisting the urge to shudder, I said, "Thanks, but I'm seeing someone."

"Don't see him anywhere around now. I'm sure I can show you a good time." He winked, and I tugged my hand back harder, only to have his nails bite into my skin.

There were two ways this could go: (a) I could motion Joe Bob over and make him take care of this grabby ass, or (b) I could handle it with grace and dignity—and a pressure point along the neck with my forefinger and thumb.

"Let go." I readied my free hand for option B and scanned the room. Joe Bob was outside, his dark, bald head the only thing I could see through the dimmed-out glass door.

"That's no way to treat your customers, now is—"

He fell back, his stool crashing to the floor. Max was there, his arm around the guy's neck and his eyes like a Category 5 hurricane. "Leave. Now," he hissed through clenched teeth. The power emanating from his tall form was like a shot of lightning on a pitch-black night.

"He's not interested." Aubrey casually leaned against me with a huff, as though there wasn't a fight ready to break out five feet in front of us.

"What the hell are you talking about?" My gaze frantic, I glanced back and forth between her and Max and the guy he had pinned to the wall.

Before she could answer, Joe Bob came storming into the bar.

"No, no, no, no. Not again!" I raced out from behind the bar, déjà vu fierce, just in time for Joe Bob's elbow to collide with Max's eye as he stepped in between the pair.

Max fell to the floor, completely off balance, bringing a table along with him.

I dropped to my knees beside him. "God, Max, don't you ever just mind your own business?" I tilted his head back to get a better look at his face, cringing at his already swollen lid.

"You're still talking to me…" He grinned at me like there wasn't a chance his eye socket was shattered.

"You just got punched in the face, and *this* is what you're asking me?" I couldn't help but laugh.

"He hurting you, Lia?"

I shook my head at Joe Bob. "No, he was protecting me. The other guy though…" I glanced around to look for the asshole, but he was nowhere to be found.

Max touched my chin and pulled my gaze back to meet his. "You good, Lee-Lee?"

God, I both loved and hated his nickname for me.

"I should be asking you the same thing." I tugged him to his feet and turned toward Joe Bob. "And you elbowed the wrong guy."

Joe Bob ran his beefy hand over his face. "Sorry, man." He looked at Max, who nodded, far too relaxed for his own good.

Max laced his fingers through mine. A jolt of electricity traveled up my arm at the intimate touch, but I ignored it and pulled him behind me. Along the way, I took off my apron and filled it with ice behind the bar, tying the ends together with the extra hair tie hanging around my wrist. It was the only time I let go of his hand.

"In here." I motioned for Max to go first into Patricia's office, and then shut the door behind us.

"Big guy in there's got quite the elbow shot." Max chuckled and propped himself up on top of the desk.

I frowned and moved closer to press the makeshift ice pack to his eye. He winced but didn't push me away. "He was just doing his job." The skin around his eye was already an ugly red and swollen. But what bothered me the most was the nonchalant smile on Max's lips the entire time he sat there looking at me. I shifted from foot to foot, unnerved as always by being this close to him.

"You've got to stop doing this." I finally took a step back.

He took over the ice duties, a scowl on his face. "Stop what, protecting you? This place is a piece of garbage, and I don't get why you subject yourself to this when—"

"At least I *have* a job." I huffed and looked down

at the black-and-white tile, too chicken to watch his reaction.

"What's that supposed to mean?" he asked.

"It means at least I'm *trying* to…you know, make something of myself."

His lip curled. "By working here."

I nodded, suddenly defenseless.

"You're kidding me, right?" His words angry, cold. Not at all what I expected.

"What's there to kid about? I mean, God knows you don't take the initiative to keep a job for longer than a month."

Besides his lack of life motivation, Max didn't understand what it was like to have to work for money. From what I'd learned over the course of the past year, he was swimming in cash since his father's death. Always aloof, Max never took anything seriously. Never seemed to *want* to make something of himself either. He lived in his own personal state of *fuck off* ninety percent of the time. Whether it mattered or not, I hated that about him, especially when I knew that, deep down, he really was a smart, funny, incredible guy with loads of potential to do whatever he wanted, be whatever he wanted.

I looked up from the floor, finding fire in his eyes and a cruel tilt to his lip that had me cringing.

"You have no idea what I've been through in life." He stood, the wood of the desk creaking beneath him. "Like, how I lived on the streets of Nashville for nearly a year with my ma just so we didn't have to fucking stay with an abusive, alcoholic father?" He dropped the ice on the desk and the apron split open, letting pieces fall and scatter on the floor.

I cringed, regret sucker punching me square in the stomach. "I didn't know." I reached for his arm, but he jerked away. "I'm sor—"

"You also didn't know that I dropped out of high school just so I could get a job and help take care of my mama."

I stared at his chest and then focused my shame on the floor once more. He wore a pair of leather-strapped flip-flops, khaki shorts, and a dark-blue polo tonight. He was the epitome of a relaxed guy with no issues. Yet everything he was telling me contradicted that impression.

Did I not know the real Max after all?

"Then there was the time my father beat me so bad I wound up in the hospital for three days. Had to get my jaw wired shut, but I didn't dare say what happened for fear he'd hurt Ma worse than me."

"Max, please—" Tears clouded my vision.

"Doesn't matter." He looked past me toward the wall. "You've passed judgment. No point in revoking it when I know how you really feel." He crunched through the ice mess on the floor as he headed toward the door. I watched, my eyes dripping tears as I imagined the cold cubes beneath his feet becoming my heart.

"Max, wait." I held my breath.

He stopped, one hand curled over the doorknob.

I counted to five in my head, trying to gain the courage I needed to speak. A simple *I'm so sorry* or *I didn't know* or even *You never mentioned that to me before* would've been perfect. Yet before I could say anything, he turned back around to face me, his eyes filled with regret as he said, "I won't be back after tonight. Trust me."

I leaned my head against the wall and stared up at the

lights for a good five minutes after he was gone. There, I cried for Maxwell, for the boy who'd gone through so much. Then I cried for my own idiot self. For my hardened heart and inability to hold back my anger. I hated who I'd become these last five years. Hated that I couldn't be old me *and* new me combined. Old me never would have said the things I did to Maxwell. Old me would have had a heart, been open and understanding… Old me wouldn't have passed judgment.

Then again, old me had nearly ruined her—*our*—life.

CHAPTER

Lia

THE CARINTHIA RIVER FEST WAS ONE LOCAL TRADITION I could get behind. I'd been attending every May for as far back as I could remember. I loved everything about this event. The smells, the sounds, the food and carnival rides, even the sketchy ones. Craft booths sat to the left side of the bike path we walked down, while to our right, playground equipment and picnic tables filled the space. Boats and Jet Ski engines echoed along the Mississippi River, both making waves that crashed on the rocky edges of the shore.

This festival marked the beginning of summer, everyone in the community coming together to celebrate our small town's biggest hubbub. Normally, I relished this time, the warm spring air, the sight of geese and ducks herding their babies into the water.

Yet for the first time in all the years I could recall coming here, something was missing. And as much as I hated to admit it, I knew it was the fact that Max—who was currently ten steps ahead of us, nose buried in the hair of one of his zillion admirers, acting as though I no longer existed.

It'd been a week and two days since the two of us had our falling-out at Jimney's. Nine long days I'd spent trying to figure out how to bring up our conversation and apologize for being a bitch and saying what I did. Nine even longer days of him avoiding me every time I stopped by his place. Now we were finally in the same vicinity, yet every time I opened my mouth to talk to him, he'd run off and flirt with some random girl, or—worse yet—pretend I wasn't alive.

Not only was it pissing me off, but it was making me binge eat carney food.

"Jesus, Sis, you hungry?" Collin laughed and pointed a finger just below the V of my vintage blue Spider-Man T-shirt. "You're a mess." Blue eyes like mine crinkled at the corners in amusement. I was more than thankful he was oblivious to the tension between me and his best friend. I'd never want to mess up their friendship, no matter what kind of beef Maxwell and I had.

Frowning, I looked at my shirt, noting the blotch of ketchup that'd just annihilated the front. "Shit."

"Language," Colly mumbled, nodding his head back at my niece, who was sitting on his shoulders, squealing as she pointed a finger at the Ferris wheel to our right.

"Sorry." Like a petulant child, I slammed my corn dog stick into a nearby garbage pail, then crossed my arms as I looked again at Max.

The girl he was suddenly so accommodating to had her head tilted up in a laugh. Gorgeous brown hair fell down her back, curling at the ends, kind of how mine used to. Her body had curves for miles, while I was flat as a board, with A cups and no ass. Didn't matter though. I wouldn't dare compare myself to one of Max's conquests.

"Leave her be." Addie told Collin, tucking her arm through mine. "She's had a long day."

That I had. I'd picked up some extra hours at Java Java's and was up at the crack of dawn baking baguettes and scones yesterday and today. Normally, this wouldn't be an issue, but the fact that I had been working at Jimney's as well really put a damper on all things sleep. Still, that wasn't my only reason for being so off-kilter.

"I want cotton candy. Pink." I pouted, lip puffed out like Chloe's.

"You're gonna be sick." Addie laughed.

I looked at my closest girlfriend and deadpanned, "Bring it."

"Do you think you might be binging for a reason?" she whispered in my ear, jerking her chin in the direction of my current state of woe.

I frowned. "No."

"Liar." She grinned knowingly, then steered me toward the sweets trailer, while Collin and Gavin headed inside the carnival, along with my niece, claiming the need to win some stuffed animals for Beaner.

In the window of the battered trailer sat promises of all things fatty and delicious. Deep-fried Twinkies, funnel cakes, ice cream, candy apples, and most importantly, cotton candy.

Pushing my money away when we approached the open window, Addie gave the worker a twenty, buying my cotton candy and a funnel cake for herself.

"You know you can make this all go away by walking over to him now. He won't turn you away when Collin is right there," she said.

"I've tried all evening, if you haven't noticed." We headed into the festival to find the guys, the two of us shoving food in our mouths like our lives depended on it.

"What happened between you two?" Addie used her finger to scoop up some powdered sugar.

"Long story that ends with me calling him out on his constant lack of employment and him walking out on me." Though our issues had started before that, I couldn't bring myself to admit how long I'd been hurting. Not out loud, at least.

"Lia…" Addie shook her head, her voice filled with sadness.

"I know, I know." I tore more cotton candy off the stick and popped it in my mouth, not even able to enjoy it. "But he's been coming into the bar and fighting with any guy who even breathes at me wrong." I scrunched my nose. "It's annoying and he wasn't taking the hint, so I had to improvise other ways to get him to go."

"And how old are you again?" Addie quirked a brow.

"Don't remind me." I groaned. "It was stupid and I was being a fool, end of story."

Silence passed between us as we made our way through the crowd toward the guys and Chloe. Just when I thought the subject had been dropped, Addie piped in again, the forever fixer on an obvious mission.

"Has something happened to make him feel the need to be so protective of you lately?" She pulled me to a stop and searched my face. "Is it Travis? I know you two broke up, but I never got the whole story."

My cheeks grew hot, yet the answer wouldn't come. If she found out I'd spent the night in jail, she'd tell Collin. Neither she nor my brother needed my extra drama when they'd just figured out their own.

"No, everything's…" Before I could reply with another lie, Max walked right into our path toward Collin, Gav, and Chloe.

In all my very ashamed glory, I watched, lips curling into a frown, as he shoved a small piece of paper into his pocket. It was a phone number, no doubt. The stupid grin lighting his profile made that fact well known. I gritted my teeth, finding it extremely hard to believe that he'd put his overactive sex life on hold when he'd been so actively flirting with everything in a skirt tonight.

"Lia?"

"Huh?" I blinked, meeting Addie's questioning stare again. "Oh. No, nothing's happened. I'm fine." I waved her off, almost forgetting what she'd asked. Instead, my gaze drifted back toward Max. "Max is just…"

Protecting me?

Annoying me?

Making my head spin with thoughts I shouldn't be having when I needed to be getting my shit together? My debt. My diploma. Then, somewhere along the way, my life too.

"Never mind." I waved my answer away and started toward our group.

With a sigh, Addie followed, greeting my brother with a kiss on the cheek. He and Gavin were riled up in a head-to-head battle of Skee-Ball.

With his hands in the pockets of his khaki shorts, Max made goofy faces at Chloe before turning to face

Addie, not me. "Gonna go get some beers for the boys, Short Stuff. You up for one?" His hair stuck up at all different angles as he ran his fingers through it. He looked like porn star meets Abercrombie model, and I absolutely hated it. I hated it because looking at him made my insides dip and my lady parts warm. Max was too insanely gorgeous for his own good. That was one fact I could never deny.

"Nah, I'm good." Addie looked at me, her eyes wide as she jerked her head toward Max. "*Lia?* Do you need anything?"

I frowned, my insides still doing twists and dives like an Olympian on the high board as I met Max's stare. "Yeah, um…I'll take—"

"I'll be right back then." With a salute aimed at his friends and a wink directed toward Addie, both while completely ignoring me, Max took off, practically skipping over to the beer tent.

"Jerk," I grumbled under my breath, watching him go.

Addie laid her head on my shoulder, stuffing her mouth full of funnel cake as she said, "He's in love with you, and you hurt his feelings. He doesn't know what to do with himself."

An unladylike snort slipped out of my nose as I shoved more cotton candy between my lips. "Max Martinez wouldn't know love if it bit him in the ass." And with me at that? Hell no. Not possible.

My crush on Max had been innocent at first. I'd barely remembered what he looked like the night he carried me out of that frat house, but I'd memorized the warmth of his arms. The way they'd promised me safety when, moments before, I'd been ready for the world to

suck me away completely. It was classic hero worship
that had lasted the entire time he was overseas with my
brother and Gavin. But at the same time, remembering
his heroics had helped keep me focused on my healing.

It took months for the nightmares to go away. Months
for my broken hand to heal—the one I'd gotten when I
tried to fight back against my attacker. My attacker had
once been the cute guy down the hall in my apartment
building. He'd been flirting with me for weeks before
I'd finally caved and went out with him that night.

It was a mistake I would forever regret.

He told me I was beautiful. Then kissed my cheek,
only to hand me a laced drink at a party I never would
have gone to, had I not been sucked into his green eyes
and oversweet demeanor. My only saving grace was
that he had been too drunk to get his body to work the
way he'd intended it to. If he'd been sober, there's no
doubt in my mind that I wouldn't have been able to
fight him off.

To this day, trusting the opposite sex wasn't something I could do easily. Travis had obviously not helped
with that matter. It's exactly why I'd hardened myself.
Why I'd quit college after my attack when I'd only had
three more months to go. Why I'd gotten my tattoos,
dyed my hair, set out to change myself altogether. It's
also when I decided that I would never again be put in a
position where I might need a rescuer.

But the second Max got off that plane last summer,
after his time as a marine ended, my crush on him had
intensified to something far more. He was the only guy
I saw. The only guy I thought about. The only guy I
wanted to see. It was dangerous but thrilling. He was

safe, forbidden, something I could love from a distance that wouldn't hurt me.

But then we became fast friends. Friends, which suddenly wasn't enough for me. I wanted Max, and when I'd finally felt safe enough to open my heart, I'd made that known to him the best I could.

At least I'd *thought* I had.

"How do you know Max wouldn't change with the right woman?" Addie asked, breaking me out of my thoughts.

"Those kinds of men never change." I cleared my throat. "And besides, he looks at me like I'm a sister." *But he sure as hell kissed you like a lover*.

"I don't see that."

I nudged her shoulder as we walked back to the guys. "Then you must be blind."

She nudged me back. "You know, Max is a lot like your brother used to be. Collin had a strict no-serious-dating policy when I first met him. That changed, so who's to say you can't be that girl to change Max's way of thinking?"

I scowled. "And who says I'd even want to be that girl?" *Liar*.

"Because I've seen the way you two are when you're together."

"Friends…" I dragged the word out and glared at the gravel beneath our feet. With a little extra huff, I kicked some loose pieces to the side. "That's *all* we are." All we would be too.

"Nope. Something way more."

I huffed again. "Please. Enough with the idealistic coupling, Addison. Max is so not boyfriend material."

"And that, my dear, sweet Lee-Lee, is the truth."

I jumped in place, then looked up to find the man himself right there in front of us, two beers in hand. He handed me one, a smug grin on his stupid, handsome face, and my heart skipped another beat over the fact that he *had* been listening to me after all.

"Thanks." My lips twitched as I took the beer. Our hands grazed, and I failed to ignore the jolt of electricity that raced up and down my arm. *Goddamn chemistry.* "I thought maybe you'd gone deaf when it came to whatever I said."

His smile fell, the seriousness I rarely saw burning bright in his stare. "I'll always hear you."

Our eyes held for a long moment, then another... An apology was there on my tongue, ready to be said once and for all. I needed him in my life, at least as a friend. "Max, I—"

"Thanks for the beers, Max." Collin walked in between us, breaking the moment. He put his hand on Max's shoulder, drawing his attention away from me.

My heart dipped into my toes.

"Come and show us how it's done, would ya?" Gavin shoved Max's other arm, then motioned toward the Skee-Ball machine, while Chloe wiggled in Collin's arms, reaching for me. I couldn't even muster the strength to take my favorite kiddo in the whole world.

Addie grabbed her instead, likely sensing my turmoil. She tugged Beaner close just in time for the guys to race toward the game, a three-way match soon underway.

My throat burned as I swallowed, but I couldn't look up from the ground.

"Just friends, huh?" Addie snorted.

I shoved the last bit of my cotton candy into my mouth, then crunched the paper funnel into a ball as I said, "Not gonna happen."

"Surrrre it's not." She grinned.

Chloe wiggled, wanting down. The second she was on her feet, she took off toward Collin, grabbing at his leg.

I watched my brother pick her up, my cold, lifeless heart going warm at the sight. Then I zeroed back in on Addie, whose eyes were still on my face. I scowled, wondering what she saw when she looked at me.

"I'm a lot different than my brother, just so you know." For some reason, I needed her to understand this.

She touched the tat that lined my left shoulder. "You have the ink and piercings and hair to prove you're physically different, yeah"—she tapped the side of my forehead with a gentle smile splitting her lips—"but not so different up here."

"Collin and I want different things in life."

Her eyebrows arched. "You sure?"

My brother was made to be a parent, a leader even, while I was made to do something else. That didn't mean kids and marriage were out of the question; I just didn't think I wanted them for a long while yet.

"Absolutely sure."

Most of the time I loved to play the carefree card, but I was also driven. Ready to make something of myself when, for years now, I'd been hiding behind a mask. Though it had taken me five years to get a four-year degree in education. My new life goal was to be a teacher, preferably one who worked with middle-school kids. I'd done my student teaching in a seventh-grade ELA class and loved every second of it. At that age, kids were tough as hell to handle, brutally honest, and kind of fun too. Yet, they also had an innocence to them that reminded me of myself now. Someone who wanted so much, but had no real idea how to achieve it just yet. Pretty weird that I could relate to twelve- and thirteen-year-olds, but really, I wasn't ashamed. This truly was the only career where I could see myself making a difference in someone else's world.

The job market in Carinthia wasn't clamoring for new teachers, sadly. Same went for some of the surrounding towns as well. That's why I'd secretly sent my résumé to various middle schools across the state this past week. The only ones who knew this were my mom and dad. Still, I had to get my actual diploma *and* pay off the remainder of my tuition first. *Rome wasn't built in a day, Lia. Remember that.*

Addie and I watched the guys play round after round of Skee-Ball, while Chloe jumped and cheered and stole the occasional ball from each of their rows. No matter what my state in life was, I was happy the three of them had found one another.

"Here, let's get our picture drawn." Knocking me out of my woolgathering, Addie guided me toward one of the caricature sketchers who sat just outside the carnival gates. The man had a unibrow the size of Lake Michigan's shoreline, and his mustache was curled at the end, handlebar style. But his work was amazing. Charcoal sketches with colored eyes, balloon-shaped heads with movie-star hair.

"How much for both of us?" Addie asked, fishing through her purse. We sat on the stools, as directed, our shoulders touching.

"Thirty-five," the guy said, his fake French accent too thick to be believable.

I groaned and looked at my friend. "Seriously? That's too much."

"*Seriously*. We have to do this." Addie mocked me. "Look at how cute those are." She pointed to a couple with a heart surrounding their heads. Little doves swooped in the air around them, carrying heart balloons in their beaks. Had to hand it to the guy. He was talented.

"I've got this, ladies." I looked up at the sound of Max's deep voice, finding him searching through his wallet. He pulled out the money, handed it to the artist, then lifted his gaze to meet mine. A soft smile covered his bow-shaped lips, and everything inside me stirred to life at the view.

Addie faked a cough, then pressed a hand over her stomach. "Oh…oh no. I don't feel very good, guys."

I faced her and narrowed my eyes as she stood. *Don't*, I mouthed, already knowing her game.

Ignoring me, she looked at Max and said, "You'll take my place, won't you, Max?" She batted those brown eyes and twirled a lock of her dark hair. No doubt her way of getting anyone and everyone to say yes to her. "Lia here was *dying* to get her picture drawn."

Oh, the little liar…

Max nodded, immediately taking her empty seat to my right. With an extra hop in her step, Addie walked away, her ponytail swinging back and forth more the closer she got to Collin and Gavin and Chloe. I wanted to yank it out of her head.

"All right, look this way." I blinked at the sound

of the artist's voice, my body far too aware of Max's heady scent.

God, why did he have to smell so good? Fit so perfectly against me?

"You're much too stiff." The artist tsked from behind his easel. "Here, wrap your arm around zee pretty lady's waist, like so."

I sucked in a breath as Max's hand was guided along my back, ending at my side with his fingers tucked just under the edge of my T-shirt. I swallowed, shifting in my seat and instantly remembering our kiss—the way he'd worked his mouth over mine and how hard he'd been.

Warmth pooled low in my stomach, drifting in between my thighs. His touch was like adrenaline, kick-starting my orgasm-starved body to life.

"Chin on her shoulder, lips close to her ear…" I shuddered as Max followed the artist's directions to a T, the stubble on his chin igniting a stormy thunder inside me. Max seemed unaffected, his chest rising and falling at an even rate, while mine was suddenly in asthmatic mode.

"Relax," Max whispered in my ear, his warm breath grazing my neck. "I'm not gonna bite ya."

I shut my eyes and shifted once again, the ache between my thighs becoming unbearable. "I didn't want to do this," I finally murmured, refocusing on the artist.

Max laughed softly, his chest vibrating against my back and shoulder. "I know you didn't."

My eyebrows pushed together in annoyance. "Then why did you agree to sit here?"

"Because Addie wouldn't give up until I did." He sighed, far too relaxed compared to me.

I was jumping, itching, crawling with…something, yet he was unaffected. Which only further emphasized that he didn't want me the way I did him.

"Plus, she folds my underwear, remember? Gotta make sure she doesn't stick ants in them or something."

"Yeah, like Addie would ever stoop to your level." I couldn't help but grin, my nerves easing slightly.

He squeezed my ribs. "You would."

I turned to face him, our noses inches apart. "Damn right I would."

A slow nod later, he moved even closer, our bodies in sync…

My smile fell away. "Maxwell," I whispered, so lost in his dark eyes that I couldn't concentrate. The apology was there on my tongue like earlier, but the need weighing me down was even heavier. How could I ever be just friends with a guy who was likely to break my heart, no matter what we were to each other?

"Tell me why you kissed me that night." He looked at my lips, a serious glint in his eyes.

Blood rushed to my face at his out-of-the-blue question. My composure slipped as confusion took its place. Why was he asking me this?

"Because I…" I gulped. "I owed you, remember? For bailing me out and for keeping me safe from those guys."

Something shifted in his eyes. Disappointment? I squeezed my eyes shut at the thought. When I looked back at him, I knew I was imagining things, because flirty, fun Max was back, winking at me. "Well then." He cleared his throat. "That's good to know."

"What's good to know?" I frowned.

"That you still owe me."

"All finished." The artist clapped his hands, signaling he was done. I jerked my head away, trying to catch my breath, trying to balance the thoughts in my head.

"Thanks." I stood and grabbed the portrait from the artist. Part of me didn't want to look at it, but at the same time...

"Wow." Addie popped in behind me, her short frame practically bouncing as she moved to my right. "That's an extraordinary picture."

I nodded, not wanting to believe what I saw. Two people, so much like Max and me, snuggled together, looking as though there was nowhere else they wanted to be. Behind our cartoon heads was a heart, colored in pink and gray. We looked...in love?

That wasn't right.

It couldn't be.

I turned around to look for Max, wondering if that look was still in his eyes. I wanted to see it, to clarify that I wasn't losing my mind. What I saw instead had me squeezing the edges of the portrait, the paper crinkling louder than the crowd around us.

Max and his earlier brunette were walking away, hand in hand.

My stomach twisted like before, only this time, it felt as though someone had stabbed me with a dull knife. Not enough to do a lot of immediate damage, but enough to leave a lingering burn. I pressed my hand over the ache, willing the unwanted sensation away.

"You okay?" Addie touched my shoulder.

I turned to her, tears stinging the corners of my eyes. "Yeah, I'm great."

After telling the lie of the century, I hugged her, said I

wasn't feeling well, and then left the festival in a flash—
regret, fear, and desolation all haunting me worse than
the ghosts of my past.

CHAPTER

Max

Just because Lia and I weren't talking much didn't mean I'd given up on bodyguard duties like I said I would. A week later, I was back for another Thursday night shift, vowing that it'd be the last.

I knew she'd be fine without me because the girl was skilled in kicking ass. But the thought of not seeing her those three nights a week was eating me up. And whether she liked it or not, the idea of being her Superman was all I had to keep me sane now that I wasn't fucking woman after woman.

"Hey, sweetie, good to see ya in here again."

"You too, darlin'." The blond—Aubrey—was the only downer about coming here.

"Can I get ya anything?" She set her elbows on the bar top, the curves of her D cups peeking out of her white tank like they did every night she worked. She had a thing for me and made it known every time I stopped by. Too bad for her I wasn't interested.

"Nah, I'm good." I swiveled around on my stool, waiting for Lia to notice me. It was pathetic how I lived for her glances. She'd already looked once since I arrived, so I wasn't expecting anything more. That didn't mean I'd stop looking at her though.

Part of me wondered what she would do if I *did* stop coming in like she'd asked, like I told her I would. Would she care? Would she even notice? For now, I'd keep at it. Live for the moments I could have and deal with the ones I couldn't.

Midnight came and went, the night passing in a blur. I managed to fend off a few overly pushy ladies and even more innuendos from Aubrey. Fighting off women was a hell of a lot harder than picking them up.

I'd tried going home with one last Saturday after the festival, but the second I got into her apartment and had my hand up her shirt, I realized how much I didn't wanna be there. Just like the last few times I'd tried to hook up, thoughts of Lee-Lee and her blue eyes and pretty lips were all I could see when I shut my eyes—all I *wanted* to see when I opened them back up. It took the fun out of sex when you couldn't enjoy your partner.

Normally, I'd wait outside until Lia's shift ended, walk her to her car in silence, and offer to follow her home, only for her to shoot me down by saying *I'm fine*. But tonight was different. She stood across from me at the bar. Her eyes were wide, and those lips I loved were curved in a tentative smile.

"Hey, Maxwell."

My throat burned when I tried to swallow. I couldn't catch my breath when she looked at me like that—so sweet and shy—so not my pink-haired goddess with the sass piled on thick. It was the same smile I'd seen in that old picture I still carried in my wallet, the one covered in sand and nearly destroyed by the number of times I'd pulled it out to look at in the desert. Brown hair, pink hair, purple hair, tats, piercings, or unmarked skin...she was beautiful no matter what she did with her appearance.

"Just leaving, lost track of time is all." I grabbed my wallet and pulled out my tab money. A twenty for the one beer I'd nursed from eleven to one.

She pushed my hand away and said, "Think I can hitch a ride tonight?"

"Hell yes." My face went hot as shit at my quick answer. But the olive branch she was extending might not be there long. "I mean, sure. Yeah, fine, whatever you need. I'll meet you out front."

"Wait inside." She stared at the bar top. "I don't have to close up tonight, so it'll just be a couple of minutes." Dark circles lined her eyes when she looked at me again. The girl worked two jobs, all hours of the day. I couldn't figure out why she pushed herself the way she did, but if I asked, she'd probably chop my nuts off and tell me to mind my own business.

I nodded fast, like one of those bobbleheads. Not sure where this was coming from, since we hadn't said ten words to each other since the night of the River Fest.

"Okay." She smiled, and my chest got warm like my face. "Let me grab my purse." She tucked a piece of hair behind her ear, showing off five tiny ear piercings.

Ten minutes later, we were in my car, on our way to her place. For once, she didn't lean forward to turn on my radio, which was weird as hell, 'cause she couldn't stand silence. Instead, she sat in her seat, bouncing her knee up and down.

After five minutes of her rocking my car, I'd had enough. "Okay. What gives?"

She twisted her head my way, lip pulled between her teeth. "Can I tell you a secret?"

"Depends on what it is. I'm not covering for you any more than I already have."

She winced, but I looked away before I could take the words back.

"It's good news this time."

"That so?" I asked.

She shifted in her seat, going quiet again.

"Let's hear it then." I pushed on the accelerator, coasting around a van.

"I finally finished all of my classes at Western, which also means I'll *finally* be receiving my bachelor's degree."

I slapped the steering wheel, grinning, wishing I could pull her into my arms for a hug. "No shit? That's the best news I've heard in months."

The car swerved, and her quiet laugh echoed through my car. "Whoa, cowboy. I'd like to make it home alive, if you don't mind."

A thought hit me. I scratched at the back of my head, confused. "Wait. Why are you telling me and not Colly or your parents?"

"Mom and Dad know, but if I tell Collin, he'll make a big deal out of it. I don't want that right now." She picked at the cuticle around one of her nails, fidgeting again. "My brother already thinks I'm flighty enough, so if I tell him I got my degree, then he'll make jokes about me 'finally growing up.'" She shrugged. "Guess I just want to live in my own little bubble for a while longer."

"But that bubble includes me now," I said, unable to wipe the stupid grin off my face.

"Then consider yourself special, Martinez."

I did. Way more than I probably should have. "Seriously, Lee-Lee. This is important. Colly will be proud of you, just like your parents."

She sat there for a second, tapping her finger against her bare thigh, before she finally said, "It's just a piece of paper. I'll tell him eventually."

"Why, then, are you telling me?"

I pulled into the parking lot of her apartment, waiting for her to answer, when another thought hit me, this time like a bulldozer to the head.

"Wait. Is this because of what happened to you in college?"

"No." She shook her head, suddenly scrambling to get her purse up and over her shoulder.

I pushed in the clutch and parked, turning to face her as I shut off the car. "I'm sorry. I didn't mean to bring that up. What happened to you… Jesus, I wish I could take it all away. It kills me thinking you—"

"You don't need to pity me," she said.

"Is that what you think? That I pity you?"

Instead of looking at me, she turned toward her apartment, her voice soft as she said, "I'm not the same person I was back then." She paused. "I'm different. I'm finally ready for what's next in life. By doing this, going *there*, graduating too, I'm telling that girl in college goodbye once and for all."

"What happened to you, what that guy tried to do…

You know it's not your fault, right?" I leaned across the center console to grab her hand, my words making her flinch.

"I know that now." She chewed on the inside of her cheek.

"Do you?"

She nodded, then looked away as she said, "I figured since you weren't working right now, it wouldn't be an issue to drive me to Macomb on Monday to pick up my diploma." She cringed, then finished with, "I'm also not sure if my car will make the two-hour trip there and back without breaking down."

"What's wrong with your car?"

"Not sure. But now that I've finished paying off the last of my tuition, I'll be able to save for a new one." She blinked at me, innocence and fire fighting for dominance in her pretty eyes.

"Is that why you needed the loan for your bail?"

"Yeah. I would've had enough if I hadn't gotten the call that morning about owing the money for tuition."

"Why didn't you ask me for help?" I rubbed my thumb over the back of her hand.

"Because I'm not going to be in debt to you any more than I already am." She grinned but rolled her eyes at the same time. "Plus, we weren't really on speaking terms at the time."

I liked her version of paying off debts. A whole hell of a lot. But it's not like I could tell her that.

"You real sure about this? 'Cause I'm pretty sure your brother—"

"Dang it, Max. I don't *want* my brother."

I squeezed her hand tighter. "Okay. Sorry. Yeah, I'll

take you." *I'll take you anywhere* is what I wanted to say. To hell and back, the ends of the earth, the highest mountain, or the darkest dungeon. I'd die for this girl. Kill for this girl. And no matter what, I would *always* be there for her, if only as a friend.

"Thank you." She smiled. And for the first time in a long time, I felt that smile deep in my bones.

Lia

Monday morning had come and gone in a flash. Max and I had met early, driven the hour to Macomb, picked up my diploma, and then—*bam!*—that was it. I wasn't expecting fireworks or some big hoopla in honor of the occasion, but I'm pretty sure I should've felt something other than a constant ache in my chest that got worse the further into the day—and the drive home—we got.

"Why don't people play poker in the jungle?" Max asked twenty minutes outside Macomb. Cornfields stretched along both sides of the highway as I stared out the window. I often forgot how lonely this drive was, but I didn't mind the quiet, especially if it meant more time for just Max and me.

We were in his fancy Impala, the one with the rumbly motor, a red stripe down the hood, and black leather seats that stuck to every inch of my thighs. It was a total man car—the one he said he *only* took out on special occasions. I'd had no idea he *had* a second car, to be honest. But the fact that he thought this was a *special occasion* made everything in me flip like I was some ridiculous schoolgirl.

"Huh?" I asked, drawing my brows together in confusion. Max and his crazy jokes came at the most unexpected moments.

"Say *why*, Lee-Lee. Humor me."

I sighed. "Okay then. *Why* don't people play poker in the jungle, Max?"

"Because there are too many cheetahs."

He waited for me to react, his smile wide and contagious. But his adorably boyish humor had me swooning, causing my fluttering heartbeat and the tiny dancing butterflies in my belly. Damn him and his charm and good looks. The way his dark hair fell over his eyes, how his lips twitched as he waited with anticipation for me to say something. The way his entire face lit up with excitement over something so simple was an aphrodisiac in itself. Right then and there, I finally admitted something to myself. The reason I was feeling suddenly down was that our time together today was ending…and I didn't want it to. Why? Because I was terrified we'd go back to the way things had been.

"Do you get it?" When all I could do was blink at him, his eyebrows lifted as he said, "Okay, tough crowd then."

I shook my head quickly, my face going hot. "No, no, I get it. I'm just…"

Terrified of losing this again?

Terrified of losing you?

Terrified of wanting you this badly, but not finding an excuse to be around you now that I've paid off my tuition and received my degree?

Sure, I could accept his bodyguard duties, but that would be incredibly selfish of me, since I wouldn't need his protection once I quit Jimney's. But what terrified me most was that I might never be able to get over him, no matter how much I needed to.

"Just what?" He lost his smile completely, his dark eyebrows pushing together in confusion.

"Nothing. Tell me another one." I smiled at him, willing to take what I could get for now. Our moments were fleeting, but if they were all I'd ever have, I needed to cherish every one of them.

"Okay." He paused for a minute, probably to see if I'd changed my mind. "So, a pirate walks into a bar with a steering wheel attached to the front of his pants. The bartender says to him, 'Didn't that hurt?' And the pirate says, 'Aye, it's drivin' me nuts.'"

This time I giggled, partly because of his joke, partly because of his pirate voice. My lips sputtered as I tried to lock my laughter inside, but what was the point?

Max's jaw relaxed at the sound, and his eyes flitted from the road to my face in boyish wonder. "One more. Just warming up." He shimmied, shaking out his hands. The car swerved a little on the road, and I laughed even louder. "Why didn't the toilet paper cross the road?"

"Why?" My cheeks burned from the wide smile on my face.

He winked at me. "Because it got stuck in a crack."

I belly laughed this time, bending over at the waist and patting my knees. Five seconds it lasted, then ten, until finally I caught my breath and said, "Oh, Soldier Boy. You slay me."

His voice grew softer and his eyes seemed to sparkle. "You don't call me that much anymore."

I kicked my sandals off before putting my feet on the dash. "You haven't given me much of a chance to say anything lately."

He blew out a breath, the weight on his shoulders holding back his words, it seemed. Now was the perfect time for me to say what I'd been meaning to say for weeks.

"I'm sorry." I reached over and touched his knee. "For saying what I did to you that night at Jimney's. You're a good man, Max. You also have every right to lead your life the way you want to." I swallowed my regret and finished, "I shouldn't have judged you like I did."

I pulled my hand back and pressed it against my stomach when he didn't respond. Still, I kept going, turning my head to look outside. If I didn't get it all out now, then I never would. "It was wrong of me, and I'll never forgive mysel—"

"It's fine." He cleared his throat. "You were right anyway."

"I wasn't." My head spun with sorrow as I looked his way. "Max, don't you get it? You're—"

"This day, this trip? It isn't about me, Lia, so let's drop it." His Adam's apple bobbed as he swallowed, the mood in the car suddenly like a weight of bricks tied around my ankles and pulling me underwater.

When it was clear he didn't want to chat up my mistakes any longer, I decided to change the subject altogether. What I needed was to keep him talking—keep him with me in the here and now. I'd never win back his friendship by staying silent.

"How's your mom? Your little sister?"

He blinked as if coming out of a trance. "Mama and Charlotte are doing good."

"Can you tell me about Charlotte? I knew you had a little sister, but that's the extent of my knowledge."

With tentative fingers, I pressed my hand over his thigh. Like he'd been waiting for me all along, he threaded his fingers through mine from over the top. I swallowed, the warmth tingling up my arm. It was a possessive, yet intimate move, like he was trapping me there so I couldn't flee. And as I studied the back of his hard hand, the lines and curves of his skin, I knew fleeing was the last thing I would ever do.

He smiled and began to talk about the little girl he rarely saw but would do anything for. It reminded me of how I felt about my niece. I nodded and listened intently, loving his stories, loving how happy they made him as well. I didn't know much about his father, but from the sound of it, I knew Max was better off without him.

"And your mom... She's happy too?"

He nodded. "The happiest she's ever been."

"That's good, Maxwell." I turned my hand over, my fingers lacing back through his, palm to palm this time. "That's really, really good."

The rest of the trip was filled with comfortable silence broken by an occasional karaoke performance from Max. Several times I thought about keeping the conversation flowing, but I knew if I did, it might mess up what little ground we'd gained today. Not to mention I was still scared he'd blow me off again.

But the question that plagued me the most as we finished the drive home was: *Where do we go from here?*

CHAPTER 10

Max

"YOU LOOK LIKE A RUNWAY MODEL." IT WAS FRIDAY NIGHT, and Addie's best friend, McKenna, was over, side-eyeing me from the couch like I was a piece of meat.

I winked at her. "Thanks, hot stuff."

Long legs, chin-length blond hair, and the body of a ballerina with a decent rack… McKenna was hot but did nothing for me. Guess that tended to happen when you only had eyes for one woman.

I grabbed my wallet off the counter and tucked it into the back pocket of my jeans.

"You gonna take me out soon?" she asked.

"*Kenna!*" Addie elbowed her.

I laughed and shook my head.

"What?" McKenna blinked innocently and shoveled ice cream into her mouth. "He's hot."

"Appreciate the sentiment, but a pretty lady like you is far too good for a guy like me." I kissed the top of Chloe's head and then pointed at Addie. "Don't wait up. Colly—"

"Needs this, I know." She smiled so brightly that I could swear she was glowing. She and Collin were sick in love with each other. And damn if it didn't make me jealous.

I waved goodbye from over my shoulder and stepped outside, only to swing right toward Gavin's place. Not bothering to knock, I pushed open his door. He was at his desk, hunched over his computer like always. Sometimes I wondered if he ever left his house.

"What's up, buttercup? You lookin' at porn?"

"Ever heard of knocking?" he mumbled.

I grinned, ignoring him as I plopped onto the chair. "You ready?"

"You in a hurry?" He stood and shut his laptop, stretching his arms over his head.

"Maybe." More so *fuck yeah*, just not for the reasons I'm sure he was thinking.

Since our trip to Macomb on Monday, Lee-Lee and I had been getting along really well. Talking, laughing, hanging out like we'd done in the past. Only this time, the feelings I'd been keeping at bay were damn near impossible not to act upon. Add in the fact that I was obsessed with seeing her every waking minute I could, and it pretty much sealed the deal that I was suffering from insanity: the love kind.

Take Thursday night at Jimney's, for example. I'd nearly lost my shit when I saw what she was wearing. I'm not talking pissed-off lost my shit, more like lost my load in the middle of the bar with one look at her. Black strapless dress, with the three very important *s*'s that made me crazy: slinky, sexy, and sinful. It was exactly what I'd imagined seeing on the floor of my room. Then *last* night she'd worn a blue dress that was similar, only this time it was even shorter and had a zipper that ran down the front. A zipper I could all too easily see myself undoing with my teeth.

But it wasn't just how she looked that was making me crazy. There were her sweet smiles and her laughs, and the way she'd tell a story to a customer with so much expression and enthusiasm that I half wondered why she'd never taken up acting. Her heart was big, her soul was warm, and she made everyone around her, including me, feel like they'd won the lottery by being with her.

Gavin took off his T-shirt and threw it on the couch, only to dive into his laundry to grab another identical gray shirt. He smelled it, then tossed it on. "Where're we going anyway? O'Paddy's?"

I cleared my throat, hoping my voice stayed even. If either of the guys knew what I was really up to tonight, they'd call me out in a heartbeat, especially Collin.

"New club in downtown Macomb."

He scowled and ran his hand through his longish hair. "Why the hell do you wanna travel an hour away to a college town when we've got O'Paddy's right here in Carinthia?"

"New people." I shrugged. "New music."

O'Paddy's was *our* bar, the one we visited nearly every weekend during rugby season—which was less than two weeks away, now that I thought about it. But last night, I'd overheard Lia's boss tell her that she and a couple of friends were going to drive to Macomb to check this new place out. Something about Patricia's latest man toy agreeing to watch the bar for her so a couple of the ladies could have the night off. At first I thought she'd say no, because Lia didn't normally do the hang-with-girlfriends thing *or* the dance club scene. But to my surprise, she'd agreed, which had stirred my guys' night out plan into play.

Gav grabbed his keys off the table, a frown on his face. "I don't do people. And I sure as hell don't do music."

"Yeah, well, you do beer and near-naked women, right?"

He smirked at that. "Is Colly still going?"

"We're picking him up along the way."

Gavin put on his shoes, not bothering to lace them. "Then let's go."

We pulled up in front of the business where Collin worked security a little while later. The building was tall, with red bricks dominating the front. It looked like a place for suits and hooker heels.

Colly never talked much about his job, probably because he hated it. But now that he was in the academy training to be a cop, he'd grown less broody about going to work. Or it could've been the fact that he had a warm body to come home to every night.

The building wasn't holding my undivided attention though. What was next door had caught my eye. A small shop with ground-to-ceiling windows and a black over-hang. It looked out of place in the downtown area, which I liked. Oddness was my weakness.

"What are you looking at?" Gavin asked, propping his feet on my dash.

"You ever think about what you'd be doing right now if you hadn't enlisted?"

He laughed once. "No doubt I'd be rotting away at some desk job."

I frowned but didn't tear my eyes away from the *For Rent* sign hanging on the front door of the abandoned storefront. "You really think so?"

"What's up with the heavy?" Gavin leaned forward to turn down the music.

I drummed my fingers along the steering wheel. "Just thinking is all." 'Bout life and love, finding something to make me happy that wasn't necessarily sex and beer. Making something of myself along the way too. Kinda like Lia was doing.

Ever since she'd called me out on my lack of motivation and job, I'd been trying to figure out how to get my shit together and face the world like a grown man, especially since I didn't want to live off my dad's estate any longer than I had to. If only I knew where to start and what made me happiest.

Chloe made me happy. So did my friends. And Lia? Yeah, she made me happier than anything else. I loved to sing but would never pursue that. I also loved to cook—was decent at making pancakes and Mexican food, according to my family and the guys.

That sign, that building called to me for some weird-ass reason.

"If I hadn't enlisted, I wouldn't have met my only family." Gavin's face was pointed toward the window, so I almost didn't hear his words. Normally he didn't get deep like that, but for some reason lately, he'd been more emotionally fucked up than usual. I'd never call him out on his sensitive thoughts. It wasn't something we did as brothers.

"Yeah. Same here, man."

A minute later, we turned to each other, both of us shuddering. "I feel like a chick," Gavin said.

"That's because you are." I grinned and lifted my arms to protect my face, only for him to whale me in the chest instead.

"That all you got?" I choked on my laughter, knowing it'd only piss him off more. Gav and Collin could easily kick my ass if they really tried. I was a good three inches shorter than they were, with the body of a swimmer—an Olympic swimmer, I'd say—but skinny. With good abs, I'd been told. And then there was my dick. I'd been told *that* was magic. One girl had called it a wand with "special powers." I grinned at the thought, even as Gavin smacked the top of my head.

"Hey." The back door opened, and Collin slipped inside. With eyes like his sister, he glared back and forth between Gavin and me. "This is the first time in two months we've been able to do something just us guys. I'm not gonna deal with your punk asses fighting, so knock it off."

Gavin slumped in his seat, arms folded over his chest like a kid.

Smiling to myself, I started the engine and shook my head. This was gonna be a long night.

—⁓—

An hour later, the three of us were in line at a club called The Club. Collin was on his cell talking to someone, while Gavin glared at everyone who came within a foot of us.

The closer we'd gotten to Macomb, the jumpier he'd become. We kept asking him if he was all right, whether he wanted to turn around and head home, but he'd refused, snapping at us. Maybe he was having a dry spell? Then again, I hadn't seen him with a woman for a while—if ever, now that I thought about it.

"What kind of place is this that we have to wait in line?" Gavin grumbled. His fingers trembled as he ran a hand over his mouth.

"Have you seen the legs surrounding us?" I pointed out a few pairs, trying to ease the tension falling off him. "It's gonna be worth it. I'm telling ya. Maybe you'll even find someone to take the edge off." I squeezed his shoulder, grinning as he glared at me.

Collin pocketed his cell and blew out a breath. "Can't stay long anyway. I've gotta cover for someone at work in the morning. Not sure what I'm gonna do with Beaner, since Addie's got plans with Kenna first thing in the morning." He slapped Gavin along the back of the shoulder. "You think you could watch her for an hour 'til Addie's done?"

"Yeah, whatever." Gavin shrugged out of Collin's hold, pulling at the neck of his T-shirt.

"You sure you're up for that?" I asked him, not meaning anything by it.

Gavin glared at me. "Why the hell wouldn't I be?"

I held my hands up. "Whoa, there. Didn't mean nothing by it, other than the fact that the last time you watched Chloe, you kinda lost your shit."

"I'm gonna be fine," he growled, a vein popping in his neck. "That was one damn night."

He moved a foot ahead of us, stepping out of line. Collin looked at me, brows raised. I shrugged in turn, wishing I could read minds.

Twenty minutes later, tension thick between us, we were handed back our IDs and ushered inside. A black

velvet rope was unhooked—posh shit that made my skin
crawl. As we stepped inside, I frowned, taking in the
main room. The black-painted glass doors did a mighty
fine job of hiding the bones of the place from outside,
because the second we stepped through, a blast of techno
music burst through the air, followed by flashing, blinding lights and a room filled with three dance floors and
leather on every wall.

"What the hell?" Gavin pressed his hands to his ears,
his eyes racing around the room. Two steps back and
he was against the wall, crouched over and pressing his
face to his knees.

"Breathe, man." Collin crouched next to him, his
eyebrows pushed together.

"Fuck, I didn't know." I gazed around the room,
over the tops of heads, hunting for Lia. I should've been
down there with Gavin too, making sure he was okay,
but I couldn't stop looking around. This wasn't some
run-of-the-mill club. This was half dance club, half wan-
nabe sex club.

Half-dressed women and guys who looked barely
legal surrounded us. The guys in leather carried whips
and cuffs, all looking for their next victim. Same with
the girls—total kinky shit. A tall staircase led to a second
floor. People hung over the edge of a railing.

"Jesus, what is this place?" I asked, more to myself
than to the guys. No doubt in my mind, I needed to find
Lia and get her out of there now more than ever.

"Not heaven, obviously, so quit calling to the Big
Guy and help me get Gavin outta here. This was a bad
fucking idea." Collin was at my side, glaring around too.
If he knew his sister was out there in the crowd, he'd

flip. Then he'd kick her ass and lock her away, twenty-five years old or not.

"I-I can't, man. I'm sorry." I swallowed hard, with no idea how to tell him the truth.

"This isn't the time to get your fix, Max. Gav needs us." Collin jabbed his thumb back toward our best friend. He sat on the floor, arms latched around his knees with his head in his lap.

"I'm not getting my fix." I ran my fingers through my hair, torn. Help my buddy, or stay and make sure Lia was okay. I knew what Colly would want me to do, but right now he didn't need the added worry over his sister when Gav looked ready to lose it completely.

"Gavin can't *be here*," Collin reiterated. "You hear me?"

I nodded, not thinking twice as I shoved my car keys into his hand. "Go," I pleaded. "I got shit I gotta take care of here first. Serious stuff I can't talk about." My throat burned at the lie, my hands itching to grab a certain pink-haired, tattooed girl and throw her over my shoulder. "I'll catch a cab ride home later or something."

Collin hissed, "You're fucking serious?"

My jaw ached from grinding my molars, but I nodded. The words were on the tip of my tongue. *Lia. Lia's here.* It's not that she couldn't handle herself, but damn it all to hell, I couldn't stop myself from worrying about her.

"He's this close to cracking, Max." Collin pinched his finger and thumb together, leaving only centimeters between.

Chest tight, I nodded, worry for Gavin heavy on me. Worry for Lia beating me up at the same time. "Get him out of here. I'll find a ride. Don't worry 'bout me."

Collin opened his mouth, probably to rip me a new one. I was ready for it too. But then a voice sounded in my ear, and nails dug into my arm.

"Max?"

I shut my eyes, barely containing a shudder. I knew that voice.

"There you are." I swallowed the knot in my throat, ready to take one for the team as I twisted around to face Sadie, the last girl I'd slept with pre-celibacy. My arms went around her waist, and her hands went into the back pockets of my jeans. I cringed as she squeezed my ass, yet my cock didn't twitch a bit as she rubbed her barely covered chest against mine.

Still, she was the excuse I needed.

The scent of her cheap perfume and hard liquor drifted through my nose. "Ready to dance, sweetness?" I'm lucky I got the words out.

Her eyes widened at the nickname, probably because she was remembering my no-seconds rule. Either way, she leaned up onto her tiptoes and pulled my ear between her teeth before whispering, "I'm ready for anything with you." Her eyes drifted up the stairs to my right. I put on a grin, playing the role as I turned to Collin. Someday I fucking prayed he'd understand.

"Get him out of here." I nudged Sadie behind me. "Now."

Guilt racked my gut, churning my dinner as I held Collin's glare. It wasn't anger I saw in his eyes but disappointment. An emotion I hated more than any other. I'd seen it too many times in my life, which is probably the only thing that had me turning and grabbing Sadie around the waist.

"What's wrong with your friend?" She giggled, snuggling up to my side.

"Nothing. Let's go." I ushered her toward the dance floor, determined to do what I came here to do.

Find Lia.

Watch Lia.

And get her ass out of here as soon as I could.

CHAPTER 11

Lia

I'D LONG SINCE ABANDONED THE IDEA OF HANGING OUT WITH Patricia. A half hour with her and her friends doing shot after shot—and lobbing bets on who would get into one of the upstairs rooms first—had all but killed my mojo.

All I wanted to do now was dance. Spend my rare night off relaxing and having a good time.

Out on the dance floor, a pair of hands grabbed me from behind, and the overwhelming grip had me jumping at first. But with the stream of mixed drinks running through my veins, I gave into the sensation uninhibited. I was New Lia—the Lia that didn't give a shit who touched me.

"You're fucking sexy." The low voice purred in my ear. His hands moved to my ribs, rising higher and higher…

I rolled my eyes. Regardless, New Lia still had limits.

"And not for you." I turned around and winked before moving toward the other side of the dance floor.

Eyes shut, I leaned my head back and continued to move, the flash of lights blinding me even behind my darkened lids. The sensation of power raged through my body as I sucked down the last bit of the drink I'd brought out onto the dance floor. I shivered and smiled to myself. The freedom to be whoever I wanted to be surged through my system like a rainbow after a storm.

I swayed my hips to the seductive beat of the music. Around me, crowds of men and women kissed and touched as they danced. I couldn't help but watch, mesmerized by the idea of being so comfortable with sex and intimacy that it didn't matter who was watching. What would it be like for someone like me to act like that? Someone who'd only had sex a handful of times. Once in high school, once as a college dropout, and the rest with Travis. My throat burned at the thought, goose bumps skimming along my flesh. I didn't like the idea, but at the same time, maybe it was what I needed.

I could become the female version of Max.

Sweat beaded down my neck and between my breasts, causing the top of my dress to stick to my slickened skin. Being so free was a heady and powerful sensation. Nobody knew me here. I could be who I wanted to be — taunting the world, telling it to fuck off, saying I wasn't afraid. That is, until another set of hands clamped down on my hips and held me in place.

"Lia."

The scent of his aftershave crashed against my senses. My empty cup fell to the floor as I turned to face him, my mouth wide open in shock. Strands of hair fell in front of my eyes, but I saw him through the layers.

Max.

Had I willed him here with my imagination? I blinked a couple of times, knowing I wasn't *that* drunk.

He studied me under the lights, his expression guarded, our bodies unmoving but close. Dark lashes batted against his cheeks with every blink of his eyes, but he didn't speak, only looked at me with a glimmer of something I didn't recognize, along with fear, anger, and a little bit of confusion.

Annoyed with my inability to read him fully, I pressed my lips against his ear and asked, "Did you come all this way just to dance with me?"

I already knew why he'd come here. No point in arguing when it would only ruin my mood. He'd probably heard me talking to Patricia last night. Pair that with his inability to leave me alone since the night I'd been arrested, and he was undoubtedly freaking out over the fact that I'd decided to visit some kinky dance club.

When he still didn't answer me, I stepped even closer, slowly rolling my hips against the front of his jeans. I may not have been drunk-drunk, but I was feeling lonely and needy for…well, for him. Always, always him.

I barely looked him in the eyes as I moved, too lost in my actions to care. Tipsy Lia wasn't afraid of rejection, apparently.

"Come on now. Dance with me, Maxwell." I tangled my fingers in the back of his hair, reveling in the softness beneath. I rocked my hips in time to the music, dying for him to reciprocate that move against me.

I leaned forward, pressing my half-naked chest to his. To my surprise, he shuddered and shut his eyes, instantly reacting to my touch. His hands never left my waist, and his fingers never lessened their grip. In fact, never once did he move.

How long would it take for him to snap? To tell me to knock it off and drag me caveman-style out of this place. I could feel his protective instincts fighting with something unknown, something I didn't fully recognize, but was curious about all the same.

"Please," I pleaded once more. "Dance with me." I lowered my hands from around his neck and grabbed his elbows instead, pulling his arms completely around my back. Not wasting a beat, I once again wrapped my arms around his neck, the place where I was dying to belong.

His dark eyes narrowed at my move, meeting mine. They flashed with uncertainty before he gave in. And when he finally lowered his forehead to mine in surrender, I shivered at the intensity in his stare.

That's when Maxwell began to dance with me.

Hot breath washed over my mouth as he moved his lips within inches of mine. The heady sensation of the alcohol, combined with his touch, warmed me from the tips of my toes to the top of my head—and all the special places in between. Three songs passed, then four, neither of us taking a break. Sweat trickled from his temples, and my drenched hair stuck to my cheeks even more than before. We were lost in a foreign world of lust and imagination, the surroundings releasing us from being our normal selves.

For the first time in years, I let myself truly be free with the opposite sex—with the only man I could trust to whom I wasn't related. Travis had been a glitch on my radar, while Max was fast becoming my world…again.

My mind clouded as I spread my legs, taking things

further. On my silent request, his knee drove between my thighs. The barely there panties I'd picked to wear rubbed me in ways I could only describe as magic. I gasped, my fingers tightening in his hair. My breathing grew heavy, erratic, my lower tummy tight. Fingers drew me closer, and I moaned as a shot of something spectacular tingled its way between my hips.

"Lee-Lee," Max groaned into my ear, slowing his movements with the pace of the song. He pressed his lips to my neck and murmured, "We gotta stop."

I whimpered, willing us to be alone, most of all willing him to want this as much as I did. Instead of giving him what he wanted, I took what I wanted, pushing down all my inhibitions as I pressed myself even closer. My dress rode up high, my breasts nearly popping out the top of my dress. Air grazed my backside as the pads of his fingers slipped beneath, the sensation unlike anything I'd ever known.

"Stop," he begged louder, squeezing the sensitive area just below my ass. "Please, Lia. I can't do this…" Yet he didn't stop kissing my neck, didn't stop touching my legs, did nothing to prove that what he asked for was what he truly wanted.

What was he fighting against?

More than anything, I wanted to believe that his sudden need to touch and kiss me was because he'd always wanted to. But I knew better. Which meant I would take what I could get.

"I need you, Max. I need you to make me feel good." I leaned forward and pulled the lobe of his ear between my teeth. At my bold move, something inside him seemed to snap.

With a growl, he nudged me back, only to grab my hand and tug me off the dance floor. His grip on my fingers was so tight that my knuckles throbbed uncomfortably. But I welcomed the sensation, loving how I'd pushed him to some limit. The untouchable Maxwell Martinez with a rap sheet of women was affected... by me.

We landed in a dark corner, cut off from the rest of the club. My back hit the wall, and his mouth was on mine before I could ask what he was doing.

God, yes.

His knee took its rightful place between my thighs, but he somehow still managed to shield me from the rest of the room. He was always protecting me. *Forever my Superman.*

I moaned against his lips as he slowly lifted my dress at my thighs. "Are you sure?" he asked.

With a nod and not a lick of fear, I grabbed his hand and slipped it between my thighs, guiding him to the place where I needed him most.

For a moment, he froze, the pad of his finger firm against my clit as he slipped my panties aside. I gasped at the teasing sensation, moving my hips and urging him on. "Please," I begged.

"Lee-Lee, God." Need and desire battled for control in the dark pools of his eyes. Just when I thought he was ready to walk, he succumbed to the moment with a heavy sigh and lowered his forehead to mine.

Not wasting any time, I took what I'd been dying for and kissed him again, only for him to finally dip his finger fully inside me. "Max, yes," I dropped my head back as he rubbed a slow circle over my clit with his thumb. But it wasn't enough. Nothing with Max ever was. "Faster, please."

Three quick grazes later, I was nearly ready to burst, knees shaking, pressed together to keep the moment from being over too soon.

"You're so wet," he growled, biting at my neck.

"For you," I whispered, meeting his eyes again, my lips parted, my breath heavy.

One side of his mouth curled up in that cocky smile that was one hundred percent Max. "*Only* for me, yeah?"

I nodded fast, a thrill shooting through me at his words. Always for him. *Forever* for him. I kissed him again before I said, "Yes. Only you."

Seconds later, I came hard on his fingers, body limp, sagging against him, sated…so very, very sated. I tucked my head under his chin, nuzzling his chest. In his arms, I felt like I could rule the world.

Fingers found my chin, tipping my head back. "Lee-Lee, you're…" He trailed off. His face was a mask of wonderment. It seemed I was the only thing he could see. He lifted his free hand and traced his knuckles down the side of my cheek, watching the movement, studying my face…my lips, my eyes, my nose. In his arms, I felt whole. I felt real. I felt undoubtedly worshipped, and I never wanted it to end.

"You're…" He said it again.

"What, Max? I'm what?" I licked my lips, kissing his chin.

Another sigh, and then, "You're the most beautiful comer I've ever fucking seen." He leaned forward and pulled my bottom lip between his teeth, letting go with a heavy sigh.

Disappointment squeezed my heart at his words. This was exactly the Max I'd expected, so why did it feel as though I'd suddenly lost everything?

Not wanting my emotions to win out, I played along with his game. "Comer, huh?" I grinned. "Is that a new term in the Maxwell Urban Dictionary?"

"Fuck yeah, it is."

I couldn't help but laugh, though the bubble of unease in my throat wouldn't go away. Max was a filthy gentleman who I was pretty sure held the hearts of at least a million other women. I shut my eyes when he slowly slid the bottom of my dress back down. "Let's go," he said, grazing my cheek with the back of his hand once again.

The air was cool against my sweaty skin when we stepped outside. I trembled as he looked me up and down with a frown. "You're cold?"

"No, I'm fine."

Ignoring me, he pulled off his suit coat, the one he'd worn so casually over an old rugby T-shirt. "Put this on over your dress."

"But—"

He pressed his finger to my lips, tenderness in his dark eyes as he said, "You need it more than me."

"I'm fine without it. Promise."

Lips pursed, he shot me a look that said *don't*. I rolled my eyes but did as he asked, secretly loving how little I felt as the material fell just below the hem of my dress and down over the backs of my hands.

"Satisfied?" I flapped my arms like a bird, the sleeves nearly blowing in the wind. His eyes flared as he looked his fill.

My heart skipped, and my tummy flipped with excitement. Maybe, just maybe, this hadn't been a tipsy fluke after all.

"How'd you get here?" He pulled his cell out of his pocket and frowned at something on the screen before he pocketed the phone once more.

I bit my lip. "I drove."

"You *what*? I thought your car wouldn't make the trip."

I shrugged. "Well, it did." I just prayed it would get us home too.

After I handed him my keys, he headed toward the parking lot, his hand in mine once again. I reveled in the simple touch, the calloused edges of his fingers and palms curled around mine. It was an incredible sensation—one I wasn't so sure he was even aware of.

In the car, he turned over the ignition. It started right away, but the muffler crackled, puffing out. He started it again, an adorable look of concentration on his face, only for the same thing to happen. The third time, the engine stayed on, but Max turned to me and shook his head with a playful grin. "Hope you don't mind walking in the rain if this thing breaks down."

As if on cue, a spark of lightning exploded in the sky, proving that a storm was imminent.

"What were you planning on doing tonight if I hadn't shown up? It's not like you could have driven home."

My good mood faltered and I cringed, ashamed. I looked at my lap. "I'm not drunk." The truth was that I hadn't even thought about it, mainly because I was in such a head state today.

I'd received a phone call from one of the schools I sent my résumé to in Springfield, an alternative middle school that wanted to interview me next month. I was totally excited, but at the same time terrified out of my mind. This was real-life stuff happening. A real life that could mean moving away from the people I loved most. My only friends, my family. Max too. My trust level only went so far, obviously, and moving to a new city and meeting new people wasn't something I could do easily. Not even New Lia was fully comfortable with the idea.

"Fine. Don't answer me then." He pulled out of the lot and drove toward the highway, silent along the way. My shoulders sagged in disappointment. I was losing him already.

"Why come all the way to Macomb for me?" I tried to keep my voice even because the last thing I wanted was to fight, especially after what had just happened between us.

"Because I was worried about you."

Always worried…just like a brother. Exhaustion and fear had me leaning my head against the window. I shut my eyes, not wanting to think about what would happen next.

"I'm sorry." He broke the silence first.

"For what?" I blinked, looking at his gorgeous face and the way his dark hair curled just a bit over his forehead. I wanted to brush it away, to feel it between my fingers again.

"For being so overprotective lately. I just…"

"You just…?" I held my breath, taking a risk. I moved my hand over the console, leaving it there, my fingers dangling. I was suddenly fifteen again, waiting for him to make his move.

And then he did. Fingers tangled with mine as he pulled our connected hands to his lap. I leaned closer, laying my head on his shoulder. Feeling as though the world had just righted on its axis, completely syncing everything that had been wrong in the world.

"I just need to make sure you're good."

"Why?" I blinked, willing him to say what I'd been dreaming about for years. That he cared about me…that he loved me like I loved him.

"Because…because you're my best friend, Lee-Lee."

Tears filled my eyes at his words, while regret made it impossible for me to respond. Best friends…best friends who kissed, danced, touched.

Instead of responding, I let my tears fall silently, only to fall asleep to the steady pitter-patter of the rain against the windshield.

CHAPTER 12

Max

IT WAS AFTER THREE IN THE MORNING WHEN I FINALLY GOT Lia home. The power was out in her apartment complex from the storm we'd just missed driving through, but she refused to come home with me—not that I could blame her. I'd fucked up. Not only because of what had happened at the club, but because of what I'd said in the car.

It was more than obvious that Lia had feelings for me, and with the way I felt about her, I was terrified about what might come next. I needed some time and space to figure out where to go. Most of all, I needed a plan.

If I was going to take this plunge and make it official with her, I needed to prove not only to her, but also to myself that I was a worthy enough guy to do the job. She'd been through far too much in life and needed real and right and everything I was scared I wasn't gonna be good at. But for Lee-Lee, I actually wanted to try to be that guy.

Part one was already underway: stop continually screwing women. That was a hell of a lot easier than I'd thought it could be, since the woman who held my heart in the palm of her hand was the one I was trying to change for. I also had to quit being such a lazy ass. Jumping from job to job and partying when I should've been planning my life wasn't the way.

After I got those issues worked out, I had to figure out how to ease the sting in telling Collin about my feelings for his sister. Maybe if I was a better man, I could prove to him I was good enough. Then he wouldn't piss on the idea as much.

There again, he was Colly...and this *was* his little sister I was mad crazy about.

It was noon the next day when I pulled into her apartment parking lot again. Only this time I wasn't driving her crapper of a car, but something a hell of a lot more reliable. She'd likely be pissed when she found out what I'd done, but I didn't care. I had to use my money somehow, and what better way than buying her a safe, reliable vehicle to drive.

Taking the stairs to her apartment two at a time, I made it to her door in less than fifteen seconds. I thought about using the key on her ring to let myself in, but I didn't want to freak her out. So, I knocked a couple of times. When she didn't answer, I said *fuck it* and used the key.

The door creaked when I nudged it open, echoing in the bare space. I blinked and took it all in. Every corner of her tiny place. She didn't have a lot, from what I remembered of us moving her in last fall, but this? This was sad.

One couch. One chair. One old-as-dirt coffee table. The apartment was dark and smelled like smoke—not from her, but maybe the previous tenants? I scowled, wondering where all the stuff we'd helped move had gone.

The place was quiet for ten in the morning. I discovered why when I found her on the couch, spread out with her hair over her face and a pair of earbuds dangling around her neck. A soft snore slipped from between her pretty lips, and I wanted, more than anything, to touch them again with my own. Instead, I continued to stare at her, amazed by how beautiful she was asleep. She looked like a pink angel.

My heart took a wild ride in my chest at the sight of what she had on. She was still bundled up in my suit coat from last night, with the addition of Spider-Man socks covering her toes. Adorable and sexy and pretty much any guy's dream: *that* was my Lee-Lee.

More than anything, I wanted to kiss away the scowl on her lips and smooth the worry line in her forehead as she slept. And when those urges struck, I couldn't push them away. That is until I caught sight of something shiny behind her head on the couch.

A bottle of Jack.

I rubbed a hand over my mouth and crouched to grab it, worry making my gut go tight. Apparently, she'd gotten herself wasted after I dropped her off. Was it because of me? Of what happened between us?

Even through the haze of her tipsiness at the club, I'd known she was aware of what she was doing when she shoved my hand up her dress. She'd looked fucking phenomenal grinding all over me, and even more phenomenal coming all over my hand. But what I really wanted—more than life and air and anything else in this world—was to see the look on her face when I could finally slip inside her. Now I was worried I'd read it all wrong. That maybe she wasn't into me the way I was her. Jesus, what if she regretted it? I couldn't let that happen. She'd have to know how much last night—and every second we spent together—meant to me. And I'd tell her...

Just as soon as I was ready.

She moaned in her sleep, rolling onto her side. My suit coat popped open, and...I froze. Damn. She wasn't wearing anything beneath. Completely bare, one hard nipple peeked out, begging for my hands, my mouth. My throat went dry at the thought of pulling that tiny bud between my teeth. I squeezed my eyes shut and stood, taking a fast step back.

Not yet, Martinez. Patience.

Breakfast.

Yeah. I'd make her breakfast.

—⁓—

Lia

"...and he hasn't called since?"

Loud words of concern echoed in my living room, yet I couldn't open my eyes long enough to see where they were coming from.

"I'm sorry. I should've been there. I tried calling y'all this morning." Silence followed, then a heavy sigh. More than anything, I wanted to acknowledge the familiar voice, but moving was impossible. My body ached too much.

"I had things to take care of. Won't happen again. You guys are my life."

I wiped at my lips with the back of my arm, frowning as I tried to squint through my lids a little more. Sunlight burst through an open window, crashing over my face like on a tanning bed, minus the goggles. Max was here, leaning against the living room wall, one foot propped up behind him while he talked on the phone.

Beneath my head, a soft pillow caressed my cheek and the potent smell of dryer sheets made my stomach curl. Still, I couldn't help but wrap my arm around the pillow, savoring my last moments of what I was sure was pre-vomit.

Straight Jack did not sit well the morning after.

"Shit." Gasping, I sat up. My head spun as fast as the room seemed to tilt. Bile pushed into the base of my throat, threatening to make a fast appearance. I stood, stubbing my toe on the couch leg as I raced toward the bathroom.

But I wasn't going to make it.

On the floor next to my TV stand sat a planter, the leaves crumbled and dead inside. I grabbed it with fumbling fingers and hurled the contents of my stomach inside. Over and over I retched, falling to my knees when I could no longer stay standing.

"Damn it, I gotta go. Be home soon."

There was a thud, followed by a couple of footsteps. Then he was there—my forbidden dream come to life. Still, not even his soft words or the comfort of his cool fingers along the back of my neck could stop me from throwing up.

Dry heaves filled my throat after a while, my stomach too empty to lose anything more.

"I'm never. Drinking. Again."

He laughed softly. "That's what they all say."

"Can you keep it down?" Arms weak, I lifted the planter and placed it on the TV stand. "You're too loud."

"And miss out on the chance to baby you so you can owe me again?" He laughed once more. "Never."

I cringed and stood, walking backward until my calves hit the couch and I sat down. Flashes of last night came back to me, making my head spin for different reasons altogether.

The club.

Max showing up at the club.

Max and me and my spectacular orgasm at the club, which then ended in the spectacular disaster of him calling me his best friend and me falling asleep on his shoulder in the car.

All of that had led to the following:

Me, walking up the stairs of my apartment, Max hovering like a shadow, only for me to make him leave the second after he unlocked my apartment door.

Me, coming inside, then grabbing my half-empty bottle of Jack.

Me, sitting on the couch, sobbing into said Jack, only to pass out in my own mess of tears.

It was definitely not one of my finer moments.

"Why are you here?" I peered at him from under my matted hair.

With a strange gleam in his eyes, he twirled a set of keys around his fingers. "Because I had to bring your car back." Then he pointed to a plate of food I'd missed on my coffee table. "And to make you breakfast too."

I exhaled, unwanted tears coming to my eyes over

his sweetness. What sucked was that I'd messed up even worse than usual. It was becoming a pattern. Jail time, alcohol overindulgence… Golly gee, what would I do next?

"Thank you." I leaned back against the couch, not wanting him to know that the scent of buttery pancakes wasn't helping with my current state of woe. "I can't believe how stupid I was last night."

He sat next to me and brushed his knuckles against my cheek. "You just got a little lost is all. Happens to the best of us." He smiled, the right side of his mouth lifting higher than the left.

I looked at him, not sure which *lost* he meant. The lost part where I—actually *both of us*—took part in a little exhibitionism at some weird sex club, or the lost part where I came home and drank until I passed out. At this point in time, either was a viable option.

My throat burned, as did the corners of my eyes, but I refused to let my emotions win. If only he knew that the reason for getting lost was because I secretly wanted him to find me.

With that same hand, he brushed my hair off my cheek, his touch like ice against my temples as he skimmed his knuckles over the area. I shivered, not wanting to look away. Not wanting him to stop touching me either.

God strike me dead, but I was so beyond in love with my brother's best friend that it wasn't funny. My brother's best friend who considered *me* a best friend too.

When the heart falls in love, the rest of your body doesn't have much of a choice but to follow along. Which is exactly why I needed to get that job. I had to get away from Max, or I would never *ever* be able to get over him.

"Thank you," I whispered, entranced by his stare, those dark, brilliant eyes I'd dreamed of for almost five years captivating me once again. "For bringing my car back. For driving me home…" *For making me realize that I love something I'll never be able to have.*

He didn't respond to my thanks. Didn't try to make a joke about my liquor intake and my inability to hold it either. Instead, he dropped his hand from my face and reached for my fingers and elbow, helping me lie back on my pillow, only to cover me with a blanket like a toddler who'd caught a chill.

Max was right about one thing. I had lost my way. And this wasn't some overnight turn of events either. My only hope was that I could stop being reckless and start being right again. And the only way I could was by no longer letting his absence and his hot-and-cold attitude get to me.

He jerked his finger toward the door, his eyes on the carpet as he leaned forward on his knees. "I should go. Gav's run off somewhere again. Just wanted to swing by and drop off your car."

I frowned. "Do you know where he went?" I wasn't as close to Gavin as I was to Max, but I still loved him.

"He was supposed to watch Chloe because Addie had plans this morning, but he didn't show."

"What happened?"

Even as I said it, Max's words from a few minutes ago—*I should've been there*—echoed in my mind, laying a blanket of guilt over my already wretched emotions.

"He took off somewhere. Addie found a note that

said he'd be back, but he'd had an episode last night. Completely lost it at that club. Collin drove him home, but I stayed…"

"To look after me."

Max nodded, but kept his gaze trained on the floor.

I swallowed around the lump in my throat. "I'm sorry. You should have been there for him." I wasn't going to argue about being able to handle my own. Not this time. It was a moot point when, to be honest, he *had* saved me last night.

I'd been stupid. Driven to Macomb on my own, hardly spoke to Patricia all night… How I'd planned to make it back to Carinthia was beyond me.

"Just…don't hate me, okay?" He leaned over and kissed my cheek, a quick peck that didn't linger. A *best friend's* peck.

"Why would I hate you?" I asked, watching him stand.

"Reasons." He smiled one last time before he turned to leave.

Regardless of my confusion, I couldn't hold back my words, no matter what he said or did. "I'll never hate you."

After we'd said our goodbyes, the door clicked shut, the only noise throughout my lonely apartment. The quiet was terrifying with my heart in pain, so I did what I always did when I was by myself. I leaned over, grabbed my phone, and hit the button for my music.

Somewhere along the way, I fell back asleep listening to the heavy metal sounds of Vektor while pretending things were going to be okay.

CHAPTER

Max

DAY HAD TURNED INTO NIGHT BEFORE THE PHONE FINALLY rang. Max, Addie, and I hadn't bothered leaving the house all afternoon for fear we'd miss Gav's call. We all jumped up to answer it, but I was the one to pick up first, waving Addie off and shouldering past Collin in the process. On the second ring, I had it to my ear. "Gav? That you?"

"I'm fine."

I swallowed hard at the sound of the voice on the other end of the line. It wasn't my best friend—at least not the one I'd come to know. "Where are you? Want me and Collin to come get ya?"

"No," he said so quietly that I almost didn't hear him.

I turned to look at Collin. He was already reaching for the phone. Frowning, I shook my head and looked away, nowhere near done.

"You in trouble, Gav?"

A hard breath huffed from the other end. "I just... I need some time away."

"You need us, man." I leaned against the table and ran my fingers through my hair, feeling broken for my family, my brother.

"I'm sorry I flaked out on Addie this morning." He sighed. "Tell Colly I'm sorry too."

"Stop with the sorry BS, and tell me how long you're going to be gone. No, screw that. Tell us where you are. I'll come stay with you until you're ready to come home." He'd pulled this shit several times in the past few months, claiming he needed *time* to just *clear his head*. The problem was, the trips were getting longer and more frequent, and he didn't always check in like he said he would. Not to mention he'd never left right after having one of his episodes.

"Couple of days, maybe? Don't know."

"Does this have something to do with what you were looking at on the computer last night?" It was a wild guess, but I had to start somewhere.

More silence. Addie stood and carried a sleeping Chloe back to her bedroom.

At my side, Collin leaned against the table and motioned for the phone again.

Impatient motherfucker.

"All right, Gav. We're here for you. You know that, right?"

He didn't respond, just sighed, this one shuddering over the line. Without saying goodbye, I handed Collin the phone, done with trying to figure Gavin out, and more than done with trying to keep tabs on him. If the guy wanted to get away, we'd have to let him. We could only do so much.

Wordless, I grabbed my shoes and left the house, my shoulders stiff and my back tense, probably from stress. I knew where I was headed, didn't even have to stop and think about it. It'd become an addiction to serve as Lia's pseudo bodyguard while she worked. Only tonight, I wasn't going to go inside and wait. Instead, I'd stay in my car, maybe sleep a little, and then set my alarm so I could go in closer to closing time. For one, I wasn't in the mood to see Aubrey. And another? I knew the second I saw Lee-Lee again, I'd want to do every unspeakable thing to her that I'd been thinking about all day—things I'd been thinking of doing for years.

I knew this wasn't the time to worry about her. But guilt had rendered me stupid all day, and staying behind with Colly any longer at the house wasn't a good plan. What if I slipped? Told him everything? That I was more than sure I was in love with his little sister, though I was also pretty sure she wanted to tear my nuts off—if her voicemail left on my cell an hour ago was any indication.

Guess the fact that I'd bought her a new car wasn't sitting too well.

In the parking lot of Jimney's, I turned off my car and pulled my cell from my pocket. Thumbing through my contacts, I found my ma's name, tapping Send before I could talk myself out of it. Even at twenty-seven, a guy needed his mama on occasion.

"Maxwell?"

I smiled at the sound of her voice and her familiar, thick Spanish accent. "Hey, Ma."

"My *hijo*. How are you?"

I shut my eyes and leaned back in my seat. "I'm good."

"You can't lie to me. What is wrong?"

I laughed as the sound of my eight-year-old sister's voice echoed in the background.

"How's Charlotte?" I was good at changing the subject, and Ma loved to brag on our girl even more than I did.

"Charlotte has a recital next month. She asked if you were coming."

I wanted that more than anything. I missed my ma, my little sister, and even my stepdad. "I'll try. Got a few things going on right now though."

Mama went off after that, her voice heavy with emotion, paired with her accent, as she asked about Gavin and Collin. Ma was a free-spirited Mexican woman, and one of the most important people in my life. She'd never changed, no matter what we'd been through, and I was one lucky son of a bitch to be able to call her Mother.

She had had me when she was nineteen and stuck with my father for more than fifteen years, even after he'd had three affairs and told her he didn't want any more kids. Then, the summer before my senior year in high school after his *last* affair—and not long after he'd broken my jaw—we finally left him.

It was the best and worst decision we ever made.

I'd told Lia a few things about that time in my life, but nobody knew the real truth except my mama and me.

We'd gone from posh living to staying at homeless shelter after homeless shelter in Nashville for six months straight. The thing of it was, we were happier homeless than we'd ever been when we lived with my asshole cheat of a father.

During the day, I'd sing for money along the streets, while my mama played backup guitar. At night, I'd hang out at the restaurant where Ma waitressed, "interning" under the chef while she worked her ass off for tips to save money for our own place. Eventually, we got a one-bedroom apartment, and I was finally able to reenroll in school to finish my senior year—a year late.

Bottom line, we made it through unscathed and together, even though it was the hardest year of our lives. I graduated. Then Ma met my stepdad one night during a shift. He was a good guy, one who loved her and me both. He took her in and married her. She got pregnant with Charlotte a couple years later, and I got a decent job out of high school as a ranch hand on a farm not far from our house.

Still, I'd wanted to prove to my ma and myself that I could make it in life as someone more than just a farmhand. That's when I enlisted.

"Are you there?"

"Yeah, sorry." I scrubbed a hand over my face.

"Now, tell me what is wrong with you. Is it a woman? Are you being safe? Treating her right?"

"No. There's no woman."

If I told her the truth, she'd ask me what the problem was. Then I'd be forced to tell her that I was in love but didn't quite feel worthy enough to be the man that Lia needed.

At least not yet.

"Then what is it? What is the problem?"

"It's just…" I blew out another breath. "I don't have a job. I'm living off Dad's money, and it sucks."

She cleared her throat, and I could almost hear her thoughts from the other end.

Don't be ridiculous, hijo.

Your life is great.

You are perfect the way you are.

You were a marine. You saved lives.

You deserve to do whatever you want to do.

You earned every bit of that money.

Something about Gavin taking off today really messed with me, made me want to fix my own shit now more than ever. But the words that came out of my ma's mouth didn't match the ones I normally heard.

"Then do something about it. Get a job, quit being a *bebé*."

"I'm not a *baby*." I glared at my lap.

"No, not in the literal sense. You're like a nineteen-year-old boy who feels as though he has no purpose in life. Just like you were before enlisting."

"I've got purpose, Ma."

"*I* didn't say you had no purpose. Just stating things how I see them."

"Having purpose isn't the problem." I squeezed my eyes shut.

Fuck. Maybe she was right. Maybe I *didn't* have purpose. Maybe I was just *getting by* so I didn't have to think and deal with the reality of life. Maybe I was scared of the future. Maybe I was afraid to grow up because the last thing I wanted was to find out I wasn't good enough to be the person I wanted to be in the end—even if I had no idea who that person was.

I didn't have the skills to be a professional in life. I wasn't cop material like Collin, and I sure as hell couldn't handle blood and deal with dying people like Gavin did as a paramedic. Gav might have been suspended from his job, *but* at least he had one and was damn good at it when he wasn't running away.

So who was I? What was *I* good at?

"The question you need to ask yourself, Maxwell, is what do *you* want out of life? What makes you happy?"

"Family makes me happy."

"What else?"

I smiled and leaned my seat back, imagining her in the kitchen—more specifically at the stove, wearing that black-checkered apron of hers. Her hair would be up in a bun, and every time she'd nod, dark pieces would fall out and cling to her temples. For Mama, being in the kitchen was as natural as breathing. I'd do anything to be working alongside her right now. Hands in the meat, sleeves up to my elbow…the skillet sizzling with peppers, and the homemade tortillas scenting the air.

"Holy shit," I whispered to myself—at the epiphany that had just smacked me across the face.

"Maxwell, do not use those words with me."

I shook my head. "Sorry, Ma. I gotta go. Talk soon?"

She spouted off her frustrated goodbye, demanding I call her more than once a week—which I promised like always, even though most of the time I failed to keep my word.

Ten minutes after the call ended, my mind was beyond thinking about Ma. Instead, I had an old napkin pressed to my thigh and a half-busted pencil in my hand, jotting down ideas with a stupid-ass grin on my face.

Cook. I *loved* to cook. I had *fun* cooking too. And if I

could make money doing something I loved, then what more did I need?

It wouldn't be an overnight success. Opening and running a business took time and a lot of energy. I'd have to come up with a menu and a list of possible clients, book events and advertise. Hell, I'd have to find a place to actually *run* a business out of.

Maybe that building by Colly's work with the rent sign?

I grinned at the thought, writing it down on my napkin.

The one thing I did have was money. Enough to fund this endeavor. Granted, I didn't want to go crazy with expenses, because this could wind up being a failure and then I'd be broke. But if that happened, at least it'd serve my dad's memory right. A failure of a father meets a failed career. A win-lose situation I was damn ready to attack.

My face ached from smiling by the time Lia stepped outside Jimney's a couple of hours later. Part of me wanted to jump out of the car and tell her the news... but I had to tread lightly after everything that'd happened between us. Yeah, I wanted her—Collin, life, and fuck-ups be damned. But it wasn't time. Not yet. Soon enough she'd know how I felt. Soon enough she'd be proud of me for taking the initiative to do this, to make something of myself once and for all. Same went for Collin and Gav, Addie, Ma, and even Charlotte.

First though, I needed to do this for myself.

CHAPTER 14

Lia

YOGA WASN'T SOMETHING I PRACTICED ON A NORMAL BASIS. I preferred cardio and kickboxing, exercise to keep me active, yet unthinking. But every once in a while, I sought the peace yoga brought to my constantly anxious and overactive brain. It was therapy for my muscles too, keeping me limber and focused.

But this session wasn't flowing as well as the others. And that had everything to do with the *tap-tap-tapping* against the front window by very-hot Maxwell Martinez.

All eyes zeroed in on his shadow as he peered inside. He couldn't see us, but we could see him. Police glass is how the owner, Tanya, referred to it. She called it bad karma for her *clients* to be disturbed by people outside — which made no sense since *we* could still get distracted by what was out there.

Cue Max.

When it was clear he wouldn't quit his incessant knocking, Tanya finally unlocked the door to let him inside, disrupting more than just our workout. Wearing long, red gym shorts and a tight, gray tank top, he looked very much like a guy who was ready to work out…just not with yoga.

So, the question of the day was: Why was he here?

"They certainly didn't make 'em like that back in my day."

I pressed my knuckles against my lips to fight off a laugh. Cynthia, the eighty-some-year-old woman who took this class four times a week, made her thoughts known the second anyone got close to her. Apparently, she thought Max was one in a million. Can't say I blamed her.

A couple of the other ladies giggled like schoolgirls as he set his mat—*his mat?*—out on the floor, kitty-corner from mine in the back row. Everyone was far too distracted to perform the *tadasana* with the new man of the hour standing and stretching as though this was the most natural place for him to be. I knew otherwise, of course. Max had a reason to be here…but I'd yet to figure it out.

Hopefully, he wouldn't recognize me. Not with the extra layer of clothing covering my back and arm tats. I also wore a black do-rag to catch the sweat, which happened to camouflage my pink hair too. When it came to Maxwell, I wanted to be as incognito as possible right now. Childish, I know, but what was a girl with a mildly broken heart—not to mention damaged ego—to do?

After I'd left him at *least* twenty threatening voicemails over the fact that he'd *stolen* my car, only to *somehow* trade it in for a new one, I had finally decided to just say to hell with things. If Max wanted to be an

overprotective ass, then fine, so be it. I was tired of
fighting against it when *technically* I didn't mind it that
much anymore. Well, at least when he wasn't beating or
threatening someone. Or buying me cars.

But just when I'd decided to officially let him off the
hook, he'd stopped coming into the bar. Add that to him
ignoring my calls—only to text me back minutes later
to say **Sorry, I'm too busy to talk**—and I was a teensy
bit bitter.

Okay, I was a *lot* bitter. Two weeks and we'd come
full circle again, landing at the spot I thought we'd just
gotten ourselves out of.

"Hey, ladies. Sorry I'm late. First time yoga-goer here."

I rolled my eyes and stretched to my right, the burn
in my ribs doing little to distract my irritation. Seriously.
What did he think this was, a singles' bar? A place
where he could lay down a little charm on a room full of
"yoga-goers" and then expect them all to fall at his feet?

Cynthia moved her mat next to his, wasting no time.
She was a certifiable, man-eating old lady. "I'll share
my mat *and* let you follow my moves, big boy."

A low chuckle rumbled from Max's throat. "Thanks,
ma'am. Appreciate that."

I bet he winked. It was a very *Maxwell* thing to do.

"I'm not gonna lie to you fine ladies today. I didn't
come in *just* for yoga. I've actually started leasing the
building next door and thought I'd drop in, see if anyone's in need of a little catering."

I froze, even though my ankle threatened to break
from my *vrksasana*. Either my ears needed cleaning, or
Max had just said he—

"Catering, you say? What kind of food do you cook?"

My lip curled at the sound of Tanya's voice. Yoga boss-lady extraordinaire was breaking her own karma rules for this?

More than anything, I wanted to laugh. Max couldn't even commit to a woman. What made him think he could open a business?

"Mostly Mexican food. Tostados, tamales, enchiladas…"

I winced. Okay, well, the guy *was* the enchilada king, so if it was something he loved to do, that *might* make a difference. But still. This *was* Max. The forever twenty-one-year-old who insisted on taking and breaking hearts. Like mine, for instance.

"My son's graduation party is next month." A quiet blond who normally spoke to no one in class piped up in front of me. She turned to study Max. Her lips quivered as she continued. "My…my husband just lost his job. We don't have a lot of money, but if you can take payments, then maybe—"

"It would be my pleasure to help you and your family, ma'am. No money needed. Just lookin' to spread the word." A collective sound of *aww*s and gasps surrounded me. Everyone had stopped with their poses altogether, too focused on the man behind me.

Heavy footsteps padded against the floor, and I could smell his aftershave before I could see his body. He'd moved to stand next to the quiet blond, which left him almost directly in front of me. I turned my head away and shut my eyes, willing the warmth in my chest to stop stirring. Damn him and his goodness, that silver-and-gold-plated heart of his.

Words were exchanged among the other women

behind me, and when I glanced back again, most had left their positions to crowd around Max. It reminded me of a male strip joint, all the clientele looking at him with wide, eager eyes and dollar bills at the ready. The only thing missing was his G-string. Even if the situation matched the scenario, I could almost guarantee Max wouldn't take the money. The guy lived for the attention of others.

An annoying ache sat in my chest as I watched him. Clueless and bright eyed, he grinned and laughed as the women spoke and fawned over his words. He didn't seem to have any qualms about telling the world he'd started some *catering business*. Yet as far as I knew, he hadn't told anyone he was close to, including me.

Max seemed to have had made some big life decisions over the past two weeks. No doubt he'd used his dad's money to make this happen, which I'm sure was a big weight lifted off his shoulders. Part of me wondered if *my* bitchiness had helped push him to do this. The fact that I had called him out on his lackluster lifestyle would forever cling to my chest like guilt superglue. There again, if that was the case, shouldn't I be glad I'd done it?

As I took a few steps back and silently wove my way through the small crowd of people now distracted by Max, I couldn't shake the feeling that I had suddenly lost one of the most important things in my life.

Until I heard what he was saying, that is.

"...she's got pink hair. Some tattoos too...mostly flowers. Name's Lia. Does she come in here at all? Her brother said she did."

Ignoring the murmurs of the women, I frowned. I

wasn't recognizable as *that* girl in here. Here, I was Old Lia—a.k.a. Leanne. It's the name I'd registered under. My *real* name. Regardless, I held my breath and continued toward the bathroom. At this point, I was willing to hang out in a stall until he decided to leave. I wasn't ready to speak to him. Not yet.

"She sounds like a gorgeous woman," an unrecognizable voice said.

"She's *beyond* gorgeous. She's perfect."

I froze at Max's words, my hand shaking as I clung to the bathroom doorknob. I shut my eyes, willing him to keep going, scared at the same time of what he'd say if he did.

"And she's one of my best friends."

My shoulders fell, and that same ache I'd been feeling for weeks now burned hotter in my chest.

Best friends. That's all we are.

"But I think she's avoiding me. I've been trying to find her all day." He chuckled. "Guess luck isn't in the cards for me right now."

"Aww, sweetie," I heard Cynthia say. "I don't think we have anyone who comes in here with that description. But I'll be sure to keep a look out anyway."

"You sure?" The distress in his voice had me biting my tongue. "I mean, maybe you haven't noticed her? She's quiet and sits alone everywhere she goes. Maybe she's—"

"How tall is she?" Tanya asked.

"Is she pale, or is she one of those spray tanners?" Blondie from the front row asked next.

"Big boobs or small boobs…" *Cynthia?* I bit my lip to curb my laughter, even with tears building in my eyes.

"Her eyes? What color are they?" an unrecognizable voice asked.

In my head, I counted to thirty, waiting for him to answer.

"Phew…I, um… Her eyes?"

I swallowed and twisted the door handle, my wrist aching from holding on so tight. He'd known me for years, yet he couldn't even remember my *eye color*?

"Her eyes. They're…"

My chest tingled, the waiting endless torture to my soul.

"Her eyes are amazing." Max blew out a heavy breath. "So wide and blue, like fire and ice combined, then exploded to create the perfect color."

"Oh God," I whispered under my breath, pressing a hand to my chest.

"They always steal my breath whenever she looks at me. It's kind of insane, really."

My face grew hot, while my belly did loop-de-loops inside. Max made me feel like I was on crack—the chocolate kind. The kind you crave so badly that your stomach tightens with the simplest thought of it—of him. The kind you know is so bad for you, but the forbidden pull only makes you desire it more. Add words like he'd just spoken, and I was done. Gone. Completely and utterly taken.

"You love her." Cynthia said. That woman… I wanted to hug her and hit her at the same time. Because now I couldn't escape into the bathroom like I'd planned. Instead, I had to stay there and torture myself some more.

"Sure I do. Like I said"—he cleared his throat again—"she's, um, like a sister to me."

I blinked. And I blinked again. The truth so harsh I couldn't think. *Sister*…that word was even worse than *best friends*. It was truly all I would ever be to the guy who had a solid grip around my shattering heart.

Ignoring the burn in my throat, I shouldered my bag a little higher, squared my shoulders, and left.

This yoga session was over.

CHAPTER 15

Max

THIS DAY WAS ON THE FAST TRACK TO FUCK-ME-VILLE—and not the good kind where I got my dick wet.

The girl I'd hired to help with my first on-site paying gig Sunday had canceled when I told her I wasn't interested in a little side action. You just don't mess with a guy when he's trying to cook. Especially not when there's a hot oven and boiling water right in front of him.

I'd jumped back when she fell to her knees and tried to unzip my pants. She shocked the shit out of me so badly that I wound up dropping my ladle on her head. That's when the crazy chick nut-punched me and called me a tease.

Me, a tease. That was the weirdest shit I'd ever heard.

I wound up calling Collin and told him the whole thing. After he got over the shock of hearing about my business venture, then laughed for a good two minutes about my hired help fiasco, he told Addie. At least she had the decency to ask if my soldiers still worked *after* she told me she was proud of me.

Unlike Collin, Addie listened to me complain. Even gave me the idea to ask Lia for help. Not sure why I didn't think of her in the first place. Honestly? I was damn nervous about what she'd say when I finally did call, mostly 'cause I'd been ignoring her. Not on purpose; more because I was still trying to get my shit together.

It'd been exactly two weeks since I'd come up with the idea to start my own catering business. Exactly two weeks since I'd stopped going to Jimney's three nights a week. Somehow, I was able to convince myself that Lia was gonna be all right without me, but damn if I still didn't look at the clock every night she worked and wonder whether I was doing the right thing.

Collin told me she was at the yoga studio downtown— the one that happened to be next door from the building I was leasing. It was fate, in a way, except that she hadn't shown today.

Now, there I was at Jimney's again, willing to do whatever it took to make it up to her.

"Max! It's so good to see you. I've missed you." I nodded at Aubrey, only to scan the room in search of pink hair.

I was a few minutes earlier than Lia's normal shift, but I'd wanted to get there before she did. Mostly, I wanted to prepare myself to explain why I hadn't bothered to talk to her in two weeks. Tell her I was trying to put some purpose in my life...purpose that mattered. Purpose that would make her and everyone else I loved proud.

Plus, if I wanted her help, I'd have to do some severe groveling to get it.

"Bud Light bottle, please." I slipped my card across the bar top. Aubrey swiped it and tapped it against her chest. I didn't take the bait. "Set up a tab for me, would ya?"

"You're here earlier than you used to be." Aubrey licked her lips.

"Got business to take care of, so if you don't mind…" I motioned toward the card reader by the register, not wanting to be a jerk, but not caring at the same time. "And would you tell Lia I need to talk to her when she gets in, please?" I pointed at a corner table toward the back of the bar. "I'm gonna be sitting over there tonight."

Aubrey frowned, sinking her teeth into her lip after she finally handed me my drink and card. "I'm not doing tables tonight though."

"Next time then." I didn't want to be a complete ass.

Beer in hand, I headed toward the booth and burrowed down in the seat. Trying to stay focused, I pulled out my bag and set it on the table. When I said I had business to take care of, I meant it. Inventory listing was a lot of work when there was only one person to do it. Plus, I had to make sure I had everything in order for Sunday. Plates, silverware, napkins, stuff I hadn't thought I'd need to worry about.

A throat cleared fifteen minutes or so into my work. The glasses I wore when I needed to read had slid down onto the tip of my nose. I looked up and saw Lia standing to my right, hands on her hips, annoyance in her eyes, and looking as gorgeous as ever.

"Hey." My voice cracked. Not something I was proud of, but damn. Those leather pants hugged her thighs so good that all I could think about was rubbing my hands over the surface.

"What are you doing here, Maxwell?" Defeat sat in her blue eyes, and even darker lines shadowed beneath.

"Seeing you"—I motioned my hand toward the table and shook my head—"and working."

"You're kidding right? *You*, working on a Friday night?"

"Why wouldn't I be?"

"Forget it." She rolled her eyes and glanced over her shoulder toward the bar, tucking some of that wild hair behind her ear. That's when I noticed how much her hands shook.

"What's wrong?" I stood, already scanning the room for a potential threat.

She jerked her head back to face me. Her eyes narrowed like heat-seeking missiles, and I was the target. "Nothing's *wrong*. I'm just busy. It's my night for tables, and I don't have time to sit here and discuss whatever you think we need to suddenly discuss when you've been ignoring me for two weeks now."

I deserved that. "Someone harassing you?"

"No, just—"

"Who is it? Who's messing with you? He here? Is it Travis again?" I moved out of the booth and stood directly in front of her.

She sucked in a sharp breath. "Travis and I are done. You know that." She took a step back and rubbed her hand over her forehead.

"Tell me who I need to set straight." I took another step closer, stalking her in that way I knew she hated.

She groaned and tossed her head back. "Jesus, Max.

Quit with the heroics. I thought maybe you'd finally taken my advice since you haven't shown up in two weeks, but *nooo*, apparently—"

"Lia," I interrupted her. "I know you can protect yourself. It's why I've stayed away." But now I was wondering if I should've kept at it.

"Well, that's…that's good." She worried her lower lip even harder, and I couldn't help but watch and remember what it tasted like: sweet cherries and so damn delicious. "It took you long enough to realize it." She folded her arms.

"I always knew." Needing to touch her in some way, I lifted my hand and pressed it to her cheek. Probably not the wisest move since she was working, but damn… I'd missed her so much it hurt.

Her breath caught, but she didn't push me away. "Then why did you do it in the first place? Why did you constantly try to be a hero when you knew I was capable of taking care of myself."

"Guess I couldn't help myself." *I needed to be with you. Close to you. Anytime I can, anyway you'll let me.*

Another step forward and our hips were flush, my body hard where hers was soft. The noise around us seemed to fade, and more than anything else in the world, I wanted to kiss her again. "How's the new car treating you?" I grinned, unable to help myself.

Her angry scowl was like a shot of adrenaline that ran straight to my cock. I loved feisty Lia more than any other version.

"At the junkyard, thank you very much."

I jerked my head back, opening and closing my mouth. Then I saw her lips twitch, and I knew she was just fucking with me. "You're welcome, by the way." I winked.

She rolled her eyes. "You're such a son of a bitch. My old car was fine."

"No, it wasn't. And I'm a son of a bitch who takes care of the people he loves."

Her body froze. Even under the dim light, I could see her face go pale. My heart skipped a few thousand beats, unsure what I'd done to screw up.

Eventually she squeezed her eyes shut, losing that fire I adored. "Please, Max." When she reopened her eyes, the torment in her baby blues twisted me up. "You're making this harder than it needs to be."

"Making what harder?" I rubbed my thumb along her chin.

She shivered. "This, Max." She moved around me and stepped away, flinging her hand in between us. "Us."

"What do you mean *us*? Our friendship?"

"Stop being the annoying, overprotective big brother. I-I just... Jesus, Max, I'm in love with you. How can you not see it?"

The air rushed out of my lungs. "You're what?"

She nodded once and looked at the floor, blinking, her face pink. "It's why I pushed you away when you kept coming back."

Shock rendered me speechless. I knew she was attracted to me, but love?

Holy. Fucking. Shit.

"You love me?"

This changed everything.

She flinched, a small gesture that stabbed me in the gut, but I saw her nod. Just one tiny nod.

"I've got to get back to work."

She turned to leave, but I grabbed her hand. "Fuck, no, wait. I'm sorry." As she turned to face me, her hands shot up, blocking me.

"Lee-Lee, shit. I'm sorry. I-I don't know what to say. You told me you love me, and I just came here to say I'm sorry. My guts are all twisted up." Not to mention my head.

She loved me. Lia Montgomery, my purpose…*loved* me like I loved her.

She scoffed, just as the strap of her tank top slipped over her tatted arm. "An 'I'm not interested in you like that' would have sufficed."

The table full of dudes to my right stared at us, probably thinking the worst. I wanted to jam my fingers in their eyes, tell them to mind their own business. But I had bigger fish to fry.

"I've got to get back to work." She turned to walk away.

"Lia, would you just wait?" I growled, following her as she moved across the room.

"What?" she snapped, scooping up an empty tray on the table to her right. "What could you possibly say that would make this night go even better than it already has?"

"I… I'm in love with you too." There. That wasn't so hard. In fact, now that I'd said it once… "I've *been* in love with you since the day I moved to this town."

The tray she'd been holding slipped from her fingers and fell onto the floor with a crash. There was no going back. I was done fighting this thing between us, especially now that I knew how *she* felt. It just took my brain a few seconds to catch up to my heart.

When she didn't turn around, my heart started racing. My head spun too. With slow, unhurried steps, I pressed my chest to her back. "Talk to me," I whispered, keeping my hands at my sides but my chin on her shoulder.

"Don't play with me, Maxwell."

"Never." Unable to help myself, I leaned over and kissed the spot below her ear. Now that I'd said those words, everything inside me was begging to touch her. To make her officially mine in all the ways I could.

"Y-you fuck girls. Then you walk away and start all over with the next lucky contestant. You don't *love* girls. And you certainly don't *love* me."

"You're wrong," I whispered. "So, so wrong. I'm done screwing around, Lee-Lee. Done. Hell, if I'm being honest with myself, the only reason I ever chose to fuck around like that was because I was trying to get you outta my system."

A snort fell out of her mouth. "And how'd that work out for you?"

I shook my head. "Terribly."

She braced her hands on the edge of a table, her body trembling against mine. All traces of humor slipped away as she continued, "You say these things now, Max, but what happens when you decide that settling down isn't for you after all? You can't just pick me like I'm some random letter on *Wheel of Fortune*. I'm not disposable. I'm not some vowel you can purchase for one round. And I'm—"

"Everything, Lee-Lee." I turned her to face me and wrapped my arms around her waist. Lia needed to know, right here and right now, that I was no longer that guy. "You're *my* everything. Have been for years."

Tears filled her eyes, but none slipped out. "Why would being with me, loving me, change that for you?"

My smile fell. "Because love isn't about spinning some wheel and landing on the next girl to screw, or picking whatever letter you think will fit some temporary puzzle." I held her face between my hands, lowering my forehead to hers. "Love is choosing one winning *person* and enjoying them for the rest of your life."

Her lower lip trembled as she whispered, "This isn't a game show."

I couldn't help but grin as I ran the pad of my thumb over her chin. "You started the analogy. Only right I finished it." I studied her for a second longer, in awe of her gorgeous face, her strength, and that fight inside her. God, why had I waited so long to do this? Say this? Fuck Collin. Fuck the world too. This—right here with Lia—was the answer to my prayers.

Slowly, I lowered my lips to hers, not caring where we were, not caring who might be watching. I loved this girl. And I'd kiss her for a millennium just to let the world know that, game show or not, I had won this stunning woman.

Her lips were slow to respond, like she wasn't sure I was real. And if I was being honest with myself, I was terrified outta my mine that she'd up and disappear from beneath my hands. But I kept going, keeping it slow. This, right here, was my nonverbal version of *I love you*.

My eyes opened to hers, all light and filled with awe. And that right there...that look? That was her nonverbal *I love you too*.

"Lia!" Her head shot toward the bar, nearly ramming into my nose when she turned. Some guy I'd never seen before stood on the other side, buddied up with Aubrey. "Get your ass back to work."

My lip curled. "Who the hell is that?"

She sighed. "Patricia's new boyfriend. The guy's been a douche since they got together, thinking he runs everything and everyone in here."

"Is that what's bugging you tonight?"

She looked at me from under her lashes, so innocent when I knew she was anything but. "Yeah. But I've got it handled." She pressed her hand against my chest.

I pulled her closer and hugged her, determined not to make a scene. I knew she needed to deal with this on her own, but I couldn't help but get at least one dig in. "Quit. Right here, right now. You don't need this job. Find a new one."

"I can't just walk out." Her hot breath huffed against my neck.

"Why not?" I pulled back and looked at her, met with a glare.

"Because I have to do the right thing. Give two weeks, which I'm planning to do tonight anyway." She pulled away, dropping her arms to her sides like she wasn't sure where things would go next between us.

Good thing I was.

I grabbed her hand and brought it to my mouth, kissing her knuckles. "If you're worried about money, let me help. I'll take care of you until you find a new job."

"No. Absolutely not. You've already paid my bail money *and* bought me a new freaking car. I will not owe you even more money than I already do."

It was my turn to scowl. "I don't give two fucks about money. I just don't like seeing you get treated like ass."

She blew her pink bangs out of her face, but they flopped right back over her eye. "It's none of your business how people treat me."

"Fuck yes it is." I put one hand to her neck. "I'm in love with you. And love means sharing every good, bad, and ugly thing together."

She nuzzled her cheek against my hand and shut her eyes, like she was savoring my touch. But it was over just as quick as it happened.

"Three words do not give you the right to control my life and what happens in it, Maxwell."

I'd been used to taking care of my ma for so long that it was hard not being able to take care of Lia too. I knew she needed her independence, needed to make it known to herself, and to the world around her, that she was a big girl with a big world at her feet to dive into. So, I let it go.

"Fine. But we're not done talking. I'll see you tomorrow. Then after the game, we're gonna talk about this some more." I leaned forward and kissed her lips hard, just once.

"Yeah…about the game. I wasn't really planning on going because…" Her words were so soft that I barely heard them. But they said enough.

"You weren't planning on going to our first match of the year?"

"Well, do you blame me? I thought you hated me again."

"You've never missed a match."

"My parents are coming home. I'm not sure if I'll be able to get there in time." She pushed past me and headed to another table, but I grabbed her hand this time, squeezing it in mine.

"Bring them with," I said.

She lifted her chin and smiled teasingly. "Maybe."

Before I could get in another word, she was gone, off to the bar. If I were more like my best friends, I wouldn't have waited. I would've hightailed it her way, tossed her over my shoulder, and taken her back to that supply closet again. There, I'd kiss her, strip those leather pants, and fuck her hard against the wall. But I wasn't like my best friend, at least not usually. Yet Lia made me wanna be that fucked-up caveman type. A type that wasn't me.

Still, those three words had been said. And Lia Montgomery would officially be mine...or I'd work myself to death to make that happen.

CHAPTER 16

Lia

"THIS IS MADNESS, LEANNE." MOM GASPED AS SHE WATCHED the fourteen men run across the field. "How can you tell who is who with all of their heads constantly butting together like that?"

"The boys are grown. They know what they're doing." Dad squeezed my shoulder from his lawn chair. I smiled back at him from the grass, thankful to have him in my corner.

My parents had flown back from their winter stay in Arizona this morning, both of them with golden tans and a happy-go-lucky outlook on life. It was sickening how giddy the two of them were. Of course, the last thing I wanted was for them to worry about their daughter's love-life woes, which is why I'd kept up the facade of the doting sister who was dying to see her brother play rugby, when really, I couldn't take my eyes off my brother's best friend.

"You're never too old for a broken bone." Mom frowned and took a drink of her bottled water.

"It's fine. Collin's got life insurance."

Mom gasped. "Leanne Montgomery!"

"Sorry, but it's the truth."

She frowned, eyeing the tats on my arms once more. "That is *not* something you should joke about."

Frowning, I glanced toward the parking lot, praying like hell Addie and Chloe would get there sooner than later. I'd never needed them more.

The second my parents stepped off the plane, Mom took one look at me and burst into tears. Not happy tears either. Apparently, the new additions to my body—the pink hair and additional tats—had been a little much for her to take.

My transition from Old Lia to New Lia had been gradual at first. A few highlights here, a few hidden tattoos there. But throughout the past year especially, my body had craved more. At first, it had only been a ruse, something to help hide who I once was. Now though? I felt powerful with the ink, sexy with the pink hair too. It was a win-win for me...just not one for my mom.

"So, tell us when we get to see this mysterious Addie," Dad asked, leaning forward in his chair. He looked identical to Collin: black hair, same build, and two dimples that adorned his cheeks when he smiled. He, at least, didn't seem bothered by my new appearance.

"Soon, Daddy. You'll love her." I smiled and searched the field for my brother. At least he had to do the girlfriend intro thing. That would definitely take the heat off my back.

My parents had *loved* Amy, Chloe's mother, and were heartbroken when she passed. Now that Collin had a new girl for the first time since he'd gotten home from his tours, our parents were insanely curious to meet the person who'd swept their son off his feet.

"How's the job at the coffee shop coming along? Have you been getting more hours in now that you've gotten your degree out of the way?" Mom asked, leaning forward to grab her water bottle off the ground.

I chanced a look at my dad, finding his gaze on the field. His eyes were narrowed a bit, proof that he hadn't told my mom about my bartending gig. It wasn't so much that I was ashamed of it, but that I didn't want Mom to worry. She'd be worse than Max and Collin combined if she knew I'd become an employee at our town's nastiest bar. Dad only knew because Collin had told him, but like me, Dad knew Mom would freak out about it, so he'd kept it a secret for me. And for her.

Out of everyone in my family, Mom was the one who had seen me at my worst after I dropped out of college and moved back home. There were days when I'd refused to get out of bed. Days when I wouldn't eat. The nightmares when I *could* fall asleep had kept her awake as much as they did me. I'd put her through hell, not that I could help it, which is why I did my best to shelter her about my current status.

Dad knew I could handle things now. That my job at Jimney's was only temporary until I could finally land a real job as a teacher. I'd given two weeks' notice last night, just like I told Max I would.

I couldn't continue to work there, especially now that Patricia's newest psycho was acting as the boss. He'd hit on me and called me a skank in one night. Something Max would beat him bloody for if he knew. I'd taken care of it though by letting the air out of the boyfriend's truck tires before I left the parking lot after work. I was evil when I wanted to be and sweet when I had to be. It was a decent combo of awesome, I'd say.

The good news was that I'd paid off the last of my tuition and garnered some savings to help get by for a bit. Not just from tip money at Jimney's and my measly salary from Java Java's, but also because I'd sold quite a few of my personal possessions. I knew things would be okay, that once I made a steady income, I could replace material items.

"Leanne, did you hear what I asked?" Mom put her hand on my arm. When I looked up, I found her gaze on my face for the first time in at least an hour.

"Yeah, sorry. Work is great, Mom." I cleared my throat and chanced a look across the field. Off to the side, Max stood, his hands on his hips, his eyes on me. I gave him a slight wave as I said to Mom and Dad, "I'm gonna use the restroom really quick. Be right back."

I quickly grabbed the jersey sitting under Max's bag a few feet ahead of me on the grass, wondering what he'd say when he saw me wearing it. Mom had been glaring at my tats enough for one day, so I hoped she'd be less freaked out if I covered them up.

Leaning against the back of the brick building that housed the bathrooms, I texted Addie, asking where she was. Seconds later, she sent a text.

Not going to make it. Chloe fell asleep, and I don't want to wake her up.

Frustrated I wouldn't have them as my backers, I blew out a breath and pocketed my cell. I pulled Max's jersey on over my shirt. It was long, landing just above my knees, but it did the job I needed by covering my shoulders and arms. I rarely cared what I wore, but today was different. I felt dirty, though I knew my mother didn't really think that about me.

Five minutes of fidgeting went by, and the uneasy ache squeezing my stomach refused to go away. I covered my face with my hands and shook my head, hating that I wanted to hide.

"Lia. What're you doing?"

I looked up, finding Gavin's imposing form standing in front of me. His brows jumped curiously over his green eyes as he searched my face.

I was glad he was home. But we all could see a change in him. He was more subdued than before, quieter but less angry too, which was strange. None of us could quite wrap our heads around his constant disappearing act, but because he was Gavin the super secret-keeper, we let it go.

On a sigh, I leaned my head back against the wall. "Um, would you believe me if I said I was taking a piss?"

"Girls don't *piss*." He nudged my shoulder with his own as he moved to stand at my side. The game must have ended, which meant Max would likely be looking for me soon. I wanted that more than anything, but at the same time, the pressure of dealing with the parentals *and* him was almost too much to deal with.

"You of all people know that pee and piss are the same, Mr. Medical Man."

Not taking the bait, he frowned, studying me in that unnerving Gavin way. When he pursed his lips, the scruff he'd developed over the past few weeks moved as well. He was so oddly attractive, in that younger Josh Duhamel way—Josh Duhamel meets Charlie Hunnam—that even I got a little light-headed around him.

"This about your parents?"

"How did you know?" I folded my arms over my stomach, nervous for some reason.

He kicked his cleat against the wall we were leaning against. "You seem off today. Figured it was either Max or that."

"Why'd you think it had something to do with Max?" I held my breath, not sure what to expect for an answer. Gavin was a very studious man. Aware of his surroundings and the people in them as well. He was a reader, I guess you could say. The fact that he was also best friends with Max didn't hurt.

"Because love's complicated, that's why." His eyebrows scrunched together, and he looked at me as though the answer was simple.

"Love, huh?" I couldn't help but grin. "Nobody *I* know is in love." At least, nobody he needed to know about right now. I rolled my eyes at his serious demeanor, then shoved him a bit. He didn't budge, a huge, massive force that never failed to awe me. "You're something else, Gavin St. James."

His lips twitched like he was fighting a smile, something he didn't do too often. "As are you, Little Montgomery." He paused. "Seriously though. If you ever wanna talk about stuff"—he shoved his hands into the pockets of his black rugby shorts—"I'm pretty good at listening."

"Thanks, you." I leaned forward and wrapped my arms around his waist. I wasn't much of a hugger, but Gavin looked like he could use one.

He laid his head on top of mine in a surprisingly affectionate move, wrapping his arm around my back. I smiled. I often wondered if Gavin was hugged much as a kid. I knew he'd been through a lot growing up, but I also knew he wasn't one to display his emotions and affection much.

Footsteps skidded to a stop on the cement, a sweaty-looking Maxwell being the culprit. "Shit, sorry, I..." His eyes narrowed in accusation as he looked back and forth between Gavin and me.

"Hey, man." Gavin's arm stayed wrapped around my waist for a few seconds longer, then he pulled away. His voice was coy, happy even, but nothing about him seemed rushed. I, on the other hand, reacted like I'd been caught doing something wrong—shaking knees and goose bumps galore. "Lee-Lee was cold."

I stiffened.

Max did too.

Oh God, Lee-Lee? Gavin did not just call me by Max's nickname.

"*Lee-Lee?*" Max's lip curled, right on cue. "*Lee-Lee* was cold? The girl who wears miniskirts and flip-flops and crazy short dresses in the freezing cold?" He folded his arms.

"Yep." Gavin stepped around me. "See you on the side of the pitch, Martinez." Then he pinched me in the ribs before leaning in to kiss my cheek. One squeeze of his hand on Max's shoulder later and he was gone, his ginormous body exuding nonchalance that should not have been there...but totally was.

He'd just left me to the wolves. And I could almost guarantee he'd done it on purpose.

"So, this is how it's going to be now, huh?" Max moved forward, taking Gavin's place at my side. His face was expressionless, but his eyes flashed with uncertainty, jealousy too.

I frowned, taking a step closer to him. The bathroom door was just to our right, and I wondered what he'd do if I shoved him inside and kissed him a little bit. Max was the most adorable jealous man I'd ever seen.

"What do you mean?" I blinked, playing innocent.

He scowled down at the cement and slid his hands into the pockets of his rugby shorts. "Come on, now. You know what I meant."

My lips twitched. I pressed a finger under his chin and lifted his face. "You're not jealous of Gavin, are you?"

"No." He shifted in place and shrugged.

"Liar." I pulled my lower lip between my teeth to hide my smile.

He scowled and reached for me, tugging me close by the bottom of his jersey. "What's this, by the way?" he asked, changing the subject.

"The coat of armor against my mother." I folded my arms, losing my good mood. "She's not too hip on my new ink, apparently."

"I like seeing you in my jersey." He pressed one hand on my hip and used the other to trace one of the tats peeking out from the neck of his jersey. "I also love Mrs. M, but if she doesn't like your tats, then screw her."

"Easier said than done." I snorted.

He narrowed his eyes. "Those tattoos are everything you are as a person now, Lee-Lee. And represent everything I'm in love with."

Tears filled my eyes at his sweet words. The kind of tears that had me smiling at the same time. Only Max could rock my world with a few simple words, making me feel as though something that was so big and imposing seconds before was minimal. A glitch in the road of life.

"You're amazingly charming when you want to be, Maxwell." I moved closer, wrapping my arms around his neck.

He dropped his chin, wiggling his eyebrows as he said, "Charming enough for you to want to get in a quickie inside the bathroom?"

I laughed, then stood on my tiptoes to kiss him. "You're also incorrigible."

"Can't blame a guy for trying, right?" He nuzzled my neck and wrapped his arms around my waist.

I shut my eyes and sighed. Max's arms were my new comfort, and in them, I felt as though I could take on the world and say stuff I wouldn't normally say. Not that I was afraid to speak my mind. But I wasn't one for the serious emotional stuff, all of which had been plaguing me since last night's declaration.

As much as I'd have loved to jump into bed with him, to start this relationship off with a literal bang, I realized that a lot of things were still unsaid between us. Things I needed him to clear up before we took that next step.

"You good?" he asked, pulling back, uncertainty now clouding his eyes as they roamed over my face. "I was kidding, by the way. There's no rush to…you know…" His cheeks went pink, a very un-Maxwell quirk. "We've got our whole lives to be with each other like that."

"*That's* not going to be a problem. Trust me."

Thankfully, the fact that I was attacked in college never kept me from wanting intimacy with a man. It took some time to emotionally heal from that night, but I was left more with my mistrust in the opposite sex than anything.

"Then what is it?" He pulled his arms from around my waist and cupped my cheeks. "What's wrong? Tell me."

I blew out a breath, knowing there was no way around telling him. So, I just spit it out. All three words. "I'm terrified, Max."

Max

I blinked, taken aback by her words. "Of me?"

"No, no. Not you, per se, just *this*." She motioned a hand between us. "Us."

I blew out a breath, relieved I hadn't done something to fuck up already. "Oh. Well, hell, Lee-Lee. Don't worry. You're not the only one who's scared." I dropped my hands from her face and grabbed her hands instead.

"As far as I can tell, you're not scared of anything." She shrugged, chewing on her bottom lip.

I tapped the end of her nose with a finger. "And that's exactly where you're wrong."

I was scared for a lotta reasons when it came to us. What if I fucked up without meaning to? What if I unintentionally hurt her? And most of all, what if she decided I wasn't what she wanted after all?

"How so?" she asked. "Tell me so I don't feel like the only fool here."

I swallowed, willing to admit all my flaws if it made her feel even a little less terrified. "I'm not perfect,

Lee-Lee. I'm inevitably gonna fuck something up. But you're the first—the *only*—woman I've ever wanted to try to be better for. You get me?"

"I get you." She smiled, but didn't hesitate to add, "But there's one more thing you need to know."

"What's that?" I asked.

"I know about your business." She reached up with her free hand and brushed a piece of my hair off my forehead. "And I want you to know that I'm so proud of you."

My heart grew about ten sizes at her words. For the first time in four years—maybe even longer than that—I almost felt worthy of something other than drinking, sex, and rugby. And damn, did it feel good.

"I'm sorry I didn't tell you about it right away."

"I'm not your keeper." She folded her arms. "You don't have to tell me everything all the time."

"No. But you're half the reason I wanted to do this in the first place. You should've been the first person I told."

"Because of what I said…" Her face went red, and shame gathered in her eyes. I hated seeing it there.

"You said what I needed to hear." I leaned forward again, pressing my forehead to hers. "I needed to prove to you that I wasn't some slacker who fucked around with things in life anymore."

"Why?" Her voice was soft and smelled like peppermint.

"Because I'm fucking crazy about you." I lowered my mouth, kissing her forehead, only to pull back and say, "I *love* you."

She smiled, a slow curve of her lips that had me almost falling to my knees in devotion. "I love you too."

"Fuck yeah." I dropped my hand from her face and wrapped both arms around her waist. She squealed as I hiked her legs up around my body, then giggled as I spun us in circles.

"Maxwell Martinez, I never thought I'd see this day." She sighed against the curve of my neck, fingers running through my sweaty hair with slow strokes in the back.

"And all it took was you." I pulled back just enough to kiss her, sealing the deal while getting a taste of her sweet lips. She moaned, and I'm pretty sure I did too, only for a whistle to sound from the pitch, signaling the start of the next match. I didn't want to let her go. It was the first time in months that the draw of the game, the time with my guys, and the promise of competition didn't pull me in.

"I've got a catering gig tomorrow. My first *paid* job. Think you can spare an afternoon and be my assistant?"

She kissed my chin, then my cheek. "I would be honored."

"Then afterward, maybe we could go to your apartment and hang out, watch movies or something."

"Like a date…"

"Yeah. A date." Not that it was an ideal one.

"Sure." Dark-as-sin lashes batted against her pink cheeks as she glanced up at me. "And if you need any more help over the next few weeks, I can be that girl for you, since I only have one other job now."

"You really quit Jimney's?" Excitement had my heart beating faster. I set her down on the ground again but kept hold of her hands.

"Yep. Figured I'd overstayed my limit there anyway." She scrunched up her nose.

"So what…you wanna work with me full-time then? At least 'til you find yourself a better-paying job? Because I could use another set of hands for a lot longer than a few weeks."

"I'd love to help. You, me, doing the chef thing…"

"The chef thing, huh?" I couldn't help but grin.

Gone was any hesitation. In its place was a woman who knew exactly what she wanted. And for some reason, she wanted me. I'd always been the fucked-up, goofy kid who didn't take things seriously. But now? Seeing her look at me this way? It made everything disappear. Made me feel like I was important. Most of all, she made me feel like I had some sort of purpose. And that was the most incredible feeling I'd ever had.

CHAPTER 17

Max

HAPPINESS CAME IN THE FORM OF LIA GRINNING WHILE wearing a white apron as she tied up garbage bags and did dishes inside a church kitchen. Happiness was also watching her and knowing she was mine.

"That's it, Enchilada Man. Catering gig number one is done." She winked at me, tying the last of the garbage bags as she set them by the exit. Rubbing her hand over the yellow bandanna she wore on her head, she smiled wide and moved my way.

"Enchilada Man, eh?" I grinned, yanking the last of the foil off the roll to cover the leftovers. I planned to take them to the women's shelter near my building.

"I think I like this pet name stuff. Can I call you Burrito Hottie?" I walked around the table and wrapped my arm around her waist.

"Hmm… I think I'd like it if you called me the Tostada Princess instead. I'm filled with layers that you can peel off and eat one by one."

"I can deal with layers." Balls tight, knees weak, I scanned her body, appreciating the perfection of her dress and wondering at the same time what was underneath. It was yellow, maybe gold, and definitely not the type of thing I was used to seeing her in. Still, as with all the other dresses she wore, I'd kill to see it on the floor of a bedroom—hers or mine, didn't matter which.

I yanked her closer by the waist. Screw the fact that God was probably frowning on us. I wasn't scared of hell if it meant I got to kiss this pretty thing in my arms again. "Fuck, you've got beautiful lips."

"I do, huh?"

Nodding, I leaned forward, ready to show her how much I loved them, only for a cock-blocking granny to enter the room at the same time.

"Um, excuse me?"

My brows shot up as I turned to face today's employer with her tiny nose and wide eyes. She ogled me from behind her glasses, a flirty grin on her red-painted lips. She was the first one to hire me for a paying gig after walking by my building one night. She'd mistaken it for a flower shop. Cock-blocker or not, I owed her. Not only for today, but because I'd gotten two other jobs from her fellow quilting friends.

"Forget something, ma'am?" I asked.

She tipped her head to the side, and her grin grew even wider. "I just wanted to thank you again for everything. The food was so delicious, and everyone was very impressed with your services." She took a step closer, nearly knocking Lia out of the way. "And I wanted to say too…if you're ever in the market for a baker to make desserts, don't hesitate to call me." She bit her bottom lip, leaving a faded stain on her teeth. "I can make a mean brownie when I want to."

Lia smothered her face against my shirtsleeve, squelching a laugh. I pinched her and she squeaked instead, but still held her knuckles against her mouth.

Once the lady finished ogling me, she took off, a little extra shake in her hips.

I turned to Lia again. "You're insane, woman."

She walked around to the other side of the table, owning every move she made. If sexiness could be patented, my girl would be the reigning queen.

"It'll always be like that for you, won't it? The parade of women, all ages, throwing themselves at you in some way or another..." She walked back around the table, grinning.

"That bother you?"

She shrugged, tossing some more garbage into the can. "Maybe. But it's not a deal breaker."

The memory of her calling me a man whore ran through my head. But I figured if she was really bothered by women coming on to me, she'd say something.

She zipped up the bag we'd brought along for the plates and silverware. "There." She looked back at me, one eyebrow raised and a half smile on her lips. Those lips were purple today—bright purple like the new color she'd added to the underside of her cotton-candy-colored hair. I couldn't take my eyes off her.

"What're you looking at, Soldier Boy?"

"Nothing. Just like looking at you and knowing you're mine."

She rolled her eyes, shouldering the bag. "I'm not *anybody's*."

"Sure you are." I lifted the rest of my stuff and cradled it in my arms as we headed toward the door. "You're mine to kiss and touch. And I don't plan on sharing you, unless of course you initiate it."

She laughed but didn't dismiss the idea. "So, a threesome is okay, then? Like, I could call Gavin and ask him to—"

"Fuck no." I shuddered, opening the back door with my shoulder. I'd driven the Charger today, feeling like my lady needed a carriage.

"I was kidding. Relax." She laughed, the sound so spectacular I couldn't help but watch her. Head thrown back, eyes shut...

Stunning.

Inside the car, she turned to me as I started the engine. It rumbled and purred, making me wanna rev the thing and race it down the road.

"Don't worry. I'm not up for threesomes either, in case you were wondering." She winked, but I couldn't shake the rock lodged in my chest.

What if this thing brewing between us wasn't anything but a good time for her? Something to tide her over—maybe help her get over Travis. Jesus, this insecurity bullshit wasn't fun.

"You're thinking an awful lot over there." She reached across the console and squeezed my hand. Taking it up another notch, I interlocked her fingers with mine, palm to palm, the anxiety inside me easing at her touch.

"Just...happy is all." I blew out a heavy breath, lying, but not knowing how else to explain my feelings.

"Happy looks good on you, ya know." She leaned her head back against the seat, eyes half-lidded.

I stroked my thumb over hers. "You've always been the one to make me the happiest."

She turned toward the window. "Then it's obvious you've led a pretty boring life."

I frowned. "Don't do that."

"Do what?"

I turned down her street, trying to pull in my frustration. The last thing I wanted was to fight with her. I might have kissed her lips, laid claim to her mouth, but that didn't mean I'd laid a full-on claim over her heart yet. Love was just a word in the scheme of things.

"I give you a compliment, and you follow it up with something negative."

She shook her head, and a chunk of her new purple hair fell out of the back of her bandanna. My finger twitched, wanting to brush the hair off her neck.

"That's what I do, Max." She shrugged. "Get used to it."

"So, you don't *want* me to compliment you? Because I'm not sure if I can do that."

I turned to look at her just in time to see her frown. Her response never came though, and I didn't push for it. The ache in my gut said not to. That something bad would happen if I did. More than anything, I wanted to stop the car right there in the middle of her street, pull her onto my lap, and tell her how stupid she was being. Because when a guy is trying to win the heart of a woman, compliments happen. It's part of relationship building. I might not have been all that experienced with commitment, but I knew a beautiful woman deserved a compliment any chance you could give her one.

"I'm pretty tired tonight. Probably won't be much fun." She yawned when I pulled into a parking spot near her apartment building.

My shoulders tensed as I put my car in Park. Was she trying to push me away again? "No problem. We'll just order some pizza instead of cooking. Maybe watch a little Netflix."

"You want to Netflix and chill with me, Maxwell?"

She smirked, her arms folded under her tits. I looked at them, then looked at her face. "Yeah? So? I'm tired as hell too and would like nothing more than to get you naked and kiss you all over."

"You're... Ugh." But I saw her grin, and those gorgeous cheeks turned pink too.

Then when she stepped out of my car and headed toward the trunk, I knew I'd won.

Inside her apartment, she flicked on the lights and tossed her bag onto the floor. "I'm going to take a quick shower. There's alcohol in the cupboard next to the microwave and pizza menus in the top drawer." She tried giving me a little smile, but it didn't reach her eyes. "Go ahead and order whatever you want."

Nodding, I put the leftovers inside the fridge, then tugged off my shirt. It stank of old lady perfume and Mexican food—a combination I didn't like much.

It didn't take me long to find the menus. She had next to nothing in the drawers, except for the occasional plastic piece of silverware.

Once I'd dialed and ordered, I started snooping around. I'd only been in Lia's place twice, and once was when she'd moved in a year or so ago. Before that, she'd been staying wherever she could crash, which always bugged me. I didn't know why until now. She was reckless back then, didn't seem to worry about anything. Even before I realized I was half in love with her, I hated thinking she was unsafe.

After everything she'd been through, you'd think she would have been a little more careful about what she did, where she stayed, who she lived with.

She'd started watching Chloe during the day while Collin worked, and with what he paid her, along with her job at the coffee shop, she made enough money to move into her own place. Not sure what her plan for money was now that she'd quit Jimney's. Even if she said no, I'd pay her for the catering gigs she helped with.

Once I'd thoroughly hunted through the space, I headed back to her bedroom. A small, beat-up futon shared space with a few blankets and pillows scattered all over. Apparently that was where she slept. I frowned at the thought of her living this way, but she didn't seem unhappy, and I wouldn't judge.

"Jesus, Max, what're you doing in here? You scared me."

I turned, my body going stiff at the view. Wrapped in a towel, blue eyes wide, with her wet hair dripping down her bare shoulders, Lia stood in the doorframe, studying me.

"Nice bed." I grinned, motioning toward the futon I was ready to toss her onto.

"Thanks…?"

Instead of running to her, wrapping my arms around her waist and kissing her 'til I lost my mind, I fell back on top of her blankets with a grunt and folded my arms behind my head. My feet hung over the edge, my elbows too.

"You're welcome." I motioned toward the nineteen-inch dinosaur TV. "Now, hand me the remote, please."

When she didn't move, I sat up higher to look at her better. She tugged the top of her towel up and bit her bottom lip. I stared at her naked legs, one eyebrow arched, waiting.

"Um…" Her cheeks went red again. For a girl with as much attitude as she had, Lia sure did blush a lot. "Do you think you think you could wait out in the living room or something?" She crossed and uncrossed her ankles.

I raised both my eyebrows this time, feeling no shame as I let my gaze wander over the exposed tats on her shoulder and neck. "Nope. Thinking I'm good right here."

The pink-and-black tattoos reminded me of a picture I once saw at an art show in Tennessee—a Japanese tree tunnel, I think it was called. Pink flowers on the ground, pink flowers cascading over the tops in the trees… exotic, gorgeous, stunning, and just like her.

"Fine." Her voice cracked. "Don't say I didn't warn you."

And then she did the opposite of what I expected her to do. She turned around and dropped the towel onto the floor, showing off the finest ass I'd ever seen in my life.

Lia

"DAMN, LEE-LEE."

"What?" I grinned, secretly high-fiving myself. "I'm just looking for some clothes."

Max groaned. "Warn a guy the next time you decide to go commando."

"I did warn you. But you were too stubborn to leave."

Laughing, I searched through my top drawer, fingering the silk of my panties until I finally found *the ones*. They were white and bikini cut with a pink bow on the front and two barely there strings on the sides. I called them my bridal panties because they reminded me of something a bride would wear on her wedding night.

"You act like you've never seen a girl's naked ass before."

He grumbled "Fuck me" under his breath and said out loud, "Well, usually the ass I'm looking at belongs to a girl I'm not interested in seeing. I'm a boob man usually...though that may be changing after this."

My heart raced, and the sweat dampening my palms had me opening and closing my fists. When Max got nervous, his ridiculously sexy Tennessee twang would surface. It made the space between my thighs warm, which terrified the hell out of me. No doubt in my mind that I wanted Max, but what if he decided I wasn't good enough? Tonight wasn't about the future though. Tonight was about fun. Just hanging out, seeing where things went between us, that was all. We'd done the love declaration, but that didn't mean we were diving into this as though we were days from getting married.

Hands shaking, I tugged the panties up and over my thighs, then leaned down and grabbed a T-shirt from the drawer below. It was midriff length and green, with the phrase *I'm the kind of dirty you can't wash off* written across the front. After pulling on a pair of matching sleep shorts, I turned to face Max.

A nearly inaudible moan sounded from my futon as his gaze drifted over my body. Knowing that I affected him this way gave me the courage to be the seductress I didn't think I could be.

"Did you order pizza?" Feigning innocence, I sat at my vanity with the oval mirror and ran a brush through my damp hair. The ends curled up slightly, probably because of the new color, but it worked, making me look like Marilyn Monroe.

"Pizza?" Max asked, his voice thin.

I stole another quick glance over my shoulder at him as I stood. Flat on his back with an arm draped over his eyes and a massive bulge in his pants, he looked like he was dying.

I cleared my throat. "I'm gonna grab some liquor."

"Lick her?" He shot up.

My lips twitched. "Yeah. *Liquor*. Like, the stuff you drink from a bottle?"

He quickly put his feet on the floor to stand. "Shit, sorry, I forgot. I'll grab—"

"It's fine." I smiled, placating him. "I've got it."

For once, he didn't argue or throw the chivalrous card at me, nor did he move from the futon. When I got back to the room, two Solo cups in hand and a bottle of Boone's Farm tucked under my arm, he was still in the same spot, but this time his head was down and he was muttering something under his breath.

"Max."

He lifted his head, watching me with hooded eyes as I set the cups on the cardboard box I used as a nightstand next to my bed. My heart thrummed in my ears as I popped the cork and began to pour. Chancing another look in his direction, I found his gaze on my chest, his lips parted.

"You're gonna make me drink alone?"

"I'm not drinking that. Don't you have any beer?" His eyes trailed over my body again, like he couldn't help himself.

"It was part of a Christmas gift from Collin last year. It's all I have. Sorry."

"I'm gonna have to teach your brother some tact when it comes to gift giving, because this stuff tastes like shit."

I didn't complain. Alcohol was alcohol to me. But it *was* fun to play along and get Max all riled up. "I'm not about to waste something as delicious as Boone's Farm, Maxwell. It's the classiest drink on the planet." I sat on the edge of the bed, handing him his drink while keeping a good hold on mine.

"Cheers." I lifted my cup toward his, wasting no time as I downed the fizzy stuff in ten seconds flat. My throat burned and I shivered, but the sweetness on my tongue had me licking my lips. I poured another cup, glancing at Max once I was finished.

His eyes were wide and focused on my mouth. "I'm so fucking turned on right now."

"You're too easy." I laughed.

He grunted, then moved forward, his lips curled higher on one side. The futon squeaked under his weight. "You gotta little…" His thick thigh brushed against my knee as he lifted his thumb to wipe the wetness off the corner of my mouth. My breath caught at the move. On instinct, I flicked my tongue out again. His dark eyes grew molten when I pressed the tip to his finger.

He cocked his head to the right and studied my mouth. "You gonna let me kiss you again tonight, Lee-Lee?"

A sizzle inched its way over my skin, down my arms and legs, between my thighs…

"Only if you want to," I whispered.

"Fuck yeah, I wanna." His eyes glazed. "I wanna do a lot of things to you, but kissing is where I need to start."

Our eyes stayed locked, the ever-present chemistry crackling between us. My face and neck warmed. It reminded me of heat lightning in the summer, but feeling it instead of seeing it. The humid air, the intensity of thinking it was so close, yet so far away…

Not thinking twice, I leaned forward, going straight for his mouth. But his palm stopped me short, pressed between my breasts. My chest heaved. The space between my thighs grew hot and aching and far too frustrated.

"Tell me something first." He set his still-full cup on the table, unnervingly calm.

My face grew hotter, whether from embarrassment or the alcohol, I didn't know. "What's that?"

He moved even closer, as though drawn to me, like I was to him. "When was the last time you were properly made love to by a man?" He touched my knee with his hand, slowly moving it up my thigh until he reached the edge of my panties.

Goose bumps danced across my inner thigh. "I-it's been a while."

He trailed his fingers down my cheek and over my chin, utter devotion in his gaze. "I don't want to push you. Ever. I do something wrong, take something too far, you tell me, got it?"

I nodded, not willing to let Old Lia work her way tonight. I wanted Max to push me to my limits. Love me like he'd loved all the other women he'd been with. So I sucked in a slow breath and leaned forward, whispering over his mouth, "I've dreamed about you touching me nearly every night for years now. So, go ahead, Soldier Boy. Work your magic."

"Woman." He threw himself back on the futon, pulling me on top of him. I straddled his lap, rolling my hips against his. "You're killing me."

"Nah." I tugged at the end of his shirt. Both of his hands went to my thighs as he zeroed in on my panties. "The dick dies along with the dead body, and you feel very much alive to me."

He growled low in his throat, then tugged me close

for a kiss. Moaning against his lips, I continued to rub slow, tantalizing strokes against his zipper, my breasts heavy against my shirt. He lifted a hand and palmed one, a tentative movement that was more of a tease than anything else.

He moved his other hand to my back, splaying his hands out against my spine. Over and over, he trailed his lips across my neck, my throat, my chin. "Gotta see your beautiful body."

He tugged my top up with one hand—higher, and higher, and higher… "Gorgeous." The shirt was off and he pulled back, trailing his finger over my tats.

"I wanna spend all night kissing every bit of this ink, you know that?"

In one sweep, he moved to lay me beneath him, only to drop his lips to the underside of my breast. "And these, damn…" He nuzzled his nose around my nipple just once, inhaling. "They're perfect."

I moaned, arching my back as I ran my fingers through his hair. I needed more. I needed it all. But Max was gentle, worshipping the space and ink surrounding my breasts with only his hands. Just when I felt like I was on the verge of cracking, he finally touched my nipple. Fingers hot, he trailed them around the beaded hardness. He squeezed lightly, then tugged, the pinch going straight to the center of my body. I ground my hips up, seeking relief, and he grumbled his appreciation, finally latching onto the peak of my breast with his lips.

"Max…" I moaned at the wet sensation, needing more, but needing him to stop at the same time. Parts of my brain were growing fuzzy and out of control. An unfamiliar warning voice popped into my ears.

Stop while you're ahead. I tried to push it down, but it wouldn't go away. *You're not his first rodeo, cowgirl. This is what he thrives on in life, remember?* My eyes popped open and I stared at the ceiling of my bedroom. As good as this felt, as much as I wanted to keep going, I realized things were happening too fast. Not that I didn't want a Mighty Max O again. It's just that the what-ifs of him and me taking this to the next level were suddenly too overwhelming.

Stupid, logical Old Lia and her even stupider brain.

"Max, wait…" I pushed his chest, catching him off guard, only for him to fall onto the floor with a thud. I cringed and jumped down beside him. "Crap. Are you okay? Did I hurt you?"

His lips twitched in spite of the moment. His voice crackled as he said, "I might need a Band-Aid."

There was a knock on the front door. The pizza man, most likely. When I was sure Max wasn't going to pass out, I helped him sit up and then move to the futon.

"A Band-Aid?" I winced. "Are you bleeding some-where?" I scanned his body, just as another knock sounded. He sighed. "It's my knees, Lee-Lee."

I crouched down in front of him and pulled the legs of his jeans up. "Like, what, rug burn?"

"Yeah." He reached over and trailed a thumb over my chin. "I think I scraped them when I fell for you."

Because I couldn't help myself, I laughed and leaned into his touch before kissing his lips just once. "You're truly made of magic, Mr. Martinez." When all he could do was stare back at me with wide, puppy eyes, I patted his cheek and stood, then hunted around the room for some decent clothes to put on.

CHAPTER

Max

SOMEWHERE BETWEEN PIZZA AND A BOTTLE OF BOONE'S Farm, Lia and I had fallen asleep.

I'd barely been able to concentrate on whatever movie she'd picked off Netflix. Between my throbbing hip—the one I'd gotten after I fell off her futon—to my forever raging hard-on, I was a mess. Luckily sleep had won out, giving me a little reprieve.

She stirred against my side, and I immediately opened my eyes. I wasn't one to sleep soundly. At least, not since my time in Afghanistan. We'd always have to be on alert back then, and some habits a man couldn't change.

It was still dark out, no telling what time, but I knew we hadn't been out long. She got up and sat on the edge of the futon. For some reason or another, she was shaking, her head buried in her palms. Not wanting her to know I was awake, I stayed still and watched her, keeping a healthy distance. Lia said she didn't wanna be rescued, but I wasn't sure how far that went.

An advertisement danced across the TV screen, and the rumble of a thunderstorm echoed in the distance. Occasionally a flash of lightning lit up the room, showing the hourglass outline of her waist. She wasn't wearing a shirt. She'd told me her preference was to sleep naked, and I wasn't going to complain. A beautiful, unclothed Lee-Lee was my new favorite thing in the world.

A few minutes passed until she finally stood, wearing nothing but those tiny panties. I wanted to reach out for her, pull her close, but decided at the last minute not to. I wasn't really sure why she was up, or upset. A bad dream, maybe? I could relate.

She headed out of the room, gone for a few minutes. I heard the water in the kitchen sink run and figured she was getting a drink.

Eventually she came back, in time for a loud thunderclap to echo in the room. She squeaked at the noise, running toward the futon, and I couldn't help but laugh.

"Sorry." She sat next to me, curling back under the blankets and against my chest. "I didn't mean to wake you."

I snuggled closer, wrapping my hand around her warm waist and settling my chin on her shoulder from behind. The futon was uncomfortable as hell, but the discomfort was worth it to be close to her. "You afraid of a little thunderstorm?"

Quiet filled the air. She didn't respond. I frowned, leaning up on one elbow so I could look at her face.

Her eyes were open, unfocused on the ceiling. "Terrified, actually."

Another flash of lightning. I put my hand on her cheek and pulled her face toward mine. "Wanna talk about it?"

A shrug. "It rained that night."

I fisted my hands. "In college."

"Yeah," she whispered with a nod, her gaze now locked with mine. "I remember my roommate telling me not to go. That it was supposed to get bad outside."

I didn't remember much about that night, other than finding her, carrying her out, and then taking her straight to the hospital. But now that she'd mentioned it, I did remember the way my rain-soaked hair had stuck to my forehead as I stood in the ER waiting room with Gavin.

Blinking the memory away, I refocused on her face. "I wanted to kill him."

She flinched, but didn't pull her gaze from mine. "You wouldn't have found him. He took off that night. Never came back to school, to his apartment either. I-I didn't even know his last name."

"You could have found out. Pressed charges... Ruined him." *Like he almost did you* is what I wanted to say but didn't.

She frowned, not because she was upset, but more like she was thinking. "I was dumb. Scared. I just wanted to forget it ever happened." She sighed. "My parents were already so worked up about Collin leaving that I didn't want to add more issues."

"I'd say that was a hell of a lot bigger issue than Collin leaving."

She blinked and gave a small, sad smile. "Not to me it wasn't."

"Come here. I'll always keep you safe from storms."

She grinned but did as I asked, laying her head on my chest. "Thank you," she whispered, so softly I could barely hear her. But I did. I always would.

After a while, her breathing evened out, only for a small snore to escape her lips.

—◦◦◦—

Lia

I didn't wake Max the next morning. Instead, I quietly slipped out of bed, took a shower, and got dressed and ready for work. It was Monday morning, and I had to be at Java Java's early to help Betsy with the baking, something I normally loved. Except for today.

More than anything, I wanted to lie next to him and brush his dark hair away from his eyes until he woke and kissed me into oblivion. Then, maybe, I'd have the guts to do what I was regretting we hadn't done last night.

Soon, I told myself. *Very soon*.

Betsy pulled up into the spot next to me by the coffee shop, taking in my sleepy state through the window. "Come along now," she called. "Let me make us some tea."

I nodded and opened the door with a grin, wordlessly following her inside. I felt high on life, regardless of the fact that I'd had to leave Max.

Like always, Betsy's steps were cautious, and her hands shook a bit more than usual, but I wasn't going to comment on it. She was worse about taking care of herself than I was sometimes.

Inside, she flicked on the lights, then shut and locked the door behind us. I headed straight to the kitchen to get to work, never tiring of this routine. I loved the Java Java Hut. Leaving it someday would likely break my heart.

"Did you wash your hands?" She motioned toward the dough.

"Yep. Always."

Side by side, we readied and baked the morning pastries, her soft country music a welcome sound in the quiet.

My thoughts skipped to Max, wondering where he was, what he was doing, or if he was still asleep in my bed.

Before Max, more than anything else in my life, I'd wanted calm, peace, and focus. But *with* him, things were already taking a different road, one I hadn't thought I'd ever travel, but in no way one I wanted to avoid. The dips and curves of a roller coaster ride, the high of stepping onto a plane, knowing your life is at another person's mercy. It was a little bit terrifying, but a whole lot of incredible.

"So, Ruby told me you've got a job interview next week."

Until that inevitable crash and burn came around, full force. *Ruby and her big mouth*.

"Yeah, um, I received the call last week. They want a formal interview with me this coming Thursday."

"We're so proud of you, dear. You deserve the very best."

I smiled and hugged her close, inhaling the scent of flour and sugar in her hair. I'd worked there for years, and the only employees Betsy had were me and her daughter. She'd have to hire someone new if I got another job, something I'm pretty sure she wasn't looking forward to. But Java Java's was never my forever career. She'd known that from the beginning.

The job in Springfield, on the other hand, was exactly

what a forever career entailed. An alternative junior high, a.k.a. "safe school," was where I'd be working as an ELA teacher. Most of the kids attending the school had behavioral disorders, which would likely test me at times, but I could totally deal with it. I'd work there for the mandatory four years until I became tenured by the state. Then, after that, I could move back home again, find a job that was either in Carinthia or close by.

Before I knew this thing between Max and me was a possibility, I'd told myself I would take the position if offered, no matter what. I would never make something of myself if I didn't take chances, and what better chance would I have than this? At the same time, what would happen between us once I left? I shook my head, refusing to go there. Things were so fresh and new that I refused to spoil all my happiness with what-could-bes right now.

"You've got something you want to talk about, girlie?" Betsy stopped in the middle of kneading and looked at me, then past me toward the front of the store.

"Just tired."

"You look like you're suffering from a broken heart." She hummed under her breath.

Far from. "I've got a few things on my mind, but nothing to keep me from making the best croissants you've ever tasted."

Not taking the bait, Betsy frowned and asked, "Does it have anything to do with the fact that your brother's been pacing the front of the store for the past five minutes?"

I whipped my head toward the glass door. Sure enough, Collin was out there, running his hand through his hair, doing exactly as Betsy said he was. Worry for him, my niece, and Addie pulled me out of my thoughts.

I needed to go out there, but with the amount of work we still had to do before opening, I couldn't help but cringe as I pointed to the door and asked, "Do you mind? I won't be long."

Betsy motioned her chin toward the door. "Go on. Take your time, dear."

A minute later, I flipped open the door lock and stepped outside, the warm morning air caressing my cheeks.

Collin's eyes grew wide at the sight of me. "I've been looking all over the place for you."

I frowned and pulled out my cell phone. It was off—probably dead. "Everything okay? Why are you out so early?"

"Got training at the academy in an hour."

"Java Java's doesn't open until—"

"She won't marry me."

I jerked my head back. "Who, Addie?"

"Who else would it be?"

I took a step closer, grinning like a fool, which was probably not the reaction he was hoping for. But Collin didn't realize how big this was. Rejection or not, my brother had come a long way over the past year. "You really asked her?"

He nodded. "Last night. Chloe was asleep and I took Addie out on the porch for a picnic. Had her favorite wine, some strawberries, even used the red checkered blanket from the first time we first had sex—"

"Oh my God, please don't." I pressed my hand over my ears, singing *la, la, la*.

He knifed his hand through his hair again. "Shit, sorry. I'm just… I'm a mess."

Sighing, I leaned against the front bumper of his

truck. "Tell me what happened. Start from the beginning, minus the sex-capades, please."

"She freaked out. Told me she wasn't ready. That with her mom being sick and only being at her new job for a few months, it wasn't the right time to think about marriage. She said she wanted to be settled first."

"What's the issue, then? She didn't technically say no, just that she wants to wait a bit."

He shook his head. "I *love* her. She loves me too. We live together, and she's already asked me about becoming Chloe's legal guardian. I even called a lawyer to see what the process would be. All that's left is marriage, and that seems like nothing compared to everything else."

I squeezed his shoulder. "She loves you. She'll come around."

He pinched the bridge of his nose but managed a nod. That was something at least. Normally it took Collin a lot longer to get over his little "man tantrums."

He frowned, leaning against the bumper of his truck at my side. "Why are you here so early anyway? I stopped by your place, thinking you'd be still asleep, but you didn't—"

"You stopped by my apartment?" I froze.

"Yeah. About twenty minutes ago."

"And I wasn't there…" I blinked and then frowned at the sidewalk. Either Max didn't answer the door on purpose, or he was asleep and didn't hear it, or he'd already left.

"No shit, you weren't there." He tugged off my hairnet. I shoved his hand away and frowned. When I didn't respond, he asked, "What's up, Sis? Travis bothering you again?"

I shook my head, wishing it were that easy. Because the new complication of Maxwell and me wasn't something Collin could know about yet. I was sure he wouldn't be that upset, though we'd have to tread carefully in how we told him. But I'd barely wrapped my head around the idea myself, which meant I needed more time before I told Collin. And now with the interview, I was pretty sure our transition into official coupledom wasn't going to go as smoothly as I'd hoped. The less drama, the better.

"No, not Travis. Just that I haven't been able to sleep well lately." That was true. Sleep and I never got along well. Last night had proved that, yet again. On top of the nightmare I'd had and the storm, I was running on two hours of sleep. Having Max there helped, but I never rested well. "And I'm always here early on Monday to help Betsy bake."

"How about that other job?" His eyebrows drew together, but I could tell he was trying to stay positive about the fact that I worked at Jimney's.

Fortunately, I had news on that front.

"Actually, I quit there. My last day is a week from Saturday."

His eyes bugged out. "You did?" Then he wrapped his arm around my shoulder and squeezed. "Best news I've heard in weeks, Sis. What're you going to do now?" He dropped his arm.

I could tell him that I had an interview, but what if he mistakenly told Max? I wanted to be the one to break it to him. Word of mouth often hurt worse than the real person-to-person explanation.

"Apply for some *real* jobs, as you so eloquently suggested I do in the past."

"What about school?" His eyebrows pulled together as he studied me. "Don't you want to finish first? Last I heard, you had a few semester hours left."

I stared at my feet. "I'm done."

"What? No, you have to finish—"

"No, Collin." I touched his arm, meeting his gaze, all while praying he wouldn't hate me for not telling him earlier. "What I meant was that I got my diploma a few weeks back. I didn't attend a graduation or anything, so it's not a huge deal."

He jumped away from the truck, only to wrap me in a big bear hug. I laughed as he squeezed, and I tucked my nose against his shoulder, fighting back my happy tears. I knew I'd been worrying everyone in my family with my lack of motivation, but the fact that he reacted like I'd given him the world made me feel like even more of a jerk for being so standoffish the last couple of years.

"Why the hell didn't you tell anyone?"

I gulped back my emotions as he put me down, his hands never leaving my shoulders. "I told Max. Just told Mom and Dad too."

"You told Max and not me?" The accusation in his voice had me cringing. God, I should've waited to mention this. If anything, I was hoping to have a job first to distract him from the news. But the best-laid plan never worked out.

"Sorry. I just knew how busy you were with Addie and Chloe and the police academy."

Blue eyes like mine stared back at me with both sadness and pride—a strange and unnerving and wonderful combination. "I get it. And I *am* proud of you, Lia.

I just wished I would've known." He stuck his hands into his pockets.

I blinked away a few tears and wiped the ones which had escaped onto my cheeks with the back of my hand.

"Why Max though, of all people? I mean, I know you two have this weird friendship…" He tipped his head to the side, his eyes narrowing in confusion.

"Because…" *I love him. And he loves me.* "Because we're friends." I cringed, realizing how ridiculous that sounded.

A frown captured Collin's face, the tension rolling off him like a tsunami of angst. I already felt really guilty. I didn't need another reminder of how wretched a sister I'd been.

"Do you want some coffee?" I nodded my head toward the door, needing to distract him. "We don't open for another twenty minutes, but Betsy wouldn't mind if you came inside. She wouldn't even make you pay."

He looked through the door, then back at me, his blue eyes softening. "Next time."

"Next time."

"You'll be at Mom and Dad's Thursday night, yeah?" he asked.

I patted his cheek. "Wouldn't miss it."

After searching my face once more, Collin walked away, waving as he got inside his truck.

"Collin?" I hollered through his open window, genuinely happy for him.

He poked his head out. "Yeah?"

"Addie's lucky to have you."

He grinned, his eyes nearly dancing. "Nah. I'm the lucky one."

CHAPTER 20

Max

THE THING I LOVED THE MOST ABOUT COLLY AND LIA'S mama? She didn't think twice about letting a bloody man inside her home. But that didn't mean she wouldn't give me the third degree and a guilt trip from hell.

I winced as Mrs. Montgomery pressed a bag full of ice against my mouth. "You're going to have to see a dentist about that tooth."

I ran my tongue over my broken incisor. "Sure thing, Mrs. M. I'll schedule an appointment tomorrow."

"Do I even want to know what happened?" She frowned and wiped a wet rag over my chin. I could've done it myself, but my hands were all sorts of scuffed and fucked from practice tonight. It'd been a tough one, but we were ready for our next tournament.

"Rugby. But you should see the other guy."

"That sport disgusts me." She scrunched her nose up, making her look more like her daughter. "No wonder Lia always tried to keep me away."

"She's a good one, that Lee-Lee." I winked and tried to stand, but Mrs. M shoved me down by the shoulder.

"Sit. I'm not done yet." She frowned at me from over her shoulder as she walked to the sink.

I'd gotten here early for a celebratory Thursday-night dinner. I had no idea what we were celebrating, but when I got the phone call to come from Mrs. M, I wasn't about to say no to a free, home-cooked meal. Since I didn't live close to Ma and Char, this was also the next best thing to family time for me.

Lia had said she'd meet me here instead of letting me pick her up at home. Something about having "things" she needed to do before going into work later that night. We hadn't seen much of each other this week, not since Sunday, which sucked. She'd picked up more hours at Java Java's to help out the owner, and I was planning menus and getting stuff ready for my next catering gig. We texted and talked every night—real dating, boyfriend/girlfriend stuff. At the same time though, I was pretty sure she wasn't being honest with me about something. Frustrating as hell, since I'd thought we'd gotten past the secrets stage. But she was Lee-Lee, the girl who didn't trust easily and wasn't used to sharing all yet. I'd ask her about it tonight, but only after I'd kissed her really good back at her place when she got off work.

"You hear from Lia yet? She on her way?"

Mrs. M walked back over with a Band-Aid and put it on my chin. "Not yet. But it shouldn't be long now. The drive from Springfield to Carinthia is only three hours, and she left right after her interview was over at three."

I jerked my head back, giving it a shake, thinking I was hearing things because there's no way Lia would have gone to Springfield today for an interview without telling me. "Uh…"

"Apparently, it went really well. The superintendent and principal offered her the position on the spot." Pride in her daughter radiated off the woman as she walked back to the counter to cut up some fruit.

I blinked, opening and closing my mouth in shock. What in the actual fuck was going on?

"She starts July 30." She turned to look at me from over her shoulder again. "But if we can find her a place to move into, we'll likely be moving her in the week before."

My face went cold, my hands too. She'd gotten a job—a job she didn't even bother telling me she was interviewing for? Sure, we hadn't defined what the two of us were yet, but when it came to starting relationships, honesty was the key. Seemed like Lia thought that honesty was one-sided.

Jesus, I wanted to hit something.

"It really is the perfect job for her, though I am worried about her being all alone down there."

I looked to the floor, my knees parted, my head hanging.

"Max? You okay?"

Slowly, I lifted my eyes to meet Mrs. M's. She'd turned around and was watching me, eyes drawn together in worry.

Not wanting to freak the hell out yet, I said, "That's real great, Mrs. M. I'm excited for her."

She pinched her lips together and nodded as she turned away again. She obviously was proud of her daughter. And, hell, I would've been too, had I not suddenly wanted to punch my fist against the table.

Why hadn't she told me about this? I'm the one who wanted her to succeed more than anyone else, but I would have liked to know about the interview in advance.

Silence filled the air. That is, until Mrs. M finally snatched my breath away with, "I know you're in love with my daughter."

My heart skipped as I leaned back in the chair. "You do?" *Well, shit*.

She laughed and sat in the chair next to mine. "It's no surprise, really. You've been her keeper since the day you two met. I've seen the way you look at her. And I know she looks at you the same way. She's just not used to relationships. She really is a good girl, but she hasn't always been dealt the best cards."

Because I was pissed as hell, I could've called Lia out myself. Told Mrs. M about her daughter's *job* at Jimney's, about how she got arrested, about how she'd been dating the biggest fucktard in the world not long ago, but I didn't. I wasn't the best guy ever, but I wasn't a douche bag either. Instead, I rubbed my hand over my forehead and stared at the kitchen floor.

"Don't worry. Your secret is safe with me."

I looked over her shoulder out the kitchen window, trying to keep myself in check. "Collin and Mr. M won't like it."

"I won't like what?" At the sound of Mr. Montgomery's voice, I whipped my head to the back door. He grinned, his eyes focused on his wife as he moved to pull her into his arms.

"Oh, you're home. How was work?" she asked him.

Instead of answering, he went in for a kiss that probably should've made me feel like a creep for watching but didn't. Her arms wrapped around his shoulders, his around her waist. Weird as it was, I loved the idea of married couples still so touchy after all their years of marriage, especially since I didn't see that growing up.

Seconds later, Mr. M pulled back to face me. "Now, what do you think I won't like to hear?"

"Oh, nothing." Mrs. M pressed her hand against his chest. "Our Maxwell is just having some lady troubles."

Mr. M grinned and walked to the fridge. He returned, two beers in hand. "Guessing you need a drink then."

Not thinking twice, I reached for one, twisting the top off with the bottom of my sweaty shirt. "Good to see you, sir."

"Enough with this 'sir' business. I'm John, always John." He patted my shoulder and then twisted the top off his own beer.

I nodded and took a heavy drink.

"And if my daughter has you in her corner, I'll never worry about her again." He winked at his wife, but then shrugged one shoulder and smiled at me. "Unless you knock her up before you put a ring on her finger."

I coughed and spit out my drink.

Mrs. Montgomery laughed. "I'm in agreement with my husband…" She leaned closer and pretended to whisper in my ear. "Unless you give me a grandson." She kissed my cheek.

A nervous chuckle built in my chest as I stared back and forth between the two people who'd grown to be like pseudo parents. I loved them almost like I loved my mama and Charlotte.

"But you better move fast." He tsked. "Because our girl might just run before you can catch her. This job opportunity is pretty spectacular." He grabbed a tray full of hamburgers and hot dogs off the counter. "Gonna start the grill." He kissed his wife again and stepped outside, whistling as he went.

"What were you saying about my husband and Collin not wanting you to be with Lia?" She smirked and took a step back, leaving me shaking my head. "Why don't ya head outside? I'll make you some sun tea. It's much better than that nasty beer you boys insist on drinking."

I needed the fresh air to clear my head, so I didn't argue. But I also wasn't in the mood to get grilled more by the man whose daughter I wanted—even if he did seem cool with the fact.

CHAPTER 21

Lia

"...AND HOW LONG HAVE YOU AND MY SON BEEN DATING?" Mom took a bite of her brownie, a grin lighting up her face as she chewed.

"I'd say about eight months now?" Addie cleared her throat, not meeting Mom's eyes as she stood up from the couch in their living room. Hands trembling, she rubbed her palms down the front of her colorful skirt. Poor girl was all sorts of nervous. Probably even more than I was. Granted our issues were over two different things, but still.

"Well, I'm certainly pleased you've stolen his heart. He needs a good, strong woman in his life after everything he's been through. As does Chloe. She's lucky to have you." Mom stood and wrapped Addie in a powerful hug.

And just like that, my brother's girlfriend was an official member of the Montgomery clan.

"I'm going to see if Chloe's doing okay. She was up

half the night with an upset tummy." Addie pulled back, her hands twisting with nervousness. Apparently, she didn't do the parental meet and greet that often, most likely because of her own nonexistent relationship with her parents. But I'd say she handled herself like a pro. Mom was already wholeheartedly in love with her because of the way Collin doted on her. She wanted him happy, just like I did, and knowing that someone could help make him that way was all she could ask for as a parent.

Sparing us a smile, Addie slipped out the door that led to my parents' back porch like her feet were on fire. Seconds after, Mom turned to me, wearing a wide, hopeful smile. "Do you think she's pregnant?"

The possibility of more grandchildren made her all but dance a fertility jig.

"No idea."

She clapped once, then said, "Now, let's talk about this thing between you and Max. What's been going on? He seemed pretty upset earlier this evening about you moving away."

"He *what*?" And there it was. The real reason he'd been avoiding me all night. *Crap, crap, crap.* I shut my eyes and hung my head. "Did you tell him about my interview, Mom?"

"I mentioned it, but I didn't... Oh dear. He didn't know, did he?"

I looked at her again, finding her hand over her mouth. "He does now."

"Oh, Leanne. I'm sorry."

I cringed and looked away, trying to hold back my scream. It wasn't her fault. She didn't know I hadn't told anyone. But Mom *also* wasn't supposed to know there was something going on between Max and me.

"We're just friends, Mom. It's fine." My voice shook, the lie so clear I could taste it on my tongue.

Before she could reply, Max came into the living room using the same door Addie had left through. Angry eyes met mine before flashing sweetly at my mother. "Care if I steal Lia away for a minute?" he asked her, not me, which I'm pretty sure meant he was ready to spank my ass or worse…

Mom shot me a look, silently asking *Are you okay with this?* I nodded and smiled, knowing I couldn't avoid the conversation any longer. If only I had told him the truth. As I'd said to myself on Monday, word of mouth hurt worse than anything else.

After Mom headed out to the porch, I blew out a breath, just in time for Max to put his hand on my lower back. I jumped in place as he leaned in to whisper, "Follow me." Then he dropped his hand and headed out of the room, not even bothering to wait for me.

God, this was worse than I thought.

My fingers curled into fists, yet I couldn't stop the shivers of unease that slithered through me. "Max, wait a sec." I bit my lip.

He froze, a hand on the wall.

"I'm done waiting." He spun back around, hurried my way, bent over at the waist, and shoved his shoulder into my stomach.

"Hey!" I squealed as he lifted me, my legs dangling over his chest. "Put me down."

Ignoring me, he powered through my parents' house and landed at the coat closet by the front door. "This looks to be as good a place as any." He whipped it open, looking both ways before walking us inside.

I blinked, trying to adjust to the blackness as he shut the door from behind.

He plopped me onto my feet. With his hands still wrapped around my waist, he said, "Why didn't you tell me about your interview?" His demeanor changed so suddenly that I could barely catch my breath.

"W-why are we hiding in the closet?"

"Don't try to change the subject, Lia. Did I fuck up or something to make you not wanna tell me? Are you having second thoughts about us?"

"No, no. That's not it at all." I grabbed the neck of his shirt and held tight, wishing I could see his face. "This was all me and my stupidity. I'm so sorry. I should have told you. I just…I chickened out is all."

His eyelashes fluttered against my cheeks as he moved in close. Lips brushed over my skin, not kissing, but touching as he sighed. "I thought I did something. I mean, I was pissed you hadn't told me, but I kept thinking you'd changed your mind about us. Scared the hell out of me."

"I'm sorry," I apologized again, pressing both hands to his face. "I never meant for you to find out this way."

"I forgive you." He pulled my hands off his face and flattened them over his heart. "I will *always* forgive you."

Beneath my palms, his heartbeat fluttered and I shut my eyes, shame washing over me. He touched his forehead to mine and whispered, "But, Lee-Lee, you feel this? My heart?" He rubbed his thumbs over the backs of my hands. "Do you feel how fast it's racing?" I swallowed hard but nodded. "It only beats for you.

No other woman will ever make it speed up like this. Which also means you're not the only one who can get hurt in this relationship."

"I'm a hypocrite. I wanted honesty, but I didn't give you the same. I get it." Tears filled my eyes, and I was thankful it was too dark for him to see me. "It won't happen again. I promise."

"Just tell me things, Lee-Lee. Keep the communication going. That's all I'm asking."

I swallowed around the lump in my throat, saying what I needed to say before I grew too chicken to admit it out loud. "I'm moving, Max. I got the job. I...I'm moving to Springfield."

He kissed my lips, just once. "I want to be with you, Lia. I *love* you, and I don't care how far apart we are. If you'd told me about this earlier, I would have said the same thing and meant it."

"What if you decide I'm not important enough to have a long-distance relationship with? I mean, what if you change your mind down the road about us?" I asked, worrying my lower lip.

Boxes went flying as he urged me back against the wall. "Don't even think I'll be the type to walk away if shit gets tough. You hear me? I've never wanted to commit to a woman until you, and you can damn sure bet I'll work my ass off to make it work, no matter how far apart we are." He fell to his knee before me and nuzzled his face against my stomach.

Tears stung my eyes, and my throat burned with a trapped sob. The *okay* was on the tip of my tongue. Any girl would be an absolute fool to say no to someone like him. Max was a good man, but could I push past my insecurities and fears to take a chance at being with him? Could I have things both ways? Find myself *and* love him too?

"Please, Lia. I'm down on my knees, begging you to believe in this. Believe in us."

If he was willing to try, then I would too. But in my own way. "Day by day, okay? We can't think forever right now. Not yet. Because if this doesn't work out, I'm afraid it'll break me."

I felt his lips part into a grin against my stomach. "Day by day. We'll take it slow." He stood, leaning forward to scoop me up into a hug. "We'll make this work. I promise you."

And just like that, I believed him.

CHAPTER 22

Max

IT WAS LIA'S LAST NIGHT AT JIMNEY'S, AND I COULDN'T have been happier.

Gav, Collin, Addie, McKenna, and I were all going out to celebrate, and we were gonna be doing it at Jimney's.

"Hot date?" Addie leaned against the doorframe with a smug smile.

"With you, maybe." I tapped my razor against the sink.

"You're getting awful pretty for a casual night out."

I grinned behind the towel I was wiping my face with.

"Who is she?" A serious expression passed through her eyes. "The girl you're getting all dolled up for?"

"Nobody you need to know about just yet." I headed past her and went into my room. Inside my closet, I grabbed the first thing that didn't stink like ass and yanked it on, while Addie stood watching me, her eyes narrowed with suspicion. The woman was on to me, which would've been okay, had Lia not wanted to wait to tell everyone we were together. She'd said she needed time to prepare her thoughts in case her brother wasn't good with the two of us hooking up. Not gonna lie, I was just as scared as she was. Probably because I had a lot to lose if Collin wasn't okay with her and me being together.

"You haven't been around much this week. Everything okay?"

"Everything's been good. Promise. Just busy with the new business." And spending my nights with Lee-Lee. Holding her in my arms, kissing her with every breath I had in me… We hadn't done anything *but* kiss since that Sunday night in her room, but like I'd said to her that day at the rugby game, I wasn't going to push it. We had all the time in the world for more.

"You sure?" Addie grabbed a few pieces of my laundry off the floor and stuffed them into the basket. She was always cleaning and taking care of us. "Because word on the street is you and Lia are hooking up."

My arms went stiff, as did my back. I looked up from my tennis shoes, my eyes wide. "Who told you that?"

She grinned. "Nobody. Just a wild guess."

I followed her out of the room and down the hall. Gavin was still next door, pouting about something like always. I was headed there first. Colly was taking Beaner to his parents' house for the night. It's the first time we'd all gone out together—us guys, Lia, Addie, and her friend, Kenna.

"It's not true."

Addie shook her head and laughed. "Don't worry. Your secret's safe with me."

In the kitchen, I stared at Addie's back, losing the

fight. The woman was maddening. "Seriously, Short Stuff. Lee-Lee would kill me if Collin found out before we had a chance to tell him."

She rinsed off a few dishes and then glanced at me from over her shoulder. "I won't."

"Liar. You tell Colly everything."

She opened her mouth, only to snap it shut before she said, "Do not."

I rolled my eyes. "If anything, keep it a secret for Lia's sake. If he finds out—"

"Your secret's safe with me." She zipped her lips and feigned throwing an invisible key away. "Just don't hurt her. Please."

I let go of a breath. "Never. She's my world."

A smirk covered her lips. "Good. Because I'll kick your ass worse than Collin if you do."

There was no doubt in my mind that was the truth.

<hr />

An hour and a half later, we were walking into the bar: me, my boys, and Addie and Kenna. Willie Nelson blared from the speakers, the country crowd in full swing tonight. Tight jeans and short skirts filled the dance floor, reminding me of home. I grumbled under my breath, locking my eyes on the old jukebox across the room. The music would have to change *now*. I listened to Willie enough when Collin sang it to Chloe. My version of good music was Aerosmith, meshed with a little Lynyrd Skynyrd and the occasional Alabama tossed in when I was missing home.

Certain moods called for certain music, and knowing I was about to see my girl made me into a different kind of man altogether. Which is why I beelined toward the juke-box, not bothering to tell anyone where I was heading.

Satisfied I had at least fifteen good early-nineties love songs picked out, I grinned and turned around… And there she was, like she'd been plucked from a garden full of pretty flowers. Lia. My girl.

No, not my girl. My woman.

With her eyes locked with mine, her lips pulled up into a half grin, she looked like she was weak in the knees as she pressed her hands against the top of the bar from the other side. And as I moved around the tables and through the crowd of loudmouthed people, I realized something.

Lia made me weak-kneed too.

CHAPTER

Lia

I WAS ALIVE WITH ENERGY, SERVING CUSTOMER AFTER customer, happier than I'd ever been working at Jimney's. I refused to admit that the playlist on the speakers was making me this way, but the music Max had chosen—the slow, cock rock of Guns N' Roses, mixed with God only knows who else—was no doubt the reason I felt the way I did.

I plucked a few limes from the bowl beneath the bar and grabbed the saltshaker from my left. Tossing my apron on the counter, I hollered at Aubrey about taking my half hour—not that she'd listen.

I approached the table full of my favorite people, only to hear Addie squeal, "Lia!" She jumped up, knocking her chair to the floor. It was apparent she wasn't pregnant, considering how much she'd been drinking. Mom would be disappointed.

"I miss you." Just barely giving me the chance to set

the tray on the table, Addie slammed into me, her arms around my neck.

"Whoa." My eyes went wide, zeroing in on my brother. "Maybe these extra shots aren't such a good idea."

Collin chuckled from over her shoulder, then leaned back to listen to something Gavin was saying.

"I know your secret." Addie giggled against my ear and patted my head at the same time. "It's about time you bashed that man's meat monkey."

I stiffened. Bashed the what? On instinct, I searched the room for Max.

"I won't tell your brother though." She squeezed me tighter, almost cutting off my oxygen supply. "Promise."

I pulled back, but her glazed stare told me not to push. I'd never seen Addie this drunk before. It wasn't a pretty sight. Red-rimmed eyes, slurring words... She was a mess.

"Have a seat, lady. It seems I have some catching up to do," I said, settling her on my brother's lap, all while trying to ignore the tug of guilt in my stomach. If she knew about Max and me, then it was only a matter of time before Collin found out. It's not that I didn't want him to know. I just wanted to be the one to tell him—at the right time.

Addie happily obliged, snuggling against my brother's chest like it was where she belonged. Seeing her and my brother so in love only pushed me to want what they had. Things between Max and me had been so easy this past week, almost like it had been before we stopped talking to each other. Except now we got to kiss. A lot. And holy Jesus, did I love to kiss Max.

"Where's Max?" I asked, searching the room.

"Dance floor," Gavin grumbled, jutting his chin out.

"Hey, that's mine." Addie leaned forward, grabbing Gavin's arm as he reached for her glass. The drink tipped, spilling all over his pants.

"Christ, Addie. Sober up." Gavin shot out of his seat and took off toward the bathrooms.

"Wow. He's a piece of work tonight." I sipped on the soda I'd brought over for myself, knowing I couldn't drink on the job. When I turned to look for Max again, my jaw dropped in shock.

The guy who'd vowed a commitment to me just a week ago had another woman—Addie's best friend— falling all over him on the dance floor.

"Asshole," I hissed, not caring who heard me or what I looked like as I took off toward the back of the bar. Max called after me, but I ignored him because of my one-track mind and suddenly pissed-off mood.

Needing space, I pulled open the back door that led to the alley. The smell of greasy food and garbage from the Dumpster smacked me in the face, drawing the anger down over me like a curtain.

He was just dancing.

He told me he loved me. That he wanted me.

Day by day...that's all this is.

He's not Travis, stupid. He's Max. Max won't hurt you.

I'm not sure who was trying to do the convincing— New Lia or Old—but either way, it crushed me.

Hands braced against the side of the building, I inhaled through my nose and out through my mouth. My stomach knotted with nerves and anger, and the edges of the bricks dug into my palms. Angry tears clung to my lashes. I quickly wiped them away, not wanting anyone to see the damning evidence on my cheeks—and hating even more that I couldn't stop them.

What was wrong with me? Why was I freaking out over this? Not even with Travis had I been this emotionally wicked, and I'd caught him having sex with another woman.

Granted, I never truly loved Travis.

But I did love Max. More than anything.

Just when my insides began to ease, when I thought I had this unexplainable feeling inside me figured out and under control, Max came bursting out the door. "Hey, what's wrong? What happened?" He flew toward me, pulling me into a tight hug.

I couldn't help but lean into him, though my words spoke otherwise. "I'm fine, Max. Just…go back inside." I cringed and looked to my right, hating the crackle in my voice.

I was jealous, bottom line. And I *really* needed to get over it.

Despite my request, he rubbed his nose across the side of my neck. Then he dropped his arms from around my waist, only to brace them against the wall by my head. "No. I'm not going to just *go inside*. Not until you tell me what's wrong."

I squeezed my eyes shut, knowing I needed to get this off my chest now. Otherwise, it would eat me alive. "Fine, you want to know what's wrong with me?" I huffed. "I-I didn't like that…that *thing* that just happened inside." I folded my arms in between us, needing distance.

"Didn't like what thing?" His eyebrows drifted together in genuine confusion.

"The dancing, you…Kenna, all…that…" God,

apparently jealousy was making me incoherent. Stupid Max and his stupid spell over me. It was so much easier *not* caring.

But so much less amazing, Lia. Don't forget that.

He blinked. "Are you jealous?"

I nodded once and looked at my feet. No point in refuting the truth.

A soft sigh slipped from his mouth before he whispered, "It was just a dance, Lee-Lee. That's all. Kenna wanted to make someone jealous. My eyes were on you the entire time, if you didn't notice." He tucked some of my hair behind my ear, and I lifted my face to meet his eyes.

Deep down, I knew that. But hearing him say it meant the world to me. It also proved how much more I had to learn about real relationships.

Water pooled just beneath a rusted spout to my right. A light drip echoed in the space, as quick as the *thud, thud, thud* of my heartbeat inside my ears. Slowly, Max moved his hands around my back, tucking his fingers under my shirt and holding them flat against my spine.

"I'm sorry," I whispered this time. "This is all just... weird and new and...not my forte."

A slow, unnerving grin lit up his face as he said, "Just so you know, jealousy makes you all kinds of sexy." He tickled my ribs, then pulled his hands out from beneath my shirt.

I lowered my forehead to his chest and mumbled. "It's not a fun experience, that's for damn sure."

"Tell me about it."

The rumble of the music inside Jimney's sounded distant from the other side of the wall, the only sound between us for minutes. More than anything else, I wanted to stay right there, ignore everything inside, and be in a bubble that consisted of only us. It was easier to figure out this relationship stuff when nobody else was involved.

"I'm sorry if I hurt your feelings, Lee-Lee." Max kissed the top of my head.

"And I'm sorry for being such a newbie at this." I leaned my head back to look up at him. "I'm confused and scared and…not any good at being a girlfriend." I shut my eyes, trying to calm my overactive emotions. "I didn't feel this way with Travis, and he's the only guy I've ever officially *dated* before."

Max leveled his forehead with mine and whispered, "It's okay, 'cause I'm not too good at this either, remember?" I nodded. "We're taking this day by day. There's no rush to a finish line. We have our whole lives to find out what happens next."

I nodded, gripping his wrists. The scent of his warm cologne filled my nose with every breath I took, calming me even more. "You make me feel something I'm scared of feeling."

"What's that?" he asked.

"Reality."

He hugged me to his chest, dropping his chin to the top of my head. "The good kind or the bad?" I heard him gulp and felt the increasing pressure of his hands against my back. I knew he was nervous about my answer, maybe even more than I was.

"The good." I urged him back a bit, running my fingers through the sides of his hair. It'd grown longer over the last few months, shaggier like a puppy. He reminded me so much of a boy, though he'd been through the world as a man in so many ways.

"I love you, Lia." He blinked once. "And I want to be the man you need."

"You are." Because there was no other... Never would be as far as I was concerned. "I just don't want to lose you if I'm not enough."

There, I'd said it. Wasn't that hard.

"Jesus, baby. When will you understand that you're more than enough for me?" He dropped his mouth, pressing his lips softly to mine.

I looked him in the eyes when he pulled back, trying to find a flaw in his statement. But all I could see were the love and devotion he spoke of. And desire. That was *always* there.

I knew then what I had to do. Accept this, flawed or not. Accept *myself*—and my fears most of all. If I didn't, I'd lose the one thing that meant the world to me.

Most of all, I needed Max to know that I was tired of waiting. Tired of putting our intimacy off. It was time to prove that what happened in The Club wasn't just because I'd been tipsy. It was because I wanted him. In all the ways he'd let me.

With slow, sure fingers, I lowered my hand to the button of my shorts and slipped it open. Max frowned, staring at my movements. He didn't speak, and neither did I. As much as I loved his patience and his willingness to take things day by day, I was ready for the good stuff.

I put his hands where mine were, then moved my hands to my side. He pressed his forehead to mine and nearly growled as he said, "Tell me what you want."

No regrets. No hesitation. "Touch me, Max. Show me how much you love me."

At my demand, he slowly pulled my zipper down for me, wasting no time as he slipped his fingertips into the front of my panties.

I arched into his touch, urging his hands even lower by the wrists until his fingertips caressed the center where I wanted him the most.

Kissing my neck, he moved his other hand to the bottom of my shorts and tugged them to my ankles. "Anything for you."

My breath came out in unsteady pants as he stepped on the denim. They held my legs in place, promising a quick fall if I tried to move. Slowly, he trailed his hands along the sides of my thighs, then tugged my panties down too.

"I'm gonna make you feel good now." Then he dropped onto the cement before me, laying kisses on my inner thighs.

I trembled, tossing my head back against the wall. "Oh God…"

"Tell me yes, Lee-Lee. Tell me you want my mouth on your pussy. Tell me all the things you want me to do. Because I'm not touching you until I've got permission."

"Yes… You can—"

In a flash, he pressed his nose against my nakedness, cutting me off. Inhaling once, he rubbed the end of his nose up and down my clit, back and forth—a pattern I couldn't even begin to keep track of. "You smell fucking amazing. Bet you taste just as good."

With practiced ease, he moved his hands around to caress my naked ass. Kneading the flesh, he flicked his

tongue against my center. "Oh my God, Max. W-what…
what are you doing?"

He smiled against me. "It's called foreplay, baby girl."

"No this isn't fore… Oh shit." I arched against his
face, my knees going weak.

He slid one finger inside me, curling it at the tip, only
to rub his tongue over my clit at the same time. My body
shook all over, no longer just my knees.

Max and his beautiful fast-and-slow foreplay was
everything.

"You know how many times I've imagined doing
this to you?" he whispered. When I didn't respond, he
kept going, his mouth just centimeters from my clit. It
was the best torture, the worst torture, the right kind of
torture. "I've thought about it a lot, Lee-Lee. So much
that nobody's meant anything to me since I met you.
Nobody will ever mean to me what you do."

Tears filled my eyes—not the kind I wanted to deal
with right now, not when I was so close to the blissful-
ness he promised. But still, hearing him say that unfurled
something else inside me. Something I'd thought I never
would find: vulnerable passion.

Panting hard, I shut my eyes against the wetness and
rocked against his mouth, silently begging for him to go
faster, to give me more. I tangled my fingers in his hair,
urging him this way and that, until he had me crying out
his name.

My ass was raw from rubbing against the brick building, but I didn't care. Nothing was going to ruin this for
me. Nothing was going to take the bliss away.

"Max, yessss." I grinded and rubbed a little harder,
nearly smothering him as my orgasm hit its highest point.

"Fucking beautiful." He kissed and licked my clit once more, then twice. I shivered, the sensitivity too much, but not enough. Then he stood before me, and I opened my eyes, and there in his stare was the Max I needed the most: the Max who loved me like I loved him.

My shorts were now in his hands, but the underwear was MIA—most likely in his pocket. That was just the kind of guy he was, and I couldn't, for the life of me, care. He'd just eaten me out in the alley behind my place of employment, right where Travis had fucked another girl.

Best. Memory eraser. Ever.

I accepted the shorts without the underwear and slipped them on, all while he kissed my neck, my shoulders too.

When I was dressed and ready to go back in, he pressed his palms against my cheeks and leaned forward, kissing me long and slow. His tongue trailed across mine, like he was intentionally sharing the pleasure he'd tasted with me.

"You good now?" He grinned so widely that little crinkles formed around his dark eyes.

I grinned back and then rubbed my nose over his cheek, completely at ease. "I will be once I return the favor."

Slowly, hand in hand, we slipped back down the alley toward the door, our palms caressing, our eyes never falling far from the other's face. This was the stuff of daydreams.

"Hey!" I blinked, coming out of my postorgasmic bliss as the sound of Collin's voice boomed from the end of the hall just inside the door. "Where were you guys?"

I swallowed and subtly pulled my hand out of Max's

to settle it behind my back. "I was going to the bathroom. Max too."

"Outside?" He looked behind us before shaking his head. "No matter. We gotta go. Addie puked all over the table. McKenna just punched some guy, and Gavin looks like he's not gonna be standing much longer. I'm gonna need your help getting them all home." Collin looked to Max, then back over his shoulder.

I, on the other hand, laughed. Postorgasm was seriously messing with my emotions.

"You've gotta be shitting me." Max laughed too, looking at me with a wide grin.

Seriously. We hadn't been gone *that* long.

Collin glared at me, then raised his eyebrows at Max. "Not shitting you at all. Now let's move."

Still high from the Mighty Max O, I followed them out of the hallway, only to be stopped at the bar by Max's mouth against my cheek.

"Call me when you get home tonight." He slipped his hand around my waist, splaying his fingers out flat across my stomach.

I stiffened, not used to the PDA.

"Relax." He kissed the tip of my ear.

My shoulders fell and I turned, first looking toward the table where my brother was trying to wrangle three very drunken idiots into submission. "You better go." I smiled and shook my head, my face heating as I met Max's stare once more.

Dark eyes sad, Max looked at me like he was afraid I'd disappear. Maybe I'd been a little crazy there for a while, worried about things I couldn't control, but seeing the fear in his eyes put everything in perspective.

"Are we good now?" He raised his hand to my neck, tracing my tattoos.

For the first time in a very long time, I realized my answer wasn't going to be a lie.

"Yeah, we're good." And then I leaned forward and kissed him goodbye.

CHAPTER 24

Lia

Two Saturdays after my last night at Jimney's, I woke to the smell of frying bacon and the blaring of country music, while I was tucked cozily under the comforter in my boyfriend's bed. This was the stuff of daydreams. Truly.

With a grin, I rolled over, stretching my arms out like a cat. Spending the night at his place instead of mine was definitely my new favorite activity.

He'd kissed me in all my special places, and I'd kissed him right back, making sure he didn't cry out my name too loudly when he came inside my mouth. *That* was the most erotically amazing thing I'd ever done. And I couldn't wait to do it again.

After that, we'd chatted like we'd always been able to do, talking about nothing and everything. Only this time, there was an intimacy we hadn't shared before… something that meant more to me than the foreplay we'd been taking part in for two weeks now.

My brother and Addie were gone for the weekend, off to the Mayo Clinic in Rochester to visit Addie's mom. They'd left Max and me to watch Chloe, which meant the two of us were free to be together the way a *normal* couple was, at least when Gavin wasn't around.

"Beaner, no! Do not touch that." I heard Max yell.

A crash sounded, followed by a long, squealing "Yay!" Forgetting where I was, I raced from the room and down the hall.

"What's going on in…" I froze, catching sight of Gavin standing just inside the front door.

Oh God. Why is he here?

Eyes wide, lips parted, Gav looked at me like I'd committed the world's worst felony.

Clueless that the two of us had been caught red-handed, Max kept jabbering. "Baseballs cannot be thrown inside the house, Beaner."

I held my breath and glanced at the carpet, my face so hot I was sure I was moments from melting into the floor. Shattered into pieces was a vase that I was positive had never seen the stem of a flower. Instead, packets of condoms hung between the chunks of broken glass. Ultra-ribbed and magnum-sized condoms, to be exact. Any other time, I probably would've freaked out about Chloe getting cut by the glass, but Max had it under control… and the view of my niece tossing those square packets into the air like confetti, along with Gavin's mortified expression, had my stomach tightening with laughter.

"Jesus," Max barked, jumping back at the sight of Gavin. "Knock next time, idiot."

But Gavin's eyes were still zeroed in on me, accusation heavy in his stare.

To break the tension, I took a step into the room and said, "You guys keep condoms in vases around here? Why? Are you looking to grow them with some fertilizer and water?"

Max zeroed in on my bare legs, his eyes popping before he looked at Gavin again. "Well, crap. This ain't good." He dropped his chin to his chest.

Gavin shook his head, coming out of a minute-long coma, only to scoop up Chloe and awkwardly tuck her against his hip. Unlike Max, he walked in my direction, his eyes looking everywhere *but* my T-shirt and legs. With her hands full of rubbers, Chloe spotted me and bounced.

This could've been an ad for birth control gone wrong.

I swiped my niece from Gavin's arms and planted her at my side. Blue eyes wide, she attempted to shove the foil packets down my shirt.

"I knew it," Gavin barked, taking a step back from me. He glared at Max and shook his head, not disgusted but more…worried.

Max's face went red this time. "Dude, shut up."

I cringed, rubbing a hand over my forehead.

"Nice shirt, Lia." Gavin shook his head, his eyes going light as he smirked.

I looked down and read the words on the front. *Play Rugby. Bones heal. Pain is temporary. And chicks dig scars.* This looked really bad.

"It's not like that." Even though clearly it was.

"You can't tell Colly." Max's eyes locked with mine, an apology written all over his face.

I held my breath and moved around the rest of the mess. Maybe I should've put on more clothes, but the thought of Gavin knowing our little secret had my brain short-circuiting as I sat on the couch. I settled Chloe next to my thigh, and she laid her head against my shoulder as if knowing I needed the extra cuddle.

"Fuck." Max lowered his head into his hands, scrubbing them over his face.

"Uck!" Chloe happily repeated, tossing the remainder of the condoms into the air with a giggle. Weirdly, the song "It's Raining Men" passed through my head at that moment, with both Max and Gavin dressed in drag, their heads back and smiling as condom after condom dripped down on their faces from a disco-ball-lit sky.

Warped didn't even begin to describe my mind-set.

"Care to tell me where she learned that word, boys?"

I leaned forward and looked into my niece's eyes. She batted her lashes at me, far too innocent for a kiddo who'd just dropped what was nearly an f-bomb. With a soft smile, she laid her head back against my shoulder again and yawned, only to pop her thumb into her mouth.

"She learned that word a while ago, actually." Gavin cleared his throat, rubbing the back of his neck.

Max laughed and pointed a finger at Gavin. "Thanks to Uncle Gavvy here."

"You taught my niece how to say the f-word?" I glared at Gavin.

Behind his scruffy beard, his face went red. "It was an accident. Kid's like a sponge."

"Yeah, well, when her daddy finds out, he's going to beat you." Yawning like Chloe had done, I stroked the back of her hair.

"I've got dirt on you both now. Don't forget." Gavin smirked. "You tell Collin about Chloe's new vocab, and I'll tell him about you two." He motioned a finger between me and Max, an evil gleam in his green eyes.

"Are you blackmailing me and my woman?" Max tsked, stuffing the remaining condoms into his pocket. "I may just have to kick your ass, if that's the case. Won't be pretty neither."

My woman.

Warmth ran through my chest at Max's sentiment.

"*Your woman?*" Gavin mumbled something like "Not another one" before he finished louder, "If you're gonna keep this up—which, by the looks of it, you are—would you both just do me a favor?"

I smiled, suddenly not caring that he knew, because if Gavin was on board with the two of us, maybe Collin would be okay with it too.

"What's that?" I asked.

"Don't screw on the couch all hours of the day and night like Collin and Addison do. You never know when someone's gonna stop by."

"*What?*" Max and I said in unison.

"This couch, right here, that I'm sitting on?" I asked, pointing at the likely soiled cushions. *Eww*.

Max grumbled, "That's it. I'm moving in with you." He pointed at Gav.

I shouldn't have been so surprised. My brother and Addie had no issue with consummating their relationship on every surface possible. One time, I even caught them in the garage going at it on the hood of Gavin's Suburban. If only he knew...

"I'm out of here." Gavin leaned down to kiss Chloe on the head. "Just heard that noise and wanted to make sure everything was okay."

"Where you headed so early this morning?" Max asked what I was dying to know. Gavin hadn't just *gotten up* this early for weeks. In fact, now that I was really looking at him, he looked a lot healthier. Still had a face full of hair, which was growing on me, but his eyes were brighter and there was some actual color to his skin. He looked like, well, he looked happy.

"Going to the Y."

Max flashed me a smile from across the room. "Yeah? I've been there a time or two myself lately. Got in a good workout last night, in fact. Lots of sweating and hard labor, but so fucking worth it." He lowered his gaze, staring at my legs—or, more accurately, the space between my thighs, which thankfully was covered by his boxers. *His* version of working out at the Y was most definitely *not* the version Gav was referring to. It's a good thing I was used to his dirty humor…and liked it.

Gavin tugged on his shoes, thankfully not noticing. "You wanna hit up O'Paddy's with me tonight?"

Max yawned. "Nah. Me and Lee-Lee got plans to take Chloe to the kids' museum and for pizza after."

I leaned over Chloe and made bug eyes at her, pretending his *plans* didn't affect me as much as they did. She giggled, reaching for my outstretched tongue. Max held all the good vibes of a potential father—loving, protective, and goofy. Even though having children was the last thing on my mind right now, Max definitely made me think twice about all the things I hadn't been sure I wanted once upon a time.

When Gavin was gone, Max walked over and grabbed Chloe from my lap. "You okay with him knowing?"

I nodded. "Afraid Addie probably knows about us too. She's been looking at me weird all week."

"Yeah," Max said, rubbing the back of his neck. "She kinda got it out of me last weekend."

I smiled. "She has those tendencies."

The two of us chatted with Chloe, asking her random yes-or-no questions. We laughed and she giggled, which ended with Max playing peekaboo with her.

"Whaddya say, ladies? You two up for a day out, just us three?" He grinned and tossed Chloe up into the air again. Her loud giggles filled the room like tiny bells.

"Yes. Absolutely." I nodded.

He blew a raspberry onto Chloe's stomach, then tossed her up once more.

"You're good at that." I stared back at him, seeing things I'd never seen before. Not just on the outside, but the inside too. The kindness and love I'd always known to be there were becoming clearer every second I spent with him. I'd never get enough of those two qualities.

"Good at what?" he asked.

"The daddy-uncle thing." I tickled the bottom of Beaner's toes, and she exploded into more giggles.

"I love kids. Want a lot of them, preferably an entire rugby team of boys. And one girl."

I raised an eyebrow, running my fingers through Chloe's curls as he sat her beside me. "The world's in for it, if there's even a chance of seven Maxes running around someday."

But in the back of my mind, I could see it: an entire field of soccer players, or baseball players, even. Not football, because Max *hated* football. Not rugby because that sport was killer dangerous—even though he, my brother, and Gavin lived for it. Max would most likely make his sons into superstars long before they even learned to talk. And his little girl... She'd be gorgeous, with her father's dark eyes and hair.

The one thought flitting through my mind as I watched him play with my niece was: *Does he want that with me?*

CHAPTER

Max

"YOU'VE USED ALL THE TOKENS." LEE-LEE LAID HER HEAD on my shoulder. She was my second biggest cheerleader next to Chloe.

I tossed a ball into the moving hoop. Beaner cheered again, reaching over the top of the glass barrier to grab me another ball. Chuck E. Cheese's was not just a place for kids.

"So? Chloe Bean here's doing a mighty fine job of getting us some free entertainment. Kid's a natural." I watched as she used her little hands and shoved the orange ball forward, missing the hoop by a mile.

Standing to my right, Lia looked at me with bright eyes and a smile tugging at her lips. This day—this entire weekend—with just her and Chloe and me had been fucking incredible. I didn't want it to end. There was no hiding or sneaking around. I was free to touch her whenever I wanted, which was pretty much every second she was near me. Best part was that Lia wasn't shy about touching me. It all felt so real, so domesticated. That probably should've scared me, but it didn't, because it was exactly what I wanted most out of life. And whether she knew it or not, I wanted it with Lia.

"Fine." She grinned and shoved her hands into my front shorts pockets. Chloe had her back to us, and because I couldn't help myself, I turned and grabbed Lia around the waist.

"Go digging any deeper in there, and you're gonna find all sorts of fun treasures."

She licked her lips, her fingers stroking my dick through the pockets. "Maybe that's the point."

I shivered and shut my eyes, forgetting where we were, and kissed her, so hard I didn't even see Beaner fall.

"Oh my God!" Lia shoved me away and dropped to the floor beside her.

Chloe lay on her side, crying so hard she'd gathered a crowd. I couldn't move. Couldn't even speak. She held her arm to her chest, staring back at me with fear and pain in her blue eyes. The tears ran down her chubby cheeks, which were so red she looked like a swelling apple.

"Max!" Lia kicked my shin. "Her arm…"

"Fuck." Not thinking twice, I knocked my ass into high gear and lifted Chloe's shaking body to my chest. She clung to the front of my shirt with her good arm, snot and tears soaking the material in seconds. "We gotta get her to the hospital."

Lia followed me as we raced out the door. A couple of workers tried to stop us, asking if we needed an ambulance, but I told them all to fuck off. Getting pissed when I wanted to cry was my natural reaction.

The hospital was only a few blocks away, but I didn't

want to have to put her in a car seat, and her little arm—
swollen and already changing colors—wouldn't let it
happen. So I tossed Lia my keys and sat in the backseat
with Beaner on my lap, praying to every holy entity out
there that my favorite little girl would be okay.

My eyes never found Lia's in the rearview mirror as
we drove, too focused on Chloe as I tried to soothe her
with a song. But that only made her cry harder. Never in
my life had I felt so helpless.

Somewhere during the five-minute drive, Chloe had
finally stopped crying. How the fuck that happened, I
didn't have a clue. She had to be in pain because her arm
was a swollen mess. Her dad was gonna kill me. Jesus,
what had I done?

When we got to the hospital, Lia opened the car
door. I froze for a second, not sure what to do. "Take
her inside, Max." Eyes watering, she searched my face
as I stepped out, her reaction calm, unlike mine. "I'll be
right behind you."

In the main emergency room lobby, I raced toward
the receptionist, barely holding it together as I stepped
in front of her desk. I'd seen so much bad in my life, but
I'd never been this scared.

By the time the nurses came out to get Chloe, Lia
had explained the whole situation, like the grown-up I
apparently was not. The girl who'd always needed me
to guide her through tough shit was leading the charge.
Insurance cards were handed over, forms were signed,
and by the time we got Chloe settled into a room, I was
restless and ready to jump out of my own skin.

"Max." Lia kneeled in front of me, her hands on my
knees. "I have to go with her for an X-ray."

I nodded, barely able to hear her. She looked into my eyes, looked back at Chloe, then to me once more. Swallowing hard, I watched the easy effort with which Lia moved back to her niece's bedside. She was a natural, whether she knew it or not.

"Has anybody called the parents?"

At the nurse's words, a switch flipped inside me. I was a fucking idiot. I needed to call Colly and Addie ASAP.

"I'm her aunt. I've been given permission to watch out for her this weekend. Her father is in Minnesota with his girlfriend," I heard Lia say.

The doctor, probably a young resident, looked Lia over with unguarded disgust. But Lia took it in stride, too busy cooing and loving over her crying niece to care what anyone thought of her.

So what if she was wearing shorts that barely covered her ass and lace stockings that looked like something straight out of *Pretty Woman*? Didn't matter that she had hair made of rainbows and more piercings in her nose and face than in her ears. She was a fucking rock star, *my* rock star, and that made me stand up and finally step into action.

The doc stepped back at seeing me, blinking as though I'd just appeared in the room. She took in my khaki shorts and polo shirt and said, "And you are…?" There was no disgust in her eyes this time. Instead, I recognized the telltale sign of interest as she tapped her pen against her lips.

"I'm this little girl's uncle." I puffed my chest out and wrapped my arm around Lia, who immediately relaxed against me. As selfish as it sounded, I felt a hell of a lot better knowing Lia needed me more than she'd let on. "And I plan on calling her daddy as soon as you get her out of here for an X-ray."

Eyes wide, the doctor nodded before wheeling Chloe out of the room, a nurse trailing behind her. I pressed my lips to the side of Lia's head. "I'm so fucking sorry I put her up on that damn game."

Lee-Lee squeezed me against her side and pulled back, meeting my gaze. "And I'm sorry I didn't stop you from doing it." She shrugged, but the sadness in her eyes wasn't directed at me. I knew this because she leaned in close and kissed my lips before she slipped out of the room to follow Chloe.

Seconds later, I had my phone out, dialing. After three rings, Addison picked up, giggling right before she said, "Hello?"

Collin grumbled something about hurrying up, which had me sucking in a breath. They were obviously loving all their free time.

"Hey, Short Stuff. Colly around?"

"Of course. Everything okay?"

I cringed. "Not really. But I gotta talk to Collin first."

She spoke some rushed words to my buddy just as he got on the line. "What's wrong?"

I told him. Not just about how fucking careless and stupid I'd been, but also how sorry I was and how I'd never be that big of a dumb-ass again. I went on and on and on, pacing the room and pulling at my hair, until I realized he hadn't said shit.

"I'll be there as soon as I can." And then he was gone, the phone clicking dead. I sat on a chair, one hand on my forehead as I called Gavin.

Unlike with Collin, I told Gavin every detail, including how I'd gotten distracted by Lia. "Better hope it was fucking worth it," he said, only to ask, "Does Chloe need anything?" Which made me feel like an ass because I hadn't been thinking about that.

Ten minutes later, when I was thinking the damn worst, they came back into the room. Lia sat on the bed, a bottle of water in one hand and Chloe on her lap with an ice-cream sandwich. Her little face was a mess of red skin, wet tears, and chocolate.

"Aww, Beaner, I'm so sorry." I moved to stand by her side, only to see her arm strapped to her tummy in some sort of sling.

A new voice piped up behind me. "Don't beat yourself up over this, Max. She's a tough kid." McKenna, dressed in a pair of nursing scrubs, popped into the room. Her blue eyes narrowed as she whispered something into Lia's ear.

She works here? How did I not know this?

Just then, the doctor stepped into the room, avoiding eye contact with Kenna and Lia and focusing only on me. "From what we can tell, Chloe likely will need to have surgery. Not right now, since there's too much swelling, but eventually." She cleared her throat, chin up, and stared down her pointy nose. The tension rolling off the stuffy lady about suffocated me. I snuck a quick look at Lia and found her eyes rolling as she glanced at Kenna.

"Fine, thanks," I said, distracted as I stared back at Beaner, nearly asleep in Lia's arms.

The doctor eventually left the room, taking with her the stench of bitch. Still, nothing about this night could make me feel better, knowing my sweet little Chloe Bean would need surgery.

"I'm not working peds tonight, which sucks because I would've loved to stay with this little miss." Kenna reached over and ran the back of her hand down Chloe's messy cheek, a strange look of awe passing over her features as she did.

"Thank you, McKenna. I don't know what I would've done if you hadn't walked by." Lia's voice cracked as she laid her head against Chloe's.

"Addie's my best friend. When she tells me the girl she loves like her daughter is laid up in the hospital where I work, I'm going to go looking for her." Kenna smiled at Lia and then frowned at me. "And *you*, asshole..."

I jerked my head back. "What'd I do?"

Her frown slipped into a sly smirk as she said, "If I'd known you and Lia were together, I never would've dry humped your ass at Jimney's. Way to make me look like a skank."

Lia snorted and shook her head.

I glared back and forth between the two of them. What had I missed?

Once Kenna was gone and it was just the three of us, I motioned for Lia to move so I could hold Chloe. Lee-Lee looked like she was about to fall asleep sitting up. Without arguing, she switched seats with me. Beaner was out cold, probably from pain meds, so she didn't seem to care where she went, as long as she had a body to lie on.

"You good?" I whispered, swiping the remainder of Chloe's ice cream from her now-lax fingers. Sticky gunk stuck to my hands, so I ate the rest of the thing and licked my fingers clean.

"As good as I can be." Lia shrugged, avoiding my stare.

"Liar."

I wanted to tug her onto the bed and hold her close too. Instead, she sat at end of the mattress, peeling off the water bottle's label. "I let that stupid doctor get to me though. Something I never do."

"What'd she say?" I frowned.

"She asked if I wouldn't mind waiting *outside* the X-ray room. Said since I wasn't the parent—"

"You're her *aunt*, and she's only fifteen months old. She needed you there."

Lia sighed and met my stare. "I know. I told her that. Then she mumbled something under her breath that sounded like 'white trash,' but I couldn't tell. So, I called her some names, just in case. Then Chloe started crying, and we hadn't even gotten the X-ray taken yet. That's when Kenna showed and—"

"Hey, shhh..." Because I needed to hold my other girl, I settled sleeping Chloe against the pillows on the bed, her head falling to the side. As quickly as I could, I jumped up and grabbed Lia's trembling hand, then pulled her onto my lap, falling back into a crappy recliner. She cried against me, her shoulders shaking. "Don't let her get to you."

"I couldn't help it." She sniffed. "I was already on the verge of cracking, worried about Beaner, worried about you having to call my brother. I just...lost it. Got stupid and cracked."

I rubbed her back and kissed her cheek, inhaling the scent of her strawberry shampoo. "Baby, we all gotta freak out sometimes. The important thing is you had a good reason. And that doc needed to be dealt with."

Lia's body shook with laughter this time, the noise so soft I could barely hear it over my thundering heart. I should've gone with them. I knew that lady was a cold-hearted bitch the second she sneered at the beautiful girl in my arms. Yet I'd been too freaked to do anything then.

Why was that? How could I get through two years of fighting insurgents in the desert, yet I couldn't handle seeing Chloe get hurt?

"I'm sorry I spaced out when we got here."

Lia sat up straighter, eyes watering as she searched my face. "You were scared. So was I. It was a natural reaction. When something bad happens, I either get bitchy or take charge. You, on the other hand, go catatonic." She shrugged. "It's called dealing with our demons. We all have ways of doing it. Some are active; some are not."

I leaned forward, kissing her lips this time. "I still don't like it. I'll work on that for you. You need a man who can be strong for you."

"Oh, come on, Maxwell. I don't need that. If anything, I just need a partner to be strong at my side, not for me." She brought my hand to her lips, kissing the backs of my fingers. "We're not expected to know what to do at every waking moment in our lives, you know."

"Not what I've been taught. Growing up, I had to be on defense all the time with my father. Then when me and Ma finally left him, we were still on defense, trying to make it through life. I had to be the man she needed."

Lia yawned and toyed with the neckline of my shirt. "You're not on the frontline anymore, and I'm not your mom. It's okay to let someone else be the hero once in a while."

She snuggled against my chest, and I draped my arms over her legs. I pulled her as close as I could, trying to get into that mind-set—the non-heroic kind. Love made me into that man, the one wanting to be her protector *and* the man she was in love with.

Still, I was okay with doing things her way, even if that meant sharing a little weakness with her. Not sure what that said about me as a man, but as Lia's boyfriend, things were different.

Silence stretched between us, our chests rising and falling at an almost identical pace. At one point I thought she'd gone to sleep, until she finally whispered, "If you and I had gotten together earlier in life, do you think we'd be where we are now?"

"Fuck yes." No doubt in my mind. I knew Lia was someone different from day one. It'd just taken me a while to get off my lazy ass and do something about it.

"Don't be mad." She toyed with the back of my hair, her breath a whisper against my neck. "But I don't think we would've."

My jaw locked, but I concentrated on keeping the rest of my body relaxed. I didn't like thinking like that. If I wanted something, I got it and then kept it. Sure, we would have been a hell of a lot younger and were going through some bad shit then, but everything in me believed our relationship would've panned out in the end.

"Doesn't matter." She cuddled in closer, her lips grazing my neck as she spoke. "I'm here, you're here… We're right where we belong now." She yawned again.

I held her closer. "Yes, we are." That was the one thing I knew for certain.

CHAPTER 26

Lia

THE SMALL WINDOW OF THE HOSPITAL ROOM SHOWED IT WAS nearing dawn when my eyes opened. The early morning rays of sun were just beginning to filter into the dark, white-walled space. Although I'd only fallen asleep an hour or so ago, I felt like I'd been down for days. Scratchy lids made my eyes burn, and I rubbed the edges, trying to regain my sense of the here and now.

Doing my best not to disturb Chloe, who lay asleep by my side, I slipped my leg over the edge of the bed and set my bare feet on the cold hospital floor. Beneath me, the mattress shifted and I quickly glanced over my shoulder to make sure she was still asleep. Of course she was. The girl had been through hell. And without her daddy by her side.

Guilt ate away at me when I stood to stretch. The thought of them wrapping her arm in that heavy temporary cast the night before about broke my heart. All the poor little thing did was cry out in pain, at least until the past couple of hours when a new dose of pain meds was given.

My body ached from lying in one position for a while, my limbs heavy from what little sleep I got. I blinked, catching a glimpse of my mom sleeping in the same chair Max and I had cuddled in the night before. Her pale face was a stressed mask even in her sleep, and I brushed my hand over the top of her head. I'd worried her and Dad so much with my reckless behavior. God, if they ever got word of my arrest, they'd renounce me as their daughter once and for all.

Speaking of Dad, his voice rocketed from outside the room, followed by Max's soft laugh. I couldn't help but smile at the sound. I loved how close they were.

Before pushing open the door, I grabbed my sandals. Not wanting to wake Mom or Chloe, I didn't put them on, just tucked them under my arm. The doctors thought it best for Chloe to stay a couple of nights at the hospital, just so they could keep an eye on her. And since she seemed to be in so much pain, nobody argued the fact.

Collin would be flying in early tomorrow evening, something about his plane having been grounded due to mechanical failure. I knew not being here was probably driving him crazy, but with Gavin, Max, my parents, and me all teaming up, Chloe was in good hands.

Since this was a small family-focused hospital, two people were able to stay in the room with Chloe all night. My mom and I had volunteered. Dad and Max had camped out in the lobby, while Gavin left late, claiming he had somewhere to be.

"Hey." Max's greeting was a breathy sigh, his eyes quick to meet mine.

Too tired to care about my dad's thoughts, I headed straight to Max, latching my arms around his neck. "Good morning."

I snuggled my nose against his neck, and he squeezed a little tighter, his body molding to mine.

Dad cleared his throat. "Why don't you two go home? Try to get a little rest. Mom and I will stay until Collin gets here tomorrow."

"And Addison will be here too, so he won't have to deal with this on his own." I pulled back, keeping my arm around Max's waist.

Dad sighed. "Addie has to stay behind. Apparently, her mother took a turn for the worse last night."

"Oh no." I pressed my hand over my mouth. And here Collin had to leave her alone so he could come deal with his daughter and her newly broken arm—a broken arm that had resulted from our carelessness.

Like he knew what I was thinking, Max turned to me and cupped my face between his hands. "Your dad's right. We should head out. Maybe make Beaner some cookies for a welcome-home present."

I nodded, trying to smile, but the ache buried in my throat made the action nearly impossible. "Okay."

Not bothering to say goodbye to Mom and Chloe, the two of us walked hand in hand down the hall. In the car, Max kept hold of my fingers, placing them on his lap. He cleared his throat as we pulled out of the lot. "Where do you want to go?"

I stared at his thumb as it stroked over mine. His hands were so warm and comforting, a reminder that I didn't want him to leave me today.

"I want to go wherever you go."

He blew out a slow breath. "Good." Lifting my hand with one of his, he kissed the back of my knuckles. "I wasn't gonna leave you alone, even if you asked me to."

"That could be considered stalking, you know." I smiled, secretly thankful our thoughts were in sync.

"Then arrest me, baby, 'cause I can't resist."

Shaking my head at his corny pun, I looked at him and said, "You're insane."

"And you love it."

He kissed the back of my hand once more, but the only thought running through my mind was: *That I do*.

It was Sunday, and everything was about to change again. That thought hurt my heart. This was our last day alone, which meant Max's and my temporary peace was over. The good thing was that we'd agreed to tell my brother sooner rather than later about us. Neither Max nor I wanted to keep it a secret. Still, the idea of telling Collin—especially after what happened with Chloe—made my stomach sour and twist like I'd eaten something rotten.

No matter what, I wouldn't let anything keep me from Max. I also wanted everyone to know we were together. He and I were real and right and everything I wanted. From here on out, I would do whatever I could to make that happen.

CHAPTER

Max

LIFE IS TOO FUCKING SHORT TO BE SCARED OF FINDING YOUR forever. After the last eighteen hours, I knew exactly where my forever stood: in front of my oven, dressed in a tiny tank top and my baggy boxers that hung low on her hips.

"Everything okay?" Lia glanced at me from over her shoulder, smiling as I stepped into the kitchen. I'd just gotten out of the shower a few minutes ago. I was a dumb-ass for not asking her to join me. At the same time, I'd needed a few minutes to figure out how I was gonna word the question I was dying to ask her tonight. A question that not only scared me to death, but also made my heart beat harder in excitement.

We'd spent most of the day cleaning the house so that we could all focus on Chloe when she got home the next day. Now it was time to make her some cookies.

"Yeah. I was just thinking about some stuff." I took a step into the kitchen, admiring the patch of skin exposed between the bottom of her tank and the top of my boxers.

Leaning against the counter, I watched as she yanked things out of the fridge. Milk, eggs, whipped cream… Pickles?

"What're you doing?" Smirking, I took in the sugar and flour mess, fingering the pickle jar before I propped myself up on the only clean spot I could find on the counter.

She set down everything in her hands with a huff, then turned toward me and blew a wet piece of hair out of her eyes. "Making cookies, remember?" Her lips pursed in the cutest fucking way. "I thought you might wanna show me how it's done."

"Sure thing. But this all has gotta go." I motioned toward the mess. "Don't like working in a dirty kitchen."

"What happened to the old adage? 'A good cook is a messy cook.'"

"I'm unoriginal."

She scoffed. "I've seen your work environment, Maxwell. It always looks like this, sometimes worse."

"But it's always clean before I start. That's the thing."

She rolled her eyes. "Fine, oh *master chef*. Let's clean." She popped her lips, drawing my gaze toward her mouth.

"I lied."

She frowned. "About what?"

I jumped off the counter, unable to sit still. Being near her without touching was pure fucking torture now, especially since she was mine to touch.

"Needing things clean."

"Figured as much. You're, like, the messiest person I

know, besides my brother. Dirty laundry for days, dishes soaking in the sink for even longer than that... Not to mention your room looks like someone took a sledge-hammer to—"

I gripped her waist, cutting her off. "Whoa, now. No need to get personal."

She leaned forward and kissed my lips, a quick peck that was entirely too sweet for what I really wanted. "Time's a-wasting, Chef Martinez." She faced the counter.

"Hmm, is it now..." Distracted by the soft pink of her tats, I lowered my mouth to her shoulder, licking around a vine, then a flower...until I spotted those words.

I swallowed, pulling back to look at them in full detail.

"What?" She froze.

"Why, Lee-Lee?" I traced the tattooed words: *Let me be your little bitch.*

They were ugly words for such a beautiful body, and I hated them.

Her hands trembled as she turned and pressed them against my chest. I met her stare, a warning that said *Don't even think about pushing me away.*

Like she knew what I was thinking, she sighed and looked at the floor.

"It's a reminder of that night."

I flinched. "That's one stupid reminder."

Her face went red. "Whatever. This is why I didn't want to tell you." She shoved me, but I didn't move. "Why I've never told anyone. You people keep telling me I need to talk about things, but when I do, this is what happens."

"I'm sorry." I rubbed a hand over my forehead, trying

to backtrack. "I just… Shit, I don't have a filter when it comes to this kind of stuff. Not when it kills me that I can't do something to make it better for you."

"I'm dealing with my past the best way I can. That's going to have to be enough."

I pressed my forehead to hers, needing to be close. "I wish I could find that fucker and rip his nuts off."

She smiled, but I could tell it was forced. "And leave me unable to kiss you whenever I want because you're spending life in jail?" She leaned forward even more, our noses touching. "Never."

"That'd be a damn tragedy, huh?"

She looked up at me, eyes bright—sparkling even, like the clearest lake on the sunniest of days. Stupid analogy, but true all the same. A guy could get lost in those eyes.

"The thing about this tattoo is that you only see one part. The rest is hidden."

"Where?" I looked over the rest of her shoulders, pulling down the straps of her tank, but all I could see were pink flowers and black vines.

"Here." She turned around and parted the back of her hair. "I had it done two months after that night. A girl I'd gone to high school with was dating this Russian dude who did tattoos. One Saturday, we all got stupid drunk, and he was there with his gun and ink." She shrugged. "Without anyone knowing, I went into her apartment bathroom and borrowed her boyfriend's razor and shaved the underside layer of my hair clean off."

"Damn, Lia…" At that point in time, I was hot in the desert, fighting off insurgents, learning about life and loss, thinking about a girl I'd left in the hospital with her parents a few nights before we left the States.

Had I known she was suffering… Had I known the truth…

I dug my nails into my palms. None of us knew what was going on at home, and even if Collin had, there was no way he would've told me. I barely knew his sister.

"I wanted something tough, ya know? Badass me, telling that asshole I wasn't going to be taken down." She tapped her nails against the counter she was braced against. "So for five months, the back of my head was shaved underneath, while I dyed the rest of my hair ink black. I didn't even look at the stupid thing until my mom happened to see me brushing my hair one day in my room. She cried for a really long time…" Lia rubbed her upper arms. "After she went to bed, I finally looked at it, then cried just as hard as she had, if not worse."

I pulled her hair apart to search the scalp. She let me, but the way her body trembled against mine was proof that it made her nervous. Normally, I wouldn't push her to do something that bothered her this much, but I had to see for myself what the rest of those words said.

The bottom part below her hairline said *Let me be your little bitch.*

The top part, which I read out loud, said, "I won't." For a good, long minute I stared, trying to make sense of the gibberish: *I won't let me be your little bitch.*

When the silence stretched too long, Lia laughed nervously. "Yeah…so my tattoo artist wasn't exactly fluent in English yet. And like I said, we were all a little drunk, so…" I let the hair fall away, angry she'd let someone so fucking unprofessional touch her skin like this, angry that I hadn't been there to save her—though I was starting to think she wouldn't have needed me even if I was there.

She worked through her issues, mostly on her own. She had coping mechanisms ingrained in her life to help. Yeah, she'd made some mistakes—dropping out of college, getting a messed-up tat, working in a bar that used to have hookers, punching a guy, getting arrested… But I also knew that everything she did had a purpose. And I was damn proud of her and what she'd become.

I turned her around to face me, finding her lip pulled between her teeth. "It was supposed to say, 'I won't ever be your little bitch.'"

One side of my mouth curled up into a proud grin. "My girl's a badass."

Her face was pink. "I try."

My smile fell as I whispered, "Ever think about getting it colored over to match the rest of your ink?" I traced my hand along her skin, the strap of her tank falling off her shoulder. Goose bumps scaled her neckline, and she shivered.

"Someday, maybe." She blinked. Anger, resentment, hatred, and revenge all meshed with acceptance and fear in those baby blues. It was an emotionally messed-up sight that worked on Lia, making her hard and soft at the same time.

"Now." She blew out a shaky breath and looked back at the counter. "Weren't we about to bake something?" One after the other, she plucked ingredients out of the cupboards. Stuff we didn't even need, like bread dough in a box, noodles, and Rice Krispies.

"Yeah, don't think we need all that." I nudged her out of the way with my hip.

"Hey, watch it." She smiled, only to poke me in the stomach. The air between us was a hell of a lot lighter than it had been in hours. It was just her and me... No worrying about our past, no worrying about our future. The perfect example of day by day. Just her and me, together.

"You're ticklish, aren't you, Maxwell?"

I froze, my hands lingering over the beater. "No, I'm not." I so fucking was. Hated being tickled too.

I flashed her a warning, baring my teeth. Somewhere along the way, she'd propped herself up on the counter liked I'd done. We were eye to eye.

"Maxwell Martinez, do you not like to be tickled?" She jabbed a spoon at me, and I plucked it out of her hands.

"No."

She jumped off the counter. "So..." From behind me, she pressed her soft tits against my back, only to sneak her hands under the bottom of my shirt to touch my stomach. "If I did this"—she trailed her nails down the front, and I shuddered under her touch—"then it wouldn't bother you?"

I jerked my hips back as she did it again, my breathing unsteady. "Nope." I turned around and grabbed her by the waist, only to slide my tongue across her neck.

"Eww, stop." She shoved me away with a giggle.

I smacked her ass, then pointed to the counter. "Now get your cute butt back on the counter and watch your man work."

She laughed but did as I asked. "You suck."

I poured lemon cake mix in with the eggs and whipped cream I'd put in the bowl. "Cooking is an art form. If I get distracted, I'll fuck up."

For a while after that, she got quiet and just watched me. The two-person project had soon turned into a one-person job. I liked teaching her how it was done though. And pretending to speak in a French accent put a smile on her lips that I couldn't stop staring at. For Lia, I'd always act like a dumb-ass if it meant I could see her sweet grin.

Once the cookies were on the cookie sheet, ready to be put in the oven, I turned to look at the mess, finding her eyes on mine yet again. Something shifted inside me at her look, even more than before.

I needed to kiss her. Again.

I took my time moving closer, my hands drifting up her bare thighs. She shivered but made no move to push me away. Maybe she needed this too. When I moved between her knees, I took a deep breath, thanking God for the small things—like Lia's patience, my second chance, and a few more silent hours alone.

"What do you see when you look at me, Lia?" I tipped her chin up, forcing her to meet my stare. "Tell me."

"Let's see…" She tapped a finger against her lips. "I see someone who's smart and sweet, with a great ass."

I squeezed her thighs, urging for more. "What else?"

Her smile fell a little, but the happiness in her eyes didn't budge. It was my goal to keep it there. "I see someone who'd do anything for the people he loves."

I lifted my hand, using my thumb to wipe a bit of flour from her cheek. "That it?"

Goose bumps spread across her bare arms, and I pressed my hands up higher.

"I see a friend, and an occasional smart-ass who can make me laugh."

Eyes shut, I lowered my forehead to hers. "You see all that in *me*?"

"I see more."

I pressed a soft kiss to her cheek. "I see those things in you too." And then some.

I saw her as my best friend, dressed in white, with a veil on her head and flowers in her hands. I saw her swollen and round with my son or daughter, though I knew she wouldn't be ready for either of those things for a long while. Still, the vision was there in my mind, and I knew without any doubt that I'd wait forever to make it happen if I had to.

She shook her head. "Want to know what else I see?"

"Tell me."

"I see the only man I've ever loved."

I lifted one hand and stroked the spot by her ear. "I don't know what I did to deserve you."

Tears were in her eyes, but this time I knew they weren't from fear or pain or anger. They were for me. They were happy.

"You gave me hope when I thought it was lost."

"You know, I've probably loved you since the day I came home from my last tour. Since I saw your blue eyes light up with recognition when you saw me in my gear at the airport that day."

"I saw you first." She grinned so widely that my heart skipped. "Even before I saw my brother. I felt like crap about it because he's blood, and you were like this... this fascinating memory I thought I'd conjured up. But then you weren't."

I held my breath as she continued in a rush, "You were coming down that long hallway, a backpack slung over your shoulder. Your hair was buzzed, and your face was all tan and scruffy." She stared over my shoulder, her eyes half-glazed with the memory. "You looked so handsome."

I laughed. "Hadn't slept in thirty-six hours. Not sure how I looked *handsome*."

"You smiled when you saw my dad and my mom."

"I smiled when I saw you too."

Her eyes continued that sparkle thing they did, lighting up with every word I said. "Yeah, but then you took one look at Chloe as Collin tugged her into his arms, and it's as though everything in life made sense to you again. You looked so complete for someone who'd just gotten back from war."

That day, I couldn't keep my eyes off Lia either. She'd looked so different from what I remembered. Stronger, angrier, feistier. There were bits of that pink mixed in with her black hair. But her eyes were the same. They were so big and wide and blue, and filled with love for her parents and her brother and Chloe too. I remember thinking to myself that I wanted someone to look at me the way she looked at her family—like I was all that mattered.

"If it hadn't been for that tiny baby wrapped in your mama's arms, Colly, Gav, and I probably wouldn't have made it through those first few months back home."

Her head tipped to the side. "Did you see a lot of death, Max?"

I blew out a breath, nodding. Nobody ever asked me that, probably because they didn't want to know. Not even my mama. It's not something you wanna talk about, but I'd tell Lia everything and anything she needed and wanted to know, just to keep her talking and looking at me like she was.

"More than anyone should've seen." And that was an understatement.

"I'm sorry you went through that." She stroked my cheek, trying to push my ugly memories away.

"I'm never gonna regret serving my country."

"No, I don't think you're the type that would regret much of anything."

She was wrong. "I regret hurting you."

"Hurting me?" She wasn't mad but curious. I could see it in the tilt of her head.

"Yeah, like when I blew you off over the winter. When I cussed at you for getting arrested. I regret that night I danced with McKenna at the bar too."

She rolled her eyes.

I grinned. "Say, speaking of that, how did McKenna know about us?"

Lia brushed her hands over my chest, and I tucked my fingers under the bottom of her shirt, just above her ass. "Apparently, Addie had to tell someone, and it happened to be McKenna." She ran her fingers up the side of my neck. "Kenna apologized; you know that."

"Yeah, you're right. Guess there's something to her besides a nice pair of legs, then."

"You're serious?" She narrowed her eyes.

"Sure. Legs and tits were always my thing." I reached forward and pinched her ass. "But I'm a reformed man now, baby."

"Pig." She slugged my shoulder, but her eyes glowed regardless. "But you know…Gavin has *really* big feet. And with really big feet it usually means the guy has a really big—"

With my hand full of flour and sugar, I covered her

mouth with the powder. Her eyes widened. I was a hypocrite, yeah, but Gavin's dick was not gonna be discussed right now. Or ever. "Touché, Lee-Lee. Touché."

Easing my hand away, I took a step back, my palm tingling from touching her lips, even with all the mess in between.

Eyes wide in shock, she wiped at her powdery mouth before saying, "I can't believe you just did that."

I shrugged and grinned, guilty as charged.

She growled under her breath, a finger pointed my way as she said, "You're done for, Soldier Boy."

CHAPTER

Lia

I JUMPED OFF THE COUNTER AND DUMPED THE REST OF THE flour over his head. He blinked, trying to keep it out of his eyes, but it fell into his mouth like it'd done in mine. When he moved to wipe it off his tongue, I turned to grab the sugar this time.

"Put it down." He jabbed a finger at me. "You do that, then there will be no—"

I threw it at his head, giggling as it sprinkled around him like a dusting of new snow. "Oops...sorry about that." I laughed harder, clutching my stomach. "That's gonna be a mess to clean up." I tsked and turned, plopping the now-empty container of sugar onto the counter.

Using my distraction to his advantage, Max leaped forward and pressed his hands on the counter along either side of my body.

"Damn right, it's gonna be a mess," he groaned and moved my hair aside. Some of the granules of sugar sprinkled down the back of my neck and into the front of my shirt. But I didn't care, because the second his tongue trailed over the side of my throat, my knees went weak. "And I'm gonna have the best fucking time licking you clean."

I gasped as his tongue moved across my neck, everything inside me coming alive. The motion was so erotic that I couldn't help but arch my back and reach around to grab the sides of his neck to hold him in place. He ran his hands around the front of my body, first sticking the tips of his fingers inside the front of my panties, only to change his mind and lift them up and under my shirt instead. Lips still tasting my neck, he slid his palms even higher, the tips dancing across my ribs, until he reached the base of my breasts. He cupped them in his hands, the calluses of his fingers grazing my nipples.

I shut my eyes and moaned, "Max…"

Over and over, he kneaded the warm flesh, almost as though this was his first time touching a woman, with rough palms and tender fingers, all while rocking his hips slowly against my backside.

I moaned louder.

"Fuck, Lia." My noises seemed to stir something primal inside him, while he chipped away at my carefully guarded wall, inch by inch by inch…

Using his thumbs and forefingers, he pinched my bare nipples even harder, making me gasp. The groan in his throat vibrated against my neck in turn. I braced my hands on the counter, giving myself to him.

"I want you, Max."

He froze, his breath catching in my ear. "You're sure?"

I nodded. "More than sure."

Seconds later, he leaned over my shoulder and

slipped the top up and over my head, letting it fall down my arms to my wrists.

No second thoughts. No regrets.

Breathing heavy, I let it fall to the floor.

"Turn around," Max commanded, his voice gruff and unsteady.

Doing as he asked, because *I* wanted to, I hooked my fingers in the sides of my panties and slipped them, along with his boxers, down to join my shirt.

His eyes widened as he took a step back. Up and down, he looked his fill, trailing his gaze over the length of my body. "Goddamn gorgeous is what you are."

I pulled my lower lip between my teeth, drawing his eyes back to my mouth. He swallowed, the pulse in his throat beating faster. Sucking in a breath, I jumped on the counter and spread my legs, still somehow keeping my panic at bay. More than anyone in my life, I trusted Max with my body, and because I loved him, I offered myself to him in the way he deserved.

"Lia, I…" He blinked and shook his head, only to rub a fast hand over his face. "I don't even know where to start with you."

Grinning, I opened my mouth to tell him right where I wanted him, only for him to cut me off with a smoldering kiss.

His lips battled with mine, a war of need and want raging between us. Growing braver and needier by the second, I wrapped my naked legs around his body, only to grab the edge of his T-shirt. Without hesitation, he reached down and helped me pull it off, tossing it onto the floor before collapsing against me with a groan.

The need for friction was strong, so I wrapped

my arms around his neck and climbed his body, legs
wrapped tightly around his waist. He palmed my ass,
the flour and sugar rough between his palms and my
skin. Without another word, he moved me away from
the counter, only to slam me against the kitchen wall.
Bowls toppled off the refrigerator, crashing to the floor,
but I didn't care. Nothing else mattered.

"Max, please," I whispered, never more sure of anything in my life.

"But—"

I leaned forward and sucked his lower lip between
my teeth. "Don't make me beg."

Like I'd said the magic words, he hiked me up higher
against his stomach and used one hand to undo his pants.
They fell to the floor with a clank, change and his keys
scattering all over the tile.

He said, "Fuck."

I said, "Now."

And then he was carrying me down the hall, shoving open his bedroom door, and laying me on his bed
with a flop. I giggled under my breath as I watched him
struggle to get his boxers off, only to trip over them as
he raced to his dresser to grab one of the fifty condoms
lying in a heap on top.

Then he turned to me and my smile fell, replaced with
a sort of desire I'd never known. I watched him fumble
with a condom, tearing it open so quickly I barely had
time to blink. He rolled it on, pinching the tip, and then he
was on the bed, climbing over me, legs parting over mine.

"You're sure?" He rubbed his nose over my cheek,
then brought his lips within inches of mine.

I nodded when our eyes met, afraid to admit that my

heart was beating twice as fast as normal, although fear was still trying to win me over. If I told him the truth, that this next step always managed to scare me, then he'd stop. But I didn't want that to happen. Old Lia needed to learn New Lia's way. And New Lia's way was having Max. Loving Max. *Being* with Max.

"Yes, very sure."

He kissed me slowly, biting my lip. "Not gonna last long…"

"Don't hold back." I lifted my hips up, not wanting to think, only to feel. Always feel.

Muffled grunts sounded from his mouth. "Fucking never. Never, ever."

Our eyes met, and I held my breath as he slowly slipped inside me. My body tightened, warmed too. It was a delicious, foreign, full ache that I had been craving since the day he'd walked into my world. My stomach grew hard, and my hands shook so badly I could barely hold on to his waist. Max shook too, his skin already slick beneath my palms. Yet one side of his mouth curled into a slow smile as he whispered, "To think I've missed all these years with you…" He shook his head, straining, kissing me once, then twice, moving slowly as he did.

I sucked in a brave breath and whispered back, "Then you better make up for lost time, Soldier Boy."

That's when he kissed me harder, only to say "Fuck yes" against my lips.

He drove into me with no mercy, sweat dampening his flour-coated brow, my own skin on fire. Burning me in the way I wanted. In and out he pushed, while I pulled, until everything inside me lit up.

I didn't need romance or sweet, sensual words. I just needed Max. And this… I needed lots and lots of this.

He kissed me; I kissed him back. He pushed further inside me, and I hissed, arching my spine. I clawed at his skin and he reached down, grabbing my thigh until it was wrapped tight around his waist. Flesh slapped flesh, his eyes never leaving mine as he reached one hand down between us and circled my clit.

I cried out at the contact, arching even more against him.

Below me, the cold sheets slid beneath my back, but I didn't care. Not when everything inside me was on the verge of exploding.

I trailed my fingers over his cheek and said the words I'd never tire of saying. "I love you."

"Lia, Jesus, I love you too…" He went faster, harder— and then I was falling, his fingers tangled in my hair, his breath hot against my lips. He stiffened and groaned in my ear, and everything was right.

Max gave me what I needed, and I gave back what I could give, and I knew nothing in this universe could ever keep us apart.

CHAPTER 29

Max

I WOKE WITH A START TO THE SOUND OF THE FRONT DOOR slamming shut. Thinking it was Gav, I rolled over and pulled Lia against my chest. Her hair tickled the bottom of my chin as I wrapped my arm around her naked waist. I smiled and kissed her neck, loving the way she automatically curled against me.

We hadn't bothered to get out of bed last night, other than to put the cookies into the oven and take them out. The rest of the time we spent in bed, touching, talking, making love until the sun began to rise... It was everything and then some. There was no way I'd ever be able to get enough of her like this. But I was gonna have one hell of an epic good time trying.

The door to my room shot open, cracking against the wall. "What the fuck are you two doing?"

"Colly!" I shot up out of bed, stumbling over the sheets as I stood. Behind me, Lia yipped, seeing the shadow of her brother filling the bedroom doorway.

"Jesus, man, why the fuck didn't you knock?" I covered my junk with my hands, something I wouldn't usually care about. But I'd just spent the last few hours in bed with his sister, so any modesty I could grab would be nice.

"Get out of my house." Collin looked like ass. Face pale, red eyes strained.

Lia scrambled out of bed to stand next to me, her body wrapped tightly in a sheet. Regardless of her cover, I stepped in front of her body. "Sorry to break it to you, but I live here."

"Not anymore." Collin barged farther into the room and grabbed me by the arm, shoving me against a wall.

"Stop it. Leave him alone." Lia tugged at the back of Collin's shirt, struggling to keep hold of the sheet.

Neither of us had showered after having sex, both too exhausted from the night before to move. Pasted to the crevices of her body and mine were flour and sugar from our cookie making. Though she looked thoroughly loved with her wild pink hair standing on end, I could also see the pain in her eyes from being caught. She'd wanted to tell Collin about us. Having him find out like this was a damn nightmare.

"Go home, Lia. This isn't your concern anymore." Collin curled his lip, his arm pressing harder against my throat. Even though he still spoke to his sister, the death threat in his eyes was directed at me.

I also knew he was right. Lia *was* stupid for wanting to be with me. But that didn't mean I wasn't gonna fight like hell to keep her.

"How is this not my concern, you big conceited asshole." She shoved his shoulder, but he didn't drop his hold on me.

"You even realize how stupid you're being right now?" he asked, shaking his head.

"Don't talk to her like that," I growled.

His face paled even more as he glared my way. "What right do you have... No. Fuck this." He moved his forearm to my neck, pinning me in place. It wasn't hard enough to choke me, but it was enough to prove a point. I arched an eyebrow at him, waiting for whatever bullshit he had to say next. I'd do anything to keep Lia from getting her heart broken over this. If her brother ended up not approving, I couldn't let her lose him. Yeah, but at the same time, I *wouldn't* lose Lia either.

When all Collin could do was snarl at me, I shoved him away and said, "I pay rent, and all my shit's here. This is as much my house as it is yours."

"You broke the guy code," he hissed, running a hand through his hair.

"Never said I didn't, but maybe instead of being such a dumb-ass, you'll let me expla—"

His fist flew at my face before I could finish. Then I was down, head throbbing as I palmed my eye—the same eye that'd I'd been decked in a few weeks back.

"The fuck, guys?" Gavin ran into the room, eyes wild with fear, until he glanced at Lia and her lack of clothes. He yanked Collin off me, tossing him toward the bed. Then he pointed a finger my way and whispered, "Told you guys not to fuck in plain sight."

Thank God Collin didn't hear him.

Footsteps sounded as Lia raced out of the room. Before my best friend could pummel my ass again, I was up, grabbing my shorts before I took off after her.

I'd known Collin was gonna be pissed at me. I just didn't know he was gonna go postal.

Lia was in the kitchen, already dressed when I walked in. "I-I've got to go home. My brother—"

"No, baby." I came up behind her and wrapped my arms around her waist. She melted against me, shaking. "You stay here tonight. Beaner's gonna need you here when she gets home, especially if Addie won't be here." I tried to smile, though it hurt like a bitch, both physically and mentally. "I'm gonna crash on Gav's couch and give Colly some time to cool off."

"How stupid could we be?" She swung around to face me, crashing against my chest. "We should've waited, done it at my house or something. Not here. We knew he was coming home today."

She wasn't gonna find me complaining about location, because what had happened between us the night before was fucking magic. Yeah, we could've been more careful, but I knew she didn't want to hear it. So instead, I massaged the back of her neck and lowered my forehead to her shoulder. "He'll get over it. I've seen him lose his shit like this before."

"But what if he doesn't?" She pulled back and searched my face, her eyes wet. "What if he never accepts us?"

"Then that's tough shit, because I love you and I am *not* gonna lose you."

Her big eyes welled up with more tears. I'd seen the girl cry more in the past month than I had in all the years of knowing her. I wiped the tears away with my thumbs, vowing to do everything I could to make them stay away from here on out.

She lifted her hand and rubbed a finger just over my eyebrow. "You're bleeding."

I grabbed her wrist and kissed her palm. "Wouldn't be the first time." Then I leaned closer, pressing my forehead to hers, my heart beating the hell out of my chest.

Footsteps sounded behind us just as the front door slammed shut. I cringed, knowing Collin was gone, but turned around anyway. Gavin stood in the entryway to the kitchen, dark circles under his eyes that matched the irritation all over his face. He walked to the freezer, pulling out a bag of frozen peas. He tossed it to me. "What'd I tell you two?"

Lia leaned back against the counter. "It just happened, Gav."

"Ain't gonna take it back though." I winked at her and put the veggies over my eye.

Gavin jerked his chin at me. "You okay?"

"Yup." Even though Collin punched like he had steel in his knuckles. "Where'd he go?"

"Hospital. I drove him from the airport straight there this morning. His flight got in early. That would explain why he'd shown when he did. Once Chloe fell back asleep, he had me bring him home to get his car. He's a mess right now."

"This is all my fault." Lia lowered her chin. I walked over and squeezed her hand.

Gavin frowned. "It's not just you guys or Chloe he's worried about. It's Addie too. Her mother passed this morning, and he's going crazy over the fact that he can't be there for her."

Lia sighed, the sound filled with the same regret eating away at my gut.

I pressed my hands to her cheeks. "This isn't your fault. Get that out of your head."

She didn't speak, just kept looking at the floor.

Gav cleared his throat. "Anyway, Chloe's ready to be released, so I suggest you two clean your *fucking* mess up."

I laughed because I couldn't help it. "Our *fucking mess*, huh?"

Lia shoved me, then yelled at Gavin to go home. With his hands in the air and a smug-ass smile on his face, he did, but not before saying, "I hope you two know what you're getting yourselves into, 'cause if this goes bad for either of you, it'll ruin what we have here."

My spine went rigid. Lia stiffened too. We knew we'd have to defend our feelings for each other to everyone eventually, but we'd just decided to make this thing between us happen. So maybe the best idea was what I'd been avoiding talking about since the night before. The question that'd been on the tip of my tongue ever since we left the hospital.

"We have thought about it. Matter of fact, I'm moving to Springfield with Lee-Lee as soon as things with Addie and Collin are settled." Sure, I'd planned to *ask* Lia first, but it seemed like the right response for the moment.

"You're *what*?" Lia's face paled.

"No shit?" Gavin shook his head in disbelief.

My jaw locked as I stared back and forth between the two of them.

"Not a good idea, Max," Gavin grumbled, leaving the kitchen before I could respond. It wasn't his opinion I wanted though.

"You can't be serious about this, right?" Lia glared at me. "It's too fast, Max. What happened to 'day by day'? And your business. You can't—"

"We're still taking this day by day, yeah. But my business isn't huge here." I moved forward, pressing myself against her front, backing her against the fridge this time. "I've been in love with you for years, and I'm tired of waiting. I want you, Lia. I want you all the time though, not just on weekends and holidays and vacations. I want you every night in my arms, every morning when I roll over in bed, when I come home from work, when I'm at work, when I—"

"You know I won't let this happen."

"Why the hell not?" I jerked my head back.

My throat burned as she stepped back to start cleaning the mess we'd made on the floor, but I couldn't help. Could barely breathe as I watched her jerky hands sweep the floor, clean up the ingredients, wash the dishes. "I love you. You love me. We're fucking meant to be to—"

"The answer is no, Max." She swirled around, eyes flaring.

"Why?" I growled the word, my hands balling at my sides.

When she didn't answer right away, my blood ran cold. I knifed my fingers through my hair to try to warm them, but they tingled, asleep on my hand.

She's moving.

I'm not.

She's leaving me.

She doesn't want me to come with her.

"Answer me, Lee-Lee. Tell me why I can't be there with you."

She blew out a breath. "I love you; I do. And these past few weeks have meant everything to me. But I'm not ready for more than day by day, remember? Not yet. You said you were patient, so prove it to me."

I flinched, my head throbbing from something other than Colly's punch. "What's so wrong with wanting more when I've known all along that you're my forever?"

A tear slipped out of her eye as she shook her head, wiping it away. "Because I need time to figure out who I am before I make a forever with someone else. I'm just learning how to be me again without the help of family and friends. I want to show the world, myself, and my family that I can be the girl I've always wanted to be."

A lump built in my throat, and I could barely swallow around it. Because I loved her and respected her wishes, I drew her close and said, "I get it, baby. I get it." Even though I didn't want to get it. Even though I was selfish enough to want to lock her up and keep her with me forever. I loved her enough to let her go. To be the Lee-Lee she needed to be before she could be the Lee-Lee for me too.

CHAPTER 30

Lia

TWO NIGHTS IN A ROW WITH LITTLE TO NO SLEEP MADE A woman extra weepy and a whole lot on edge. Everything about my brother was grating on my nerves this morning, from the way he dripped water on the bathroom floor and didn't bother to clean it up to the way he'd left all the breakfast dishes piled in the sink without bothering to even fill it with soapy water. It had to be the bachelor coming out of him, since Addie wasn't here. But I wasn't having it.

"Seriously, Collin? This place is a damn pigsty."

He frowned from over his cup of coffee—drinking the coffee I'd preprogrammed for him the night before so it'd be ready this morning. Not once did I get a thank-you. Mom would've been pissed at his rudeness.

"What?"

"The kitchen looks like hell. The least you could've done was maybe put the rest of the dirty stuff in the sink and wipe down the counters after spilling cereal milk all over. I spent over two hours cleaning this apartment, and now it looks like it did pre-Addie. It's disgusting."

"This is my damn house. I'll do what I want."

"And this is Max's house too. And since he and I are together now, I'll be here a lot more. And I don't want to deal with a messy kitchen." Not that Addie wouldn't fix matters when she came home, but still. I was trying to make a point.

He groaned and tossed his head back. "Jesus, you and Max don't belong together. Get that through your head."

"You know what? Screw you. Max and I have been together for almost a month. I love him. He loves me. End of story, get over it, and worry about your own life, not mine."

"The hell, Lia?" He pushed away from the table, causing his coffee cup to rattle against the wood. "A *month*?"

"Stop." I held up my hand and looked down the hall toward Chloe's room. "I have every right to pick who I love. You don't get to control that."

He stood, taking his coffee with him into living room. "You can't love him. He'll only hurt you."

"He's different with me." I followed him, my bare feet stomping against the floor with every step.

"We're done talking about this."

I snorted. "You're the one who brought it up."

He glared at me. "Chloe's finally asleep for the first time all night, and I need this time to clear my head, all right?"

I rolled my eyes. "She's only asleep because of me." Immature comeback, I know, but everything about this situation and my brother was pissing me off.

"Well, she wouldn't *be* in this position if it weren't for you and Max."

I froze, my eyes immediately growing wet. I'd known this was coming, but the timing couldn't have been worse. His words smacked against me harder than a hand or a fist ever could.

A loud cry sounded, and I moved to Chloe's door, hollering over my shoulder, "Tell me something I don't know already, asshole."

Before I could get to her crib, my brother zoomed past me, only to freeze before grabbing her. I shoved him aside, eyes widening when I found her sprawled on her back in her crib. Eyes rimmed red and filled with tears, she lay like a statue, seemingly afraid to move.

"Aw, sweet thing." Not thinking twice, I carefully scooped her into my arms and laid her against my chest. Her blond curls stuck to her wet, pink cheeks. "You okay?"

She calmed in my hold, settling right in. I laid her on her changing table as gently as I could, yet the second I set her down, she wailed and cried harder.

"Hey, baby girl. Shhh, don't cry." Collin stood by her head, rubbing his fingers over her temples as I changed her diaper. Sure, kids broke bones all the time, but being personally attached to the kid made this feel like a tragedy.

Calm and collected, Collin touched my shoulder and said, "Grab me her bear from the crib, would ya, Sis?"

I nodded, forgetting that my brother was a grade-A jackass as I did what he asked. If Collin was good at anything, it was being a dad.

Just when he'd soothed her with a singing teddy and

the hum of his own broken voice, someone knocked on her doorframe. I jerked my head back, finding my brother's eyes narrowed into slits as he focused on the doorway.

Eyes widening in shock, I found the man I was desperately in love with looking at his best friend with more sadness than I've ever seen before. Dressed in a pair of low-slung sweats and no shirt, Max looked exactly like he did every morning: casual, sexy, and absolutely delicious. But the swollen lip and black-and-blue cheek reminded me he was stepping into dangerous territory.

"How's our girl?" He cleared his throat and cracked his knuckles, clearly nervous.

For a good long and hard moment, my brother glared at him, unmoving and silent.

Deciding to break the ice first, I said, "As good as a fifteen-month-old toddler with a broken arm can be."

Max cringed as he moved to stand at my side. Not once did he reach for my hand, or even graze my skin. But somehow, I felt his love through his presence alone.

"Hey, Beaner. How's my girl?" he cooed, sending the sweetest shivers up and down my body. Collin glared at me, then at Max once more, before softening a bit when he looked at his daughter again.

Her little blue eyes nearly twinkled when she took one look at Max. Then for the first time since last night, she smiled and said, "Mas."

Unable to contain my grin, I took a step back, letting Max move in next to my brother. Collin still hadn't moved, his hands hanging onto the edge of her table. There was no way he'd push the issue in front of his daughter, which Max knew.

"How's Addie?" Max looked toward Collin, the weariness in his gaze mirroring my own.

At her name, Collin's shoulders fell, but he talked — and for now, that's all we could ask for. "She's doing all right, I guess. There's a small service on Thursday, but I'm not gonna leave Beaner to go. And Addie doesn't want me to."

That same horrendous guilt made my stomach go tight.

"I'm sorry, Colly. I-I know Addie must be hurting." Max put his hand on Collin's shoulder. My brother stiffened but didn't move to shove him off. Instead, he just shrugged.

My gaze darted back and forth between the pair, fear making me ready to grab Chloe and run, anger making me want to punch Collin in the face like he'd done to Max. Instead, I took a few more steps back, folding my arms as I waited for a storm to explode between them.

No matter what, this was my life, and if I wanted to be with Max, then I would be, no matter what my brother said or thought or did.

"I'm also sorry you had to find out about me and Lia the way you did. But I'm not sorry for wanting to be with her."

Collin scoffed. "No, I figured you wouldn't be."

I opened my mouth to speak but stopped short as I stared at their profiles. I wasn't sure if it was the unspoken look they shared or the small grin forming on Max's face, but something clicked in that moment between them, something that lifted the ten-pound weight off my shoulders.

My brother reached for Chloe, pulling her against

his chest. Her breath came out in little shudders as she settled against him.

Max leaned forward, rubbing the back of his forefinger down her cheek. One side of his mouth curled into a grin. "If it makes you feel any better, I got your parents' permission."

Collin's jaw locked. "Not surprised. They don't know you like I do."

Max shrugged. "No. But tell me something…" Max turned his head toward me, his eyes meeting mine. "When you fell in love with Addie, when you *knew* she was the one, you didn't give two shits who stood in your way, did you?"

Collin looked at me, then back at Max. But Lord Jesus in heaven, I could see his resolve and feel his resistance slipping away at the same time.

"But she's my *sister*."

"So?" Max moved to stand next to me. "We can't help who we love, man. It just happens." He smiled at me but kept his hands to himself, obviously knowing my brother's limits.

"What's gonna happen if you two—"

"It won't get to that point. Lia's my forever girl."

Tiny, dancing butterflies fluttered against the inside of my stomach at his words. Romance wasn't my thing, not because I didn't like it, but because I'd never felt the desire to experience it like I did with Max. Yet his eyes were on me, and his words running through the air sounded like poetry. It made everything I didn't think I wanted come to life.

Could it be this simple? God, I hoped so.

"Christ, you guys," Collin grumbled. In turn, I smiled

widely, knowing his acceptance was on the tip of his tongue. "Just…don't fuck with the door open anymore, all right?" He ran his fingers through his hair.

"Fu-uck." Chloe giggled.

My smile fell.

Max cringed.

In sync, the two of us turned to look at my brother, whose face had gone from blood red to pale white in a matter of seconds. "What the hell did my daughter just say?"

I blinked, my lips twisting. Max moved in closer, wrapping his arm around my waist. He laughed too, somehow getting the words out when I couldn't.

"We may have been on duty when the arm got broken, but that right there is all Gavin."

"Avvy, Avvy." Chloe looked toward the door like she expected him to be there.

"I'm gonna kill him." Collin left the room like a bat out of hell.

"Does this mean the heat's off us for a while?" Max whispered in my ear, lowering his hand to brush against my ass.

My lips curling into a smile, I reached across his waist and tickled his ribs. "I wouldn't push your luck, Maxwell."

He dragged me around to face him, his hands on my waist, a new look in his eyes. "I'm gonna take my chances." Then he leaned down and kissed me…and yeah, I kissed him back.

CHAPTER 31

Max

"She's beautiful," Lia whispered, pressing her fingers over her lips as she leaned closer to my mama.

Onstage, dancing in a black leotard and tutu, was my baby sister, Charlotte. We'd made the trip to see her, and Lia couldn't have been more awesome about it.

"She is the star. Look at her," Mama whispered, wiping at her tears. My stepdad, Tom, looked equally enamored, a huge smile on his face as he watched Char move.

It made me wonder if I'd be the same way with my own daughter someday. Then I looked over at Lia. If *she* were the mother of my baby girl, then I'd no doubt be way worse than Tom ever was.

Two months with Lia, and there I was, planning our entire future. I'd always prided myself on patience, but every day seemed like one more day I didn't want to wait to make her permanently mine.

Lia yawned and lowered her head to my shoulder,

her fingers laced through mine, palm to palm. We were exhausted, but we'd promised to have dinner with my family after this. Then we'd head back to our hotel in downtown Nashville for a night of doing what we'd gotten really good at over the past few months since that night at my house.

Her body and my body, hot, sweaty, and sliding all over each other...

She shivered like she could read my mind, then leaned back to look in my eyes. Knowing I wouldn't see those eyes up close every day after tomorrow killed me, but I loved her and supported her enough to let her go.

I just prayed it wouldn't be forever.

Once the half-hour recital was over, we met up with Charlotte backstage. One look at me and she raced across the room and jumped into my arms with a huge squeal. Her short, skinny arms wrapped tightly around my neck.

"Did you see me dance, Max?"

I tipped my head back to look into my little sister's eyes. They were the color of Tom's—bright blue—but she had black hair and dark skin like Mama and me. She was a gorgeous girl who would no doubt break a lot of hearts someday. "Yeah, I did. Next stop, Juilliard—no doubt in my mind."

She giggled as I set her on her feet. Mama hugged her hard, the strain around her eyes easing as she kissed the top of Char's head. "You did beautifully, *hija*. I am so proud of you."

"Thanks, Mama." Charlotte's cheeks turned red, but her eyes were almost dancing as she stared up at her dad and then Lia.

One weekend wouldn't be enough with my family. But it was all I could do for now. I had catering gigs scheduled every weekend for the next several weeks, while during the week, I planned on a little side cooking from my store. When Ma had asked us to visit, it worked out that on my way back home, I could drop Lia off at her new place, where her mom would be waiting to help her get settled.

Clearing my throat, I pulled my favorite woman against my side, my arm wrapped around her waist as I did my introductions. "Char, meet Lia. Lia, *this* is world-famous ballerina Charlotte Franklin."

"You've got a girlfriend with pink hair? That is so *cool*."

Lia grinned. "I have purple hair too. You just can't see it well right now."

I laughed and Ma squeezed my hand, smiling just as widely as the rest of us.

"Good to meet you, Charlotte. You dance like an angel." Lia offered her hand.

My sister shook it, awestruck and wide-eyed over the beauty that was my girlfriend. Couldn't blame her, really, because Lia looked exceptionally gorgeous tonight. Dressed in nothing like the getups she usually wore, she had on white jeans and a pink tank with sparkly straps that matched her sparkly sandals. She looked like a lady—but acted like a badass woman.

And those tats... Sweet Jesus, did I love her tats.

"Your nose and lip rings are cool too. Mama said I can get my ears pierced anytime I'm ready. But I'm scared it'll hurt. Did yours hurt?"

"Nah. They didn't hurt much at all, actually."

Charlotte reached for Lia's hand. The sight of them together did all sorts of messed-up shit to my heart—the good kind of messed up though. Ahead of us, they walked toward the exit, leaving me behind with Mama and Tom.

"She's a pretty special lady, Maxwell." Tom spoke first.

I looked at my mama next, waiting for her thoughts.

"She good to you, *hijo*?"

"She's the best thing that's ever happened to me."

Mama squeezed my arm and sniffed, probably crying again. I didn't look because that was when Lia glanced at me from over her shoulder and smiled.

Dinner passed by quicker than I wanted, but Charlotte was exhausted, and Tom and Mama looked about as drained as I felt. Lia and I said our goodbyes, and Mama hugged me like it was the last time she'd ever see me. "Don't let her get away," she whispered, then patted my arm before she slipped into their car.

Tom offered to drive us back to the hotel, but the night was cool and the streets were alive with music, so we decided to do a little exploring and walk instead.

Both hands in mine, Lia turned around, pulling me with her as she walked backward down the street. "Your family is pretty awesome."

I smiled. "I'm glad you got to meet them. My sister couldn't keep her eyes off you. I think you might be her new superstar idol." My eyebrows waggled up and down, and Lia blushed that pink I loved so much.

"Hardly. My guess is she's never seen someone with so many piercings and tattoos in all her eight years of life."

"She lives twenty minutes from this city. Girl's seen her fair share, trust me."

Lia stopped and looked up at the stars in the sky, her face lit up by the flashing bar and club signs hanging along the street. A musician with long hair sat just behind her, and I couldn't help but watch as his fingers danced over the strings of his guitar. Lia must've noticed too, because she turned, backing up to grab my hand. It wasn't fear pulling her close to me. Instead, it was fascination.

A few people surrounded him, some clapping to the beat, while others urged him to sing. But with his head down and his hair hanging over the side of his face, he seemed oblivious to everything.

"He's really good."

I nodded, an idea forming in my head. Once he finished his song and the people around him cleared out, I crouched down next to him. "You take requests?"

He didn't look at me, but I saw him nod, so I reached into my wallet and pulled out a fifty. "Can you play…" Not wanting Lia to hear, I leaned forward a little more and whispered my song choice.

The guy whipped his face up, his eyes sparkling under the club lights along the street. I grinned back, and he nodded again.

"What'd you ask him?" Lia nudged me with her shoulder.

"You'll see."

Seconds later, he started strumming the chords, his fingers slow but knowing the rhythm.

"Dance with me." I turned to Lia, pulling her close to my chest without waiting for her answer.

"What, here?" She looked around at the new crowd forming. A few people stared at us, but most eyes were on the guy playing.

"Yeah, Lee-Lee. Right here."

"You're crazy." She laughed but wrapped her arms around my neck, only to lay her cheek against my heart.

My hands tightened around her waist as we swayed, the music like a lullaby for lovers as I whispered, "I'm crazy in love with you."

She snorted, not the response most guys would wanna hear when they dropped a line like that. But I didn't need to hear anything when I could already feel her answer right there in my arms. Her hands grazed the back of my hair, and her heart beat really fast against me... Then there was a soft sigh that barely registered over the guitar sounds as I kissed the top of her head.

Come tomorrow, she and I would be apart. Me back home, her working in Springfield... But tonight? Right there in the middle of downtown Nashville, with my forever woman in my arms and the song "I Can't Help Falling in Love with You" playing on a guitar? I knew our lives were right where they should be.

———~~~———

Lia

Anticipation was supposed to make things hotter and more exciting, but I found myself hating that feeling — the way it made my skin crawl, the way my stomach clenched with every soft touch Max made. The second our elevator hit the third floor and we found the hallway leading to our room person-free, I grabbed the top of my shirt and ripped it off, only to fling it behind me against Max's face.

His bare feet scuffled to a stop behind me. "Damn, woman. I think I've finally met my match."

Grinning, with no more time to waste, I pulled him closer and unbuttoned the rest of his shirt as I leaned back against our hotel door. "Yes, I do believe you have. Now take me inside. One-up me."

I kissed him after that—climbed his body too, not wanting to wait long for the throbbing to be eased between my thighs. He urged me up higher against his waist. His shirt was still on, but his bare chest was on display, rubbing against my lacy pink bra. He tasted like wine and mint, his tongue caressing mine in a battle I was more than able to keep up with.

I moaned against his mouth as he palmed one of my breasts. He answered my begging plea by dry fucking me against the door. "Max, yes..." I threw my head back, riding him clothed, only for him to stop, drop me to my feet, and step inside the hotel room.

"Not like this." He stared down the hall. A couple was walking toward us, kissing like we'd done just seconds before. Nodding in understanding, I followed him inside and closed the door, but after that, we didn't waste another second.

My pants came off, and his did too, until all I had on were my bra and panties and him his boxers. I swallowed hard, panting as I looked over his body. He had baby-soft skin, perfect pecs, delicious abs, and two nipples I wanted to latch my mouth onto for all time.

So, I did just that, which earned me a groan and a loud "Fuck me, Lia."

He didn't have to tell me twice.

He yanked me around, my ass pressed against his erection, one of his hands buried just inside the band of my panties. With the flick of his fingers, my bra was off, joining the pile of clothing on the floor. He urged me toward the bed, whispering words of love and affection in my ear along the way.

Like I knew he would, he sat on the edge of the mattress, watching as I slid my panties to my knees, then my calves, until finally I flung them behind me somewhere in the dark room. The curtains were open, and we basked in the glow of the moon and the street-lights. Appreciation lit up his eyes as he took me in, and love filled my soul as I closed the distance between us. Wordless, I straddled his lap, sinking down on him without a second thought.

I'd gotten an IUD two days after our first time having sex, and we hadn't used anything else between us since. Because of his active sex life before me, Max had gotten tested quite often, his last results coming in clean a week after our first time in his room.

"You're so fucking beautiful" was what he finally said to get me to move. Inhaling through my nose, I did just that, opening my eyes to meet his.

Lust and love filled the darkness of his stare as he lay on the bed. I knew then that something about this moment was different—for both of us. There was a desperation that said *This is it. This is real*.

Max leaned up on his elbows, latching his lips around my nipples as I moved. He bit, then sucked, then bit, then kissed, a torturous pattern that had me crying his name.

One of his hands dug into the flesh of my ass, nails deep. He guided my movements, never releasing my breast as he did. Eyes shut, I threw my head back, pushing my chest forward, needing more but too afraid to ask—too afraid to discover what exactly that more might be.

I yanked at the tips of his hair instead, begging for a fast release. Up and down I moved, my insides twitching and throbbing.

"Lia," he growled and moved back, forcing me to meet his stare. Slowly he sat up, holding my hands like a lover would, leaning forward to whisper in my ear. "I love you." With our bodies still connected, he rolled me onto my back, taking control.

Swallowing hard, I wrapped my legs around his waist, never wanting to lose this moment, this connection. "I love you too."

The air-conditioning's blower killed the silence between us. Slowly, Max moved, taking his time, looking at me, kissing me, touching me everywhere he could.

I shivered, so cold but so hot at the same time. "Max?"

Pressing his forehead to mine, he whispered, "Yeah?"

"Faster."

He laughed. I laughed harder. Then I kissed his chin, and he hissed and groaned and lowered his lips, kissing me like this would be the last time.

And then I was falling, losing my heart to him even more, and loving. So much love, so much Max, so much more than I'd ever thought I'd have in my life.

Max was right there with me, gripping my hips as he pounded out his release. "Lia, Jesus, yes."

Holding my breath was easy. Catching my breath wasn't. If I let the air go, I'd likely say something stupid, or maybe even cry. But Max, being Max, collapsed on top of me. With hot breath panting in my ear, he asked, "You wanna do that again in a little bit?"

I laughed. "Let me recoup a little. 'Kay, Soldier Boy?"

CHAPTER 32

Max

"YOU SURE YOU CAN'T STAY FOR ONE MORE NIGHT?" MRS. M touched my shoulder, then looked back over her shoulder toward the kitchen.

Lee-Lee was in there, earbuds in and rocking out to whatever was on her playlist as she put dishes away in her cupboard. Her back was to us, and she was wearing a pair of leather shorts and an old, faded T-shirt that I'd watched her put on this morning. Wonder Woman was on the front, and the words below read *Girls Will Save the World*. I loved it.

Hell, I loved everything she put on her body because I knew I'd be the only one besides her who could take it off.

Already, my hands itched with wanting to touch her again. One quiet night in her new place hadn't been enough for me. I couldn't very well let her scream my name, not when her ma was in the spare bedroom next door.

Regret hit me in the gut as I nodded. "Wish I could." More than anything. "But duty calls." In the form of another little old lady needing a bridge game catered tomorrow night.

I kept telling myself that things were going to pick up; my client list would expand and my name would spread. But Carinthia wasn't a big town, the neighboring towns even smaller, and there were only so many old ladies who could handle Mexican food. For now, things were steady enough, I supposed. A graduation party here, one sweet sixteen there. Was it gonna be enough to keep me on track? Distracted? No, probably not.

Mrs. M sighed and patted my shoulder. "Okay. Drive safe then, and call us when you get home. Oh!" She held up a finger, a lightbulb practically dinging above her head. "If you get a chance, could you swing by my house and remind John to water my plants outside? I'm afraid by the time I get back there on Friday, they'll be goners."

"Sure thing." I winked.

One kiss on the cheek later, she was gone, using the excuse that she had to run to the store to pick up new drapes for Lia's kitchen. I knew what she was doing though, even if Lia didn't.

There was only a half hour before I had to get on the road, but I'd take it.

The door shut behind me, and nothing but the sound of dishes clanking together filled the air. One click of the lock later, I stalked my way toward the kitchen.

Toward my woman.

Lee-Lee was trying to avoid the inevitable, but if I didn't say goodbye the right way, I'd fall to my knees and beg her to let me stay for good.

My arms wrapped around her middle from behind. I tugged the earbud out and whispered in her ear, "We've got fifteen minutes."

My fingers glided up the front of her shirt, already tugging the cups of her bra down. I kneaded her tits, circling my thumbs around her nipples.

"We could make it twenty if we did it right here on the counter." She leaned her head back against me, eyes closed, lips parted.

I grinned at her ambition and pulled her around to face me. "As good as that sounds, I want you naked." I motioned toward the curtainless windows, seeing the short guy who lived next door outside walking his dog. "And I'm not really in the mood to share you with your new neighbor."

"Who is very much in love with his partner, remember?" She wrapped her arms around my waist.

I grinned, remembering all right. Some guy named Avery had jogged over shirtless the night before. Just about scared me to death. Not because I thought he was gonna do something to hurt us, but because leaving Lee-Lee here next door to some muscle-bound freak was gonna make me crazy with jealousy.

Then his short little boyfriend came out, eyed me with feigned disinterest, and introduced himself to Lia as shirtless man's fiancé. After they made us dinner and managed to make Lee-Lee laugh, I decided they weren't so bad after all.

"Let's go." I ran my palm down the side of her face and kissed her lips softly, only to haul her up so her legs latched around my waist.

In the bedroom, I didn't bother turning on the lights,

but I did manage to shut and lock the door—lessons learned and all.

Shirts went off, pants went flying, and not soon enough, I was inside her, driving hard into her warm, wet pussy.

I was home. *Lia* being my forever address.

The futon rocked beneath us, probably breaking, but I didn't care. I'd buy her a new bed if it meant I could fuck her senseless this one last time. I grabbed her hands and held them both over her head, needing to keep myself grounded, in control. Blue eyes locked with mine, and Lia moaned my name in approval. We'd both barely broken a sweat when she came on a loud cry.

I followed not long after, watching her the entire time. This was my woman, the one I'd marry someday.

"I love…" I lowered my head to hers, releasing her hands. They were on my back, stroking my spine before I could get out the "you."

Wordless after that, we kissed and said a few thousand silent goodbyes in the span of ten minutes. It wasn't enough. Never would be. I didn't want to go. I wanted to be here with her. Always. Forever. But she needed her space. I got that. I respected that. It just hurt like a son of a bitch.

We dressed and held hands, and she cried a bit, trying to hide it. I gathered the last of my stuff, praying she'd change her mind at the last minute and ask me to leave some things here at least. Maybe open a drawer and say *This is yours*.

But she didn't.

As we stood outside by my car, she hugged me close

and whispered through her tears, "Give Chloe a kiss for me, okay?"

"I will." My voice cracked as I forced a smile. I think she knew it too, because after that, her tears came faster, the goodbye still not on her lips.

"Max?" she mumbled against my neck, her lips there, touching as they moved.

"Yeah?" I held my breath, praying this was it. That she'd say *Fuck the day by day* and live in the here and now once and for always.

But she didn't do that either.

"Promise me you'll be safe and call me every night?"

I blinked away my tears, refusing to cry. "FaceTime too." I couldn't go a day without seeing her.

"Yeah. FaceTime too."

I told her I loved her, kissed her once on the lips, and then got in my car, unable to look in my rearview mirror as I drove away. I was leaving for her. I was leaving because she needed me to. I was also leaving because I loved her.

It was never supposed to hurt this bad, but the second I pulled up in front of my house later that night, something inside me started hurting worse than when I'd left her.

I squeezed my hand around the steering wheel and shoved my car into Park. The door to Gav's side of the house shot open, and if I hadn't been feeling so damn sorry for myself, I probably would've laughed at the fact that he was obviously waiting for me. He stood on the front porch, barely visible in the dark.

Pushing my car door open, I lowered my chin to block the rain and headed straight toward my best friend.

"You all right, man?" he asked as I stood on the bottom step, unmoving. Rain soaked my shirt and hair, but I didn't care.

"Good as I can be." Which was equivalent to shitty. How the hell could I do this thing called life if she wasn't there to do it with me?

I jerked my hand through my hair. "Let's go get a drink."

He nodded. "Fine by me."

The one thing that sounded appealing to me right now, besides driving back to Springfield for my girl, was to get wasted. "As long as I'm not driving. Thinking I need to get real shit-faced tonight."

The door to my side of the house flung open before I could ask Gav what his woes were. Collin looked at me for a second before asking, "O'Paddy's?" Damn, he knew me well.

"Guys' night," Gavin grunted.

Collin wrapped his arms around both of our shoulders. "Need to tell Addie first. Gimme a second." Collin grinned in a way I hadn't seen him do for a long time. He seemed at peace—happy. Which also meant his and Addie's sex was gonna get even louder than it already was. That also meant I'd be spending a lot of nights on Gavin's couch.

While Collin stepped inside, I sat on the front step, too tired to even stand, let alone go out with my boys. But I didn't want to be alone.

Gavin sat to my right, stretching his legs out. "She won't be gone forever, Max."

"Then why does it feel like my heart's been ripped from my chest?" I kicked at a groove in the wood paneling of the porch step.

"I don't know why the right thing always hurts, man. Just does."

Scrubbing a hand over my face, I processed his words. Lia needed to find her own way, so letting her go *was* the right thing to do. I was just pissed at myself for not figuring out how to make her leaving hurt me any less than it did.

"And you love her, right?"

I nodded. "She's the one. No doubt in my mind."

"Then it's worth it, the waiting and hurting. Like I said, it's not forever."

I punched him in the shoulder. "When did you get to be so damn insightful?"

He shrugged and stared at the wooden porch. "Guess I'm just wising up."

This got my attention. "Yeah? Any particular blond or brunette causing that?"

His hands tightened around his knees, squeezing. Instead of answering, he shrugged. He was hiding something big, but I was too lost in my own head to question where his was.

Collin came back outside, keys in hand. "Ready?"

Like his ass was lit on fire, Gavin stood. "Let me grab my wallet."

"What's his issue?" Colly narrowed his eyes after our best friend.

"Thinking it's a woman." I stood, then walked to Collin's truck.

While we waited inside the truck's cab for Gav,

Collin said, "Lia's doing good. Mom's got her all set up and already decorating the new place. Thinkin' Mom was pretty pissed off that Lia had let her old place get to looking so shitty. She's making up for it now."

I chuckled, though my chest ached with sadness, and kicked my feet up on the dash. "I could see that when I was leaving."

The second Mrs. M pulled the U-Haul into the apartment complex, then showed up at Lia's door with six IKEA bags in hand, I knew Lia was in trouble. And if we hadn't just christened her bedroom's walk-in closet, she probably would've let her ma have it.

"Mom's overwhelming, but she means well."

I cleared my throat, not knowing what else to say as the air grew stagnant between us. Sure, Colly had been decent to me since that day in Chloe's bedroom, but it wasn't like it had been before. Things were still strained.

Like he could read my mind, Collin blew out a breath and said, "I know we haven't talked much about you and my sister, but I wanted to tell you I'm sorry for not trusting you with her."

"If I walked in on some guy in bed with my sister, I would've done the same thing. No worries."

He cringed. "Do ya have to be so blunt about it?"

"It could be worse." I crossed my feet at the ankles.

"You're a son of a bitch." But there wasn't a fist in my nose, and he had a smile on his face. I'd call it a win.

Gavin stepped outside the house, but before he could get in the truck, Collin shocked me with words I wasn't expecting to hear. "I'm good with you and my sister being together, even though I'm not cool with how I found out."

I winced. "Yeah, still sorry about that."

"Sure you are." He groaned. "I need you to promise not to hurt her though."

Lowering my feet onto the floorboard, I turned to him, my lips flat. "She's tougher than you think she is." Punching exes, jail time… I grinned thinking back on the morning I bailed her out. "Nothing on this earth is gonna keep me from loving your sister."

He leaned forward, grabbing my hand, only to pull me in for a one-armed hug. He wasn't an affectionate guy, so that hug meant more to me than any words he could've said.

Gavin jumped inside, smelling like he'd OD'd on cologne. The two of us turned to look at him in the back of the cab. Collin's eyes went wide, and I barked out a laugh.

"What?" Gavin rubbed his hand over the top of his head, where all that hair he'd been growing was piled on top in some sort of man bun.

"You look like a pussy." Collin curled his lip.

I laughed harder. "Smell like a hooker too." Then turned to high-five Collin from over the console.

Gavin wrapped his arms around the backs of our headrests and smacked the two of us upside the head. "Drive, dickheads."

For a second, everything was right. Normal. Us. And even though the love of my life was three hours away, I knew I'd be okay for at least tonight.

CHAPTER

Lia

MY NEW NEIGHBORS WERE A TRIP.

The shorter of the guys, Ibrahim, worked at a sperm bank. He'd met Avery, the Adonis with the Tarzan hair—who worked as an interior designer—when he'd come in to donate. When Avery walked out, Ibrahim had said to him, "Thanks for coming," not meaning anything by it. He was still trying to overcome the language barrier, seeing as how he'd moved to the United States from West Africa not long before.

Apparently, Avery thought he was being a jerk and turned around to call him out on it, but instead fell instantly in love. They'd been together for six years, just moving a few weeks prior into the town house they were renting next to mine.

While I was at work this week, getting my classroom set up and meeting some of the teachers I would be working with, Mom had gotten cozy with Avery, spending the majority of her afternoons at their house

combing through *Better Homes and Gardens* maga-
zines. She didn't really need to be here, but I think she
was having too much fun to go.

Ibrahim and I would get home from work at the same
time, only to find her and Avery on our shared back
porch, drinking mimosas and giggling over random
Facebook videos together. It was a match made in
friendship heaven. I was pretty sure Mom was going
to miss Avery more than me when she left on Sunday.

"Why does your boyfriend not live here with you?"
Ibrahim asked, his accent thick. He shut off the blender.
Tonight was what he liked to call Margarita-and-Twister
Friday. In other words, he and Avery would drink mar-
garitas and play Twister. They'd invited Mom and me
over for their tradition.

The one that, according to Avery, they usually did
naked.

He handed me my third glass as I thought over my
answer to his question. Sadly, there really was no way
around the truth. "I told him he couldn't."

"Because…?" Ibrahim leaned back, setting his
elbows on the counter and kicking his feet out in front
of him.

I took a big gulp of my drink before answering. "I
wanted to find myself."

Stupidest excuse ever. I knew that now. Max seemed
to be adjusting to the idea better than I was, which I
should have expected and been happy about. Instead, I
was on day five without him and ready to give up everything just to go home, even though I was growing more
and more excited by the day about my job.

"I also didn't want to take him away from my brother

and his other best friend, Gavin. They all live together and help to raise my niece, Collin's daughter."

Ibrahim's black eyebrows rose in interest. "Sounds like a modern-day episode of that show Avery watches late at night with the three men, raising those three little girls."

"*Full House*." I laughed, having thought that myself a crap load of times. "They've been friends since boot camp, so it was natural for the three of them to move in together after their last tour in the Middle East."

"And how does the boyfriend feel about your... your..." He snapped his fingers just as Mom squealed out another laugh from the living room. She was likely three sheets to the wind from her one margarita. Poor Dad would have his hands full when she got home.

"Our separation?"

Ibrahim nodded.

"He seems to be okay with it."

He tucked his arm through mine. "You know that excuse of yours is, how do you say...bullshit, yeah?"

"Which one?" I frowned, taking another sip.

"You needing to find yourself." He tugged me toward the living room where Mom had her right foot on red and her left hand on blue. I couldn't even find it in me to laugh at how crazy she looked, not when everything inside me was breaking.

"It is bullshit." I shrugged. "But it's also too late to take back."

He looked at me, his dark eyes narrowed as he panned my face. "Nothing is too late." He winked. "You just need the drive to make it happen."

"Leanne!" Mom called from the floor, waving me

over, only to fall on her face. She rolled onto her back and laughed harder. "Come play, honey."

Avery stood and fist pumped the air, having just won the game. Seconds later, he was dancing in circles as Fall Out Boy played over his iPod.

Ibrahim chuckled under his breath, his eyes on Avery's ass. "Your mother has stolen my fiancé's heart."

"Seems so." She was amazing like that.

With a polite nod, I excused myself and walked out onto the back porch. It was a nice night, though cooler from an earlier storm. Not thinking twice, I pulled my phone from my pocket. Sprinkles of rain dripped onto my cheeks, cooling my face as I waited for Max to pick up the call. Three rings in though, and he didn't answer. I didn't expect him to. He was babysitting the neighbor's kid again, something Max did every so often to help out the grandma who was raising the boy. Likely they were too enveloped in their video games to hear the phone ring.

I sighed, resolved that we'd already had our one chat for the day, and ended the call. Leaning forward onto the railing and setting my half empty glass on the wood, I studied the stars instead of going inside, needing to think, to breathe, and most of all, to figure out what I was going to do.

The nights were the worst. Not being able to lie in Max's arms and listen to his breathing, his laughter, not making love to him either... Yet this is what I had wanted, right?

Why, Lia? Why is that?

I quieted Old Lia down with another drink.

Something vibrated in my pocket. I wiped a few stray tears from my cheeks before answering, sick and tired of crying and hurting. Sick of this day-by-day thing too. It was killing me.

I didn't bother looking at the caller ID before I said, "Hello?"

"Hey, Lee-Lee."

My lips started to quiver at the sound of his voice, and like a tidal wave of emotions breaking free, it all came out. Every tear I could make, every sob I could produce…

"What is it?" Panic made Max's voice growly, but I couldn't choke back my cries. Couldn't take a breath to tell him how broken I was without him. How I missed him so badly I couldn't stand myself anymore.

"Damn it, Lia, what's wrong? Are you hurt? Tell me!"

I sniffled and managed a small "I'm okay."

A sigh echoed from the other end, followed by muffled words and the faint sound of video game music. I squeezed my eyes shut, ashamed. I shouldn't have called. He was busy. And there I was, breaking down after some margaritas.

"Let me go get Gav next door so he can watch Diego."

"No." I shook my head, taking deep breaths to curb my sudden breakdown. "No, it's fine. I just… I miss you really bad today. That's all."

"Shit, Lia. You scared me." I heard him groan, then the squeak of a chair in the dining room as he likely sat down or stood up. "What brought this on? You were fine earlier."

"Ibrahim's margaritas?"

Max laughed, the sound sending goose bumps over my skin. "I knew that guy was trouble."

"I'm sorry." I twirled my finger around the rim of my glass, gathering the salt.

"Don't be sorry for missing me. Don't ever be sorry for that."

I wasn't sorry for missing him, that's the thing. I was sorry for being so stupid over not allowing him to move here with me like he wanted to. Admitting that to myself was the scariest thing I'd ever done. Admitting it to Max seemed impossible.

"Leanne?" Mom opened the back door, her voice laced with concern. I glanced back over my shoulder at her, just as she asked, "Are you okay, sweetie?"

I covered the phone and tried to smile as I said, "I'm fine, Mom. I'll be right there, okay?"

Her head dipped to the side, sadness overtaking her features. If she knew how bad I was, she wouldn't leave on Sunday. But Dad needed her, and I needed to learn to be on my own.

"You sure?"

"Promise." My smile must have been convincing enough this time because she went inside.

"Hey," I said on a breath, pulling the phone back to my mouth.

He was quiet on the other end, but I knew he was there. I could hear his breaths.

"Max?"

"I-I miss you too, Lee-Lee."

Another tear dripped out, but I wiped it away, pulling my lip between my teeth in case more sobs decided to slip out.

"Can you look outside for a second?" he asked.

"I'm outside right now."

"Okay," he said. "Hold on then."

A minute later, after explaining something to Diego

about hitting a left key, then a right, then the A-button, I heard the screen door to their duplex open. "Look at the moon," Max whispered.

I blinked and did just that. "I see it."

"Good. Now, know this, Lee-Lee. As long as we're both under this moon, then we're together, even if we aren't right next to each other. You got me?"

I smiled through my tears. "I got you."

"This isn't forever, right?" he asked, losing some of that Max confidence I loved.

"No, not forever at all." As soon as I saw him again, minus my margarita-fueled emotions, I would tell him the whole truth. That I didn't want to be apart. That I wanted him with me. That this day-by-day scenario sucked ass and I couldn't live with it anymore. I wanted forever with Maxwell.

And I wanted it now.

CHAPTER 34

Max

I WAS DISTRACTED. SOMETHING I'D NEVER LET HAPPEN during a match before. Whether it was from last night's conversation with Lee-Lee, or what I had to tell Collin that night, I wasn't sure. Either way, one unfocused move later, I was down for the count.

Rugby apparently wasn't my game anymore.

"Fuck, I think it's broken." I held my mangled hand to my chest, having heard the snap of a bone, maybe. Not sure who it was, but some dickhead on the other team had dug his cleat so far into my knuckles that it was like he was tunneling for hell.

Hybrid studs on a pair of cleats? Who would've thought there were idiots out there who cared so much about an intramural Saturday game.

Collin's eyes went big as he dropped down next to me. "Not gonna lie, Maxwell. It looks bad." Sweat covered his forehead, dripping down his cheek. "Gavin!" he yelled, scanning the side of the pitch. "Get over here. Now."

I panted, my chest going tight. Not real sure what Gav could do that a ride to the ER couldn't.

"Can you walk?" Gavin asked a few seconds later.

I opened one eye, finding him next to Collin. "Ain't my feet that hurt, baby cakes."

He curled his lip at the nickname, but Colly laughed. It was a good sound to hear when I was seconds away from losing my shit.

"Let's go, asshole." Gavin tugged me up on one side, Colly the other. With their arms wrapped around my waist, they both walked me off the pitch, straight to Collin's truck.

"The bones are hanging out. You see that? Fucking nasty shit," someone said.

I wasn't all that surprised to hear it, but what I was surprised about was that it didn't hurt anymore. Five minutes later and it'd grown numb, tingling down my fingers. Probably wasn't a good thing, but I'd take the relief while I could.

My eyes grew unfocused the more we moved, the world tilting at the same time. I tipped forward as we got to the passenger-side door. "Jesus, hold tight to him," Gavin said to Collin as he ran around to the bed of the truck.

Colly's arms went around my waist to hold me upright. If I wasn't worried about passing out, I probably would've accused him of hitting on me.

"Do I have something back there to cover this up?" Collin yelled to Gav.

I squeezed my eyes shut to curb the spinning. "You afraid of a little blood, Colly?"

"More afraid of what Addie will say if you get it all over my seats."

I snorted, running outta breath. "Doubt it... Short Stuff thinks I walk on magic clouds."

"Yeah, sure, keep telling yourself that."

The passenger-side door flew open, Gavin reaching for my feet to help me inside, a couple of blue shop towels in his hand.

The stupid asses were gonna lift me? Don't think so.

"Christ, guys, it's my hand, not my legs. Leave me be."

Gavin growled at me like a dog and put the shop towels over my hand. "Your eyes are dilated, and your face is turning white. If anything, you should be more worried about passing out and hitting your head right now."

I shrugged. "Meh, wouldn't be the first time."

Rolling his eyes, Gavin helped Collin get me in the truck anyway, then took off toward his Suburban.

Man, he was a moody ass.

Before Collin could shut the door, I kicked my foot out and looked him dead in the eyes, saying what I'd planned on saying later that night...*after* he'd gotten a few beers in him at O'Paddy's. "I'm asking your sister to marry me."

He laughed. "Not really surprised." This time, I let him shut the door. Guess he needed time to let it all sink in.

Once the truck was put in Reverse, I decided to break the other news. "I also was thinking of moving to Springfield in a few months to stay with her 'til her training's up."

Collin's eyes narrowed at the road. "Let's talk about this later, when you're not about ready to lose your fucking hand." He hit the accelerator and pulled out of the gravel lot.

"Seriously, Collin. It's gonna happen. Soon." I leaned my head back, trying to keep my breathing steady. Pain started to rocket up my arm, burning through my elbow, my wrist, my forearm.

"You ask her about this yet?"

I shook my head, grimacing as he hit a bump. Telling Collin and Gavin about my plans was one thing; convincing Lee-Lee to let it happen was a whole other ball game.

"You're really serious about this?" Collin said after a minute of silence.

"Yeah." My gut went tight from the whips and turns he was making. I couldn't open my eyes. Couldn't even manage a single blink. But I could say "I love her." It was the one truth I'd never get tired of saying.

I'd gotten the ring; it was buried in the bottom of my dresser at home. I'd never had an urge to go buy one, though the thought had been on my mind since the second we decided to make this thing between us the real deal. But one day when I was out, I happened to see the ring sitting in the window of the jewelry store by June's Waffle House and More, the place where Addie used to work. Pink jewels surrounded both sides of the lone diamond as it sparkled in the sun's reflection. It was simple, pretty, and all Lee-Lee.

I knew someday I'd give it to her. And someday I'd hope she'd say yes.

"We'll miss you if you decide to move, just like we do Lia, but you've got my blessing. Probably always have had."

Somehow I managed to smile, even through the pain. "Thanks, Colly. Just do me a favor first."

"What's that?"

I cleared my throat. "Don't call her about the hand." She'd just worry and wanna come home.

Collin stayed quiet for a second. No doubt weighing his options. Get reamed by me if he did call her, or get reamed by Lee-Lee if he didn't. I know what I'd choose. Lia was scary as shit when she got pissy, but also damn hot.

Still…

"Seriously, Colly. I don't want her to worry." Another shot of pain darted up my arm, and I hissed.

"Fine. I won't call."

I nodded, wanting to believe him. But at the same time, I didn't.

Lia

The second my phone rang, I should've known something was wrong. But in my half-dazed, Saturday-morning state, I didn't know if I was awake or asleep. Either way, when Willie Nelson sang to me, all I could think about was my brother impatiently waiting on the other end of the line.

I reached for my phone on my new coffee table, trying not to wake my mom. We'd been up half the night with Ibrahim and Avery. And with her long drive back home tomorrow, I knew she needed the rest.

"Hey, Brother. What's up?" I stood and headed toward my room.

"Lia, hey…" My heart stopped at his scratchy voice, the serious way he said my name.

The alarm clock in my room said 11:00 a.m. I knew they'd had a rugby match this morning, but they usually didn't end until well after noon.

"What's wrong?"

"It's Max."

I froze. "What happened? Where is he? Is he okay?"

"His hand was stepped on during a game today. Some dumb fuck on the other team was wearing illegal cleats."

A rush of air left my throat, relief running through me. Still, why would Collin sound so cryptic over a bruised hand?

"He's okay, right? Needs stitches or something?"

He sighed, and the alarm bells in my head starting to ring.

"Collin Montgomery…tell me he's okay." Knees weak, I walked back into the living room and headed straight toward the couch. At the mention of my brother's name, Mom popped up from her end, her dark eyes immediately searching my face with worry.

"Yeah, he's okay. But his hand… He can't feel anything. There are a shit ton of broken bones, damaged nerves…"

I held my hand over my suddenly cramping stomach. Oh, Maxwell…

Everything okay? Mom mouthed the question to me, fear for her son in her eyes, I'm sure.

I covered the speaker with my hand, needing to gather my wits. "Max is hurt."

She gasped. "Oh no. Do we need to go home?"

I thought about her suggestion, knowing at the same time that I had to go into work on Monday. Granted, the first real day of school wasn't until Wednesday, but

I still had so much to do. At the same time, the idea of working seemed trivial when I knew Max was laid up in a hospital, hurting.

"Okay, Sis. The orthopedic doc just went into the room to talk surgery. I gotta go. Call you with an update soon, okay?"

"Yeah, okay. Thanks for calling." I pinched my eyes shut, thinking about Beaner and her surgery from not long ago. She'd recovered fairly quickly, but this thing with Max was a whole other issue. Broken hands, torn ligaments, muscles... This would require physical therapy, and God only knew what else.

And Jesus, what about his job? His entire *business*? How could he cook with only one good hand?

I slapped the end button on my phone and tossed it onto the table. Fear and frustration had tears spilling from my eyes. I wiped them with the back of my shirt, already knowing what I had to do.

"I'll pack my stuff." Mom patted the back of my hand, also knowing what needed to be done.

Thoughts of Max's brown eyes and smile had my head spinning as I threw a few things into an overnight bag. Stupid rugby.

As we stepped outside, Mom turned to me and said, "I spoke to your father. He's at the hospital with the boys."

I unlocked my car with the key fob and nodded. "Good."

Dad had a level head, unlike his son or his son's friends. If a decision about something needed to be made before I got there, he would at least be able to provide insight.

In the car, I muttered under my breath about stupid

sports and stupid men and the stupid decisions they made just so they could feel young. I'd never been adamant about deterring the guys from playing, but now? God, I was ready to scream.

Mom chuckled under her breath, maybe even still a little tipsy from our night before. "What's so funny?" I asked her.

"Did you know that the only reason women are crazy is because men do stupid things in life to make us that way?"

I blinked, then blinked again, only for a bubble of laughter to rise in my throat. I'm not sure if exhaustion or worry had me losing it in the end, but either way, it felt better to laugh than cry.

Before long, Mom joined me, and together, the two of us laughed so hard that I couldn't help but wipe the happy tears away. We were both exhausted, likely slap-happy. But the fact that Mom could distract me when I felt like pulling my hair out reminded what she was capable of.

And what *I* was capable of.

It was a moment for me, for us as a mother/daughter unit too. Proof that we'd come a long way during the last few years. From my incident at college, to me dropping out and coming home to live, to the changes in my appearance and demeanor, to the moment Chloe was brought into the world. Amy's death had hit us both pretty hard, but Collin's arrival home had helped some. But while Mom grew stronger, I'd seemed to level out. I had no problem hiding things, but internally I felt as though I had been regressing over the past year.

Now though, times were changing. It was my turn to

grow fully and completely. Strong on the outside, strong on the inside. And sure we had a long trip ahead of us, which would ultimately lead to an injured Max, but I at least felt like I finally had a handle on life. The good things, the bad things, and all things in between. And as we drove away from my newer life to my older one, I realized something very important. Old Lia wanted back in. Old Lia was also done hiding. Old Lia wanted to mesh with New Lia once and for all.

I grinned at the thought, having no problem making a little room for her.

CHAPTER

Max

To say I felt like ass was an understatement. But really, what did I expect after just coming outta surgery?

I managed to sit up, my naked ass catching the breeze in the process. Somehow, I got my feet to the cold tile, only for Gav to yell at me about my equilibrium, or lack thereof.

I'd only been awake for about forty-five minutes, the anesthetic barely wearing off. They'd apparently wanted to get me into surgery right away, something about the only orthopedic doc in Carinthia being on his way out of town for two weeks of vacation in the Caribbean. Joys of living in a small town and all that BS meant one specialist per life issue.

What I really needed to do was call Lia, tell her I was good and not to worry—or to come. No doubt she was freaking the hell out if Collin had been the one to call her. The guy overexaggerated everything.

"I really gotta get up." I went to pull on my IV, stopped short by Collin's hand this time.

"You can't. Doc said you gotta rest. Gav was telling the truth." He sat at the foot of my bed, Chloe on his lap. Addie was in the chair next to him, frowning at me.

According to the doc, I had to get skin taken from my thigh to wrap around the bone. Grafts and whatnot. Luckily, I didn't need pins or screws, but damn it, this surgery was gonna cost me a fortune. I had my business to deal with, gigs to do. What the hell was I gonna do if I had to take time off? I had money left from my dad, but digging into that account again wasn't sitting well with me.

Collin lowered his chin to Beaner's head as she listened to Aerosmith on his phone. The cast on her arm looked like a blinged-up accessory compared to the nasty white one I was sporting. She'd had surgery three weeks ago and was already healing like a champ. I was thinking I had a longer recovery time ahead of me than she did.

"Okay, fine. Then at least gimme my phone so I can call Lia and tell her I'm okay."

"No can do." Collin shook his head.

"Why the hell not?"

"She's already on her way here," Addie answered.

My face went cold. "*What?*" She had to work on Monday. The last thing she needed was to deal with my stupid ass when she was just getting her new life up and running.

Gavin moved away from the window and leaned against the foot of the bed. He set his elbows on my food tray. "What'd you expect, man? She loves you."

"And I love her, which is why she didn't need to come deal with me."

"She'll be here soon. No point in calling now." Collin shrugged like it was no big deal she was making the three-hour drive.

"Jesus, this is all messed up. You're a liar, Colly." I pointed an accusing finger at him.

"Well, you're stupid if you think that Addie would let me keep my sister in the dark." Colly grinned at his girl, then winked at me.

I lifted my good arm to press a hand to my forehead. Couldn't even feel the bad hand at this point. "Why didn't you stop her?" I asked Collin.

"She would've come even if I told her not to." He scratched at his throat.

Likely. She was a Montgomery. They were stubborn like that.

"Fuck me," I whispered under my breath.

Seconds later, my other favorite blue-eyed girl crawled off her daddy's lap to sit next to me. "Uck bad."

My stomach tightened. "Sorry, Beaner. You're right."

I tried like hell not to laugh as she snuggled against my shoulder and frowned up at me. Her light little eyebrows were pushed together in faux anger, making her look just like Collin. Even at sixteen months, she still had more light in her eyes than I'd ever seen in anyone else's. The girl knew what was up. Knew that I was hurting too. And as she pressed her little casted arm against mine, I realized she was already a hell of a lot stronger than I'd ever be.

Addie stood, grabbed Chloe around the waist, and swung her into her arms. Chloe squealed, lightening my downer mood.

"We're going to step away from the f-bombs for a while and grab something to eat in the cafeteria." Addie leaned over and kissed my cheek. "You, Mr. Max, rest and get better." She turned and smiled at Collin, adjusting Beaner. It was then that I saw something shiny on her left hand.

I turned to glare at Colly. He was smiling at the door she'd just walked out of, looking like the cheesiest bastard alive. Happiness for my best friend, and thoughts of that ring in my drawer at home, had me itching to get out of this hospital even more. "What the hell, asshole?" I stretched my leg out and kicked him. "Why didn't you tell me you two were getting hitched?"

Colly lowered his head and shook it, a huge smirk on his face. "Happened when we were in Minnesota. She just got her ring back from being sized a couple of days ago." He shrugged nonchalantly, but it did nothing to hide the happiness in his eyes. Fact of the matter was that an amazing woman did amazing things to—and for—a man.

Leaning back against the bed with a huge grin on my face, I stretched my legs and opened them wide. Yeah, my hand was fucked, but my buddy had his forever. And hopefully, soon, so would I.

"Jesus, shut your legs." Gavin pressed the heels of his hands over his eyes.

I looked down and shrugged. "It's cold in here. What can I say?"

"Cold?" Gavin jerked his head back. "Your dick gets hard when it's cold?"

"I've got a brand of special in me you'll never have, big guy."

"I'm leaving." Collin stood from the end of the bed and nudged Gavin's shin with his knee. "Might need to grab some bleach for Gav's eyes on the way out."

"Sorry it's so pretty you've been blinded." I winked at Gavin.

He smacked me upside the head, not even caring that I was laid up in this hospital bed. It's what I loved about my boys. They never made a big deal about anything.

———ᴡᴡ———

Lia

The entire drive home was silent on the Maxwell front. Even as Mom and I pulled into the Carinthia hospital parking lot, nobody was answering my phone calls. I was exhausted and on the verge of a mental breakdown. Yet knowing I was so close to Max pushed me to get out of my funk. I didn't expect *him* to call me, but at least Addie or Collin could have called with an update. Even my dad wasn't answering the phone.

Two hours into the drive, Mom and I had switched positions. I'd slept fitfully during that last hour on the road, which only made me feel worse. Still, I loved Max wholeheartedly and would lose years and years of sleep if it meant I got to be there in person to make sure he was okay.

"You ready to go in?"

I nodded. "Yeah, just drop me off at the front door. Dad's probably at home waiting for you. You can take my car home. I'll grab an Uber to come by and get it after visiting hours are over."

Her soft, brown eyes narrowed at the clock on the dashboard. It was past seven at night. "You sure?"

"Positive."

She pulled me into a fast hug, then leaned back to hold my face in her hands. "You're a good girl, Leanne. I love you."

I hugged her once more, not holding back. I refused to cry as I inhaled the lavender scent of her shampoo. She sniffled in turn, wordless in her love as she patted the back of my head.

"And no need for an Uber. Just call Dad or me when you're ready to come back to the house."

I leaned back and nodded, already missing her.

Max's hospital room was quiet and dark when I pushed the door open a few minutes later. I'd taken time to call my principal, to explain what had happened. Said that I'd either be late on Monday or wouldn't be able to come in until Tuesday, depending on what happened tomorrow with Max. She was awesome about it, proving that I'd found the perfect beginning for a forever career.

I set my bag on the chair next to his bed. Taking a deep breath, I turned to find his dark, sinful eyes open and focused on me.

"Hey, Lee-Lee." He looked exhausted and sounded like he'd swallowed fire. But the smile on his lips and the sweet way he spoke my nickname somehow managed to lessen the burn in my throat. "You didn't have to drive all this way. I'm good."

"And miss the chance to kiss you better?" I tsked. "Never." I kissed him on the lips to prove the point, then sat on the edge of his bed. "How's the hand?" I pointed to it, frowning at the massive cast.

"Hurts a little. Luckily it's the left hand, not the right."

"A little…" I mocked and rolled my eyes.

He waggled his eyebrows. "It's a good thing I'm made of titanium."

I sighed and leaned forward, pressing my forehead to his chest. Breathing in his familiar scent made me feel like I was home.

"I gotta admit something." His voice crackled. I leaned back to look into his eyes.

"What's that?" I ran my knuckles down the side of his cheek, and he nuzzled his mouth against my hand. I opened my palm wide so he could kiss it.

"Nothing will ever hurt me worse than missing you."

I shut my eyes, shivering at his words, his touch, his simple kiss.

How was it that we had been apart for less than a week when it felt like so much longer? "I love you," I whispered against his chest.

"You better, 'cause I'm in love with you."

I smiled, blinking back tears, the happy kind. I *did* love this man. I loved everything about him, in fact. His goofy tendencies, his protective nature. The fact that I loved the way he looked didn't hurt matters either. But it was his heart that made me feel alive. Made me want to better myself, not just for my family anymore, but for him too. And because of that heart, I knew what had to happen.

I laid my ear against his chest, listening to him breathe and to his heartbeat.

"I'm gonna be laid up for a while, I'm afraid, but I'll

be good as new soon. Wouldn't think about missing my trip to see you in a couple of weeks."

The simple thought of leaving him like this hurt me worse than before. I leaned back, just enough to look in his eyes. "How will you work, Max?"

One shrug later, he lifted his bad hand. "Gonna have to master things one-handed, looks like."

"And if you can't?" Optimism was never my strong suit.

"Don't worry about me. I'll be fine." He touched my chin, stroking his thumb back and forth.

I leaned in closer. "But what if it takes a while?"

"I'm paid up on my lease at the store for a year."

"And bills?" I bit my lip. "How will you pay your bills? Or cook for your gigs?"

His face grew serious, and he stared out the window instead of at me. "Guess I'll be tapping into big daddy's money after all."

I pulled in a breath, nervous. "What if there was a different way?"

Even in the dark, I could see his gaze swing back to me. Feeling far needier than I should have, I silently took him in as well.

Feathered dark hair I adored…dark-brown eyes I'd memorized like my favorite love song…and that sly little grin, the one that managed to make everything around me feel frozen, except for my rattled heart…

God, he was sensational looking. How could I ever *not* want him with me all the time?

"I really suck at cooking, Max."

He scowled at me, but I kept going.

"And who's going to wash your back in the shower?"

I sat up along the edge of the bed and looked at my lap, my face growing hot. "I can't do life without you."

"Yes you can." He urged me onto his lap with his good hand, cradling me against his chest. "Don't say that. Don't even *think* that. This is your dream job. And I'm sorry if I worried you."

My point wasn't coming across the way I intended. So, I sucked in another big breath and laid my head back to look up at him, trying a new angle. "I got a new bed, Maxwell. Mom ordered it for me. It's huge. After she found out I was sleeping on that futon, she had a fit."

"Good." He kissed my nose. "You deserve a nice bed. That futon was a killer on my back."

"But it's going to be a *lonely* bed without you."

Half of his mouth curled up into his swoony Maxwell grin. "Then we'll have to make enough memories on it during my visits to make sure you'll never miss me again, yeah?"

I shook my head, frustrated. He wasn't getting it. Though I wasn't being clear either. So, I let it go. All of it.

"Move in with me. Live with me in Springfield. Once your hand is better, we'll come back on the weekends and do your catering gigs together. Then after I've completed my year, I'll quit and try to apply for a position closer to Carinthia. We'll move back here together."

His eyes narrowed in confusion. "But what about you getting tenured and I thought…"

There were so many ways I wanted this man, and I'd only just begun to discover them all. Apart from him, I couldn't do that, but together was another story.

"Nothing matters but us."

He sighed, looking unconvinced. I'd pushed the idea away, so there's no doubt I confused him. "Look, I have all this room in my closet and a dresser with three spare drawers. I need them filled. By you and your stuff. Your presence. I just need *you*."

He moved to adjust his bad hand, then sat up a little straighter, still with me on his lap. Eventually, he leveled our stares, pressing his forehead to mine in that way I loved. "It's a damn good thing you asked, 'cause I was thinking about sneaking into your car when you weren't looking. Hitching a ride, then permanently planting myself in your house like a protestor until you decided there was no other option."

I laughed out loud, my head tossed back. Whether it was from happiness or exhaustion, I didn't know. Either way, I had the answer I wanted. Max was going to move to Springfield. With me.

Our chests smashed together. I tangled my hands in his hair and pressed my lips to his. What had I done to deserve someone so amazing?

A minute passed, then two. Our tongues danced, and our bodies did things that hospital beds weren't made for. Touching and caressing, all sorts of naughty things that I couldn't wait to expand upon once he got out of this place.

He kissed my chin, slowly moving around until his lips were inches from mine. "Are we really gonna do this then? You're okay with it?" He tucked some of my hair behind my ear, trailing his fingers down my cheek only to stop at my chin. Fascination lit his eyes. "I don't want to rush you."

My throat was tight with emotion, but I managed to

swallow and say, "Yeah, we are. That day-by-day scenario sucked the second you pulled away from my place."

With his nose nuzzled against my neck below my ear, Maxwell shook with laughter. "You're it for me, Lia. You know that, right?"

Unable to deny what I'd known for so long, I said, "Yeah, I know. You're it for me too."

"Hell yeah." He growled low in his throat. "Now, come here and kiss me some more."

With a smile, I did just that, only to get to the point where neither of us could breathe from exertion. The sun could have been falling from the sky, or zombies could have been rising from the grave, but I didn't care. Not when I was right where I wanted to be. Forever.

Almost.

"Hold on a sec," I whispered, then straightened my legs out only to shimmy out of my shorts and panties.

No hesitation.

No fears.

No regrets.

I slipped under the covers, pulled his hospital gown up to his chest, and sank down onto his lap before he could ask me what I was doing.

There. That's better.

Once I'd adjusted to his fullness, I lowered my hands to both sides of his head and whispered against his mouth, "Think you can keep it down, Soldier Boy?"

He palmed my ass one-handed, grinding against me, urging me to move faster, when I wanted slow. "Doc said no strenuous activity for a few days." He bit at my lip, only for his heart monitor to beep a little louder. "But damn it, I need you real bad, Lee-Lee."

Equally as desperate for him, I kissed his cheek, his brows, his nose. "Well, it's a good thing we're going to be roomies, because I can't get enough of you." Slowly, I arched my back, loving him not only with my body, but with my heart.

"And it's a damn good thing I was blessed with stamina then." He wrapped his one good arm around my waist, somehow still managing to help my movements along.

I giggled and he grinned back at me, his eyes bright.

And then together we discovered just how amazing secret hospital-bed sex could be.

EPILOGUE

Gavin

Two months prior

DARKNESS TRIED TO PULL ME UNDER, AND I LEANED TO MY right to try to stay awake, only for something to smack me upside the head. A window.

"Fuck, that hurt."

I reached up and touched my scalp, attempting to shake off the haze. I was in the backseat of a taxi, next to the hottest woman I'd ever kissed. Between my knees sat a bottle of peach schnapps that she'd insisted we grab before we went back to my place.

"You okay, St. James?" she purred, reaching over to rub her hand across my forehead.

"Never been better." I smiled, looking at her, hoping to see something besides a drunken haze of lust in her pretty eyes, but that's all there was. "How about you?"

She nodded, swaying closer. "I'm peachy." Then she reached down, grabbed the bottle, and guzzled from it.

"Whoa, there." I swiped it from her and set it on the floorboard by my feet. Though a sheet of glass separated us from the driver, I didn't want to take the chance of getting caught.

Fingers tugged on the end of my beard. "This…" She licked her lips. "I'm dying to know how *this* feels."

"You're touching it now, aren't you?" I frowned, confused by what she meant.

"No, no, no. Silly…" She giggled, then tugged me down to her face. Our lips were close, our noses touching as she said, "I meant how it'd feel between my thighs."

"Holy hell." I kissed her, hard, sloppy, drunk kisses that I couldn't get enough of.

In a flash, she sat up, soon straddling me. She rode me dry like she owned me, and damn if I didn't love it like I was pretty sure I loved her.

"Touch me, Gavin."

I did, reaching down between our bodies to push her skirt up a little higher. The skin on her thigh felt like silk to my hands, and my cock jumped as she moaned her appreciation in my ear. Needing more, I slipped her panties aside, finding a kind of heat I hadn't touched in years.

The second my thumb brushed across her clit, she let out another low moan, coming alive when I needed her silent.

This woman made me crazy in so many ways. She'd been pushing me away for a month now, told me she didn't do relationships while I told her I didn't do casual. Yet here we were, weeks later, getting ready for a night I wasn't sure she'd even remember.

I would though. This was too perfect to forget.

Kisses happened, hands wandered. Her mouth on mine, my tongue grazing hers.

"I want you," she whispered.

"You got me," I groaned back, tangling my fingers in her hair while I worked her clit with my thumb.

Minutes later, we pulled up to the front of my duplex, barely taking a breath as we tucked the bottle up under my shirt, paid the cabbie, and raced to the front door. We laughed running up my driveway like we were sixteen and hiding from our parents—something I'd never done. Mainly because I didn't have parents to hide from.

"Wait." She pulled me to a stop on my front porch, her hands at the base of my shirt, her breathing as staggered and wild as my own.

"What's wrong?" I touched the side of her face, and she leaned into my palm, shutting her eyes like she was savoring my touch. I liked it. A lot.

"This doesn't change a thing," she whispered, then looked up at me. "I can't be the woman you think you need."

My heart thudded faster, my tongue thick as I lied. "No. It changes nothing."

I wanted it to change things though. I wanted her to want me the way I wanted her. Not just drunk, but sober too. All the time, all the ways, and all the days.

But if I couldn't have more, I'd settle for tonight.

"Good." She rose on her tiptoes and kissed my chin. "Now open the damn door so I can test my theory."

I frowned, scrambling for my keys in my pocket. The outside light from Collin, Max, and Addie's side of the duplex flickered on, highlighting the side of her gorgeous face.

"What theory?" I asked as I unlocked the front door.

A grin stretched her lips as she said, "That the quiet ones are always the best."

The next thing I knew, we were kissing again as we bumped into the walls of my house and made our way to my room. I heard the glass schnapps bottle shattering all over my hall when she tugged my shirt up and over my head. For once, I didn't care about order. I just needed her naked and under me as fast as I could get her there.

Clothes went flying, and soon she was right where I wanted her. I kissed her swollen lips, she kissed mine, and when I pulled back to look at her, her face was pink and burned from my beard. I kissed the skin, making my way down. In between breaths I whispered, "You're so beautiful."

I probably should've been nervous, worried I wouldn't last. Should've hated myself for not taking Max's advice to get laid more often for the sake of practice. But there I was, finding my way around a woman just fine.

Sex was like riding a bicycle. I'd never forget how to do it.

"Yes," she hissed, arching her back as I sank inside. My hands were on her naked breasts, her fingers grazing my ass. She pulled me closer, harder, urging me to go faster. Sweat stuck between us; her heeled boots, still on, scraped over my calves. I was too far gone to care about the pain.

The bed rocked beneath us, slamming hard against the wall. "Shh," I finally had to whisper when her cries grew too loud. The last thing I wanted was for Colly to come knocking on my door, bitching at me because I'd woken Beaner.

A giggle slipped through her lips, as her hazy eyes

peered up at me. "Can't help myself." She slammed her hips up, hard, her experience overshadowing mine.

I grinned and said, "That so?" Another push of my hips, relentless in their need.

She nodded, pulling her lip between her teeth to curb her moans. "You're a damn natural." Then she reached around and smacked my ass.

I froze, my cock pulsing inside her. "Did you just spank me?"

She nodded, her bright eyes holding mine. "Did you like it?"

I shook my head, not sure whether to laugh or roll her over on top of me to spank her back. "You're crazy, woman." I settled for lowering my head to her neck, then sucking until she started crying out my name again.

If she ever came back over—*God, I needed her to come back*—I'd have to be sure to move my bed to another wall.

Read on for a look at book one of the
Reckless Heart series by Heather Van Fleet.

RECKLESS
HEARTS

Collin

"Damn it, Max. How many times do I have to tell you not to mix the reds with whites when you're washing clothes in hot water?"

I tossed the laundry basket holding my newly ruined rugby jersey on top of the dining room table. It landed with a thud, knocking down one of the musical toys my nine-month-old daughter, Chloe, loved.

Raising a baby daughter with a couple of guys is a lot like being a marine. It's an intense experience that requires constantly being all-in just to save someone else's back while he manages to save yours. It smells like shit ninety percent of the time, and every time you move, another body is up in your space. But you do it because you love it. There isn't any other option but to live and breathe it. In my life, my daughter—and the guys who helped me through—were all I needed.

That, and maybe a cleaning lady.

I spun around on my untied cleats, the sound of "Mary Had a Little Lamb" playing in the background as I rushed toward the breakfast bar to grab Chloe's diaper bag.

In the hallway to my right, my roommate—and certified laundry screwup—Max stood grinning, holding my girl in his arms. Dressed and ready to go, thank Christ, she sported a tiny green Carinthia Irish Rugby jersey her aunt Lia had made for her when Max, Gavin, and I joined the intramural club a few weeks back.

"You yelling at me, Colly?" Max kissed the top of Chloe's head, probably holding her on purpose 'cause he knew I wouldn't lay into him with Beaner in his arms.

With a thumb in her mouth, she snuggled closer to her pseudo-uncle's chest, still half-asleep from her nap. My throat grew tight as I took in her gorgeous face. Lucky for Max, the anger I'd been harboring disappeared with that one look at Chloe.

My daughter was my world—my peace, my rock. And even though the past eight months hadn't been picture perfect for us as a family or as far as life went, we were good as a unit—me, her, and Max, along with Gavin, who lived in the attached duplex.

Except that none of us could do laundry to save our asses.

"What were you thinking?" Glancing at the clock on the wall, I dropped the diaper bag on the floor next to my rugby bag and grunted. "Now the thing's pink and green, which means the guys are gonna rag on my ass all day." On the table sat a stack of five diapers. I grabbed a couple and shoved them into the bottom of the diaper bag, along with a few toys.

"Where's your spare?"

"Dirty."

Max set Chloe inside the playpen by the TV, then handed her the bottle I'd made up a few minutes back that'd been sitting on the coffee table. "Dude, pink is kick-ass."

I shot him a look. "Watch your mouth."

Ignoring me, he walked over to the basket, thumbing through it for a pair of socks, taking his time, chatting like a little kid, and acting like we weren't fifteen minutes behind schedule.

"You've got the pink-for-breast-cancer thing going on, like the *Save the Ta-Tas* T-shirts." Max picked his jersey—the one that had managed to stay green and white—out of the pile, then shoved it inside his rugby bag on the floor next to mine. "Then there's pink bubble gum that never loses its flavor…" He waggled his dark eyebrows and jogged over to the breakfast nook that separated the dining room from the kitchen. He tossed two Gatorade bottles my way. I caught both, tucking them in my own bag, along with my *pink*-and-green jersey.

"*Finally*, there's my favorite reason that pink is cool. Wanna hear it?"

Not really. But I shouldered my duffel, along with Chloe's diaper bag, and waited for him to finish anyway. When he didn't say squat, I sighed and finally said, "Jesus, don't leave me **hanging**. I won't be able to sleep at night without knowing why it's *cool* to have a *pink*-and-green jersey."

With a smirk, I turned to face him again, just as he tossed me the baby wipe container. I caught it one-handed and shoved it into the side of Chloe's bag.

"Mock me now, but I'm serious. Pink lip gloss looks hot as hell when it's on a woman's lips. Especially when those lips are wrapped around the head of my—"

"Shut it." I pointed a finger at him, glancing back at Chloe. Wide baby blues stared back and forth between us, watching, waiting, almost like she knew exactly what we were talking about.

Max shot his hands up in defense while I sat on a chair to tie my cleats.

"Just saying. Pink is a good color." He winked at Chloe. "Adds character. Right, Beaner?"

Eyes damn near sparkling, she babbled something or another from around her bottle, her blond hair sprouting all over the place. Before I could bitch about Max using my daughter against me, Gavin came busting through the front door, sandy hair hanging over his eyes. Any longer and he'd have the old Justin Bieber hairstyle beat.

But then I saw what he was holding and froze, while trying to ignore the snorts coming out of Max's nose.

"New car seat's ready." Gav kicked the door shut behind him with the bottom of his foot, meeting my stare.

Max laughed harder, reaching down to grab Gav's jersey this time. He tossed it at him, a perfect shot that landed on his shoulder. Like Max's, Gavin's was also still green and white.

"What?" Gav looked back and forth between the two of us, his lip curling as he set the *hot-pink* car seat down on the floor. "Quit looking at me like that."

Teeth gritted, I stood and tied the string on my rugby shorts.

"Nice choice of seat colors, don't you think?" Max smirked, pointing toward the car seat, before he took off out the front door, car keys spinning around his finger.

I rolled my eyes and shoved my bags at Gav. He took them, trying to defend himself as he said, "You told me to get a new car seat, so I got one. Chloe's a girl, and girls like pink. What's the big deal?"

"Colly's just struggling with his masculinity today. Nothing new," Max hollered from outside on the porch.

Ignoring my asshat of a best friend, I pulled Chloe out of her playpen and smiled as I tossed her in the air. The sanity that came with being a dad definitely outweighed the occasional insanity of my two best friends.

I buckled her into her new seat. Gav had already messed with the straps, adjusting the things to the perfect size. He was a genius like that, a certified master of all things safety and organization. He'd been that way from the second I met him in basic training six years ago.

"You going to fill me in?" He grabbed his cleats by the front door and tied them to the strap of his bag.

"You don't wanna know," I said, setting the handle of the car seat, now filled with my girl, over my forearm.

Gavin grunted something under his breath, then nodded before heading toward the door. I followed, not ready to face my teammates in my fucked-up jersey but more than ready to play.

"What's this?"

I rammed into his back on the threshold, Chloe's car seat digging into his ass. She let out a happy squeal and grinned up at me, bare feet kicking the air.

"What's what?" I glanced over his shoulder.

His hand was in my bag, humor lacing his words as he said, "Think you need to borrow my other jersey." He yanked the collar of mine out, a rare grin on his face.

I shut my eyes and yelled out the front door, "It's *pink*, Max."

"Real men wear it," he yelled at me from the street before getting into his car.

Scratch my earlier thoughts. I needed my daughter, a cleaning lady, *and* a new roommate.

———

"Get the hell over here, Colly," Max yelled from where he was sitting on the side of the pitch, his hands frantic as he waved them in the air at us. A few seconds later, the whistle blew, signaling the end of the game. The guys who weren't helping to gather up the equipment jogged toward the stack of twenty-four packs set up on the sidelines, leaving me and Gavin with Jonathon, the club's owner.

"Christ, Montgomery. You're a bloody good player." Jonathon slapped me upside the shoulders, wearing a wide smile. He'd organized the team years ago when he first moved to the States from Ireland, and now he was on the hunt for someone to take it over. Think he was looking at me to do it, but I wasn't ready.

"Thanks. Felt really good out there." Normally, I played to relieve a little stress and bond with my buddies. But today reminded me how much I still needed a competitive challenge in my life.

Max yelped, then fell back onto his hands as Maggie, Jonathon's daughter, stood over him laughing.

Grinning, I nodded at the guys once more before I

ran off the pitch myself, wordless and knowing what I'd find when I got there. Max didn't do diapers, at least not the number-two kind.

"She exploded," he explained, his eyebrows raised and his normally dark face paling. He looked to Maggie, like a ten-year-old could solve his problems. She watched Chloe during games when my sister couldn't be there to do it.

Everything throbbed on my body. Neck, shoulders, back, the cleat marks on my face… But not a damn thing could take down my mood as I squatted next to my girl.

"Da, da, da, da," she squealed, clapping her hands.

Max stood and took a few steps back, already sneaking away. "Just can't do it, man. Sorry."

"He said he was going to puke." Maggie giggled, slapping her hand over her mouth.

I winked at her. "No doubt he did."

As I reached for the diaper bag, Max said, "Thanks, Colly," then took off, probably to flirt with one of the rugby groupies—the hot chicks who followed the single team members around after the games.

Gavin came up alongside me after that, running his hand over the top of Chloe's head while I stood holding her. She reached for him, but he leaned over to kiss her nose instead of taking her. The guy loved Beaner, but she terrified him to no end.

"You coming to O'Paddy's with us?" Jonathon wrapped his sweaty arm around his daughter's shoulder. Her nose curled in disgust, but she didn't move away.

"Not sure." I shrugged and set Chloe on my hip. She laid her head on my damp shoulder, playing shy as Gavin did peekaboo with her.

It was hard for me to go out after games with the rest of the team. Not when I still had to wake up in the morning to be a parent, hangover or not.

"We'll be there." Gavin nodded once at Jonathon, then at me. "Max is staying home with Chloe, and you and I are going out for once."

I raised my eyebrows. "That so?"

His face was smug with a secret. Like me, Gavin normally preferred the quiet house to a loud bar, so this was new coming from the guy who talked less than I did.

"Damn right you're going. Not a choice for our MVP to ditch out on the after-party." Another dude on the team—had to be freshly twenty-one—sidled up next to me. I barely knew him, but he was a good guy.

He tossed Gavin a beer, offering me one too. "No thanks," I said. I'd never drink with Chloe in my arms.

Jonathon laughed, head thrown back. "Ah, so glad it's not gonna be me this time. The wife would have my ass." And with that, he grabbed Maggie, along with the newbie, and headed back toward the pitch to grab the rest of the equipment.

I turned to Gavin. "What was that all about?"

"Nothing." He scrubbed a hand over his mouth, hiding a smile.

"Doesn't sound like nothing." I frowned.

"You'll see."

Before I could ask what he meant, a squeal distracted me. Chloe reached for the air, trying to grab the crispy, red and yellow leaves blowing in a swirl around us. Her blond curls blew wildly in the wind, brushing against my cheek. I inhaled, the scent of baby lotion invading my senses and calming me.

Gavin, the everyday hero, grabbed a leaf for her. He motioned at Max across the way, green eyes squinting. "How does he do it?"

Like I knew there would be, a small circle of women was gathered around our best friend, laughing and pawing at his shoulders.

"No clue." I shook my head, not jealous exactly, more curious like Gav was.

The three of us all had something we were good at. Max was a people person, always on the hunt for a new woman to entertain. He worked odd jobs, never sticking to something longer than a few months. But he had the ability to make people laugh and feel comfortable.

Gavin was the type who worked to take care of others—to keep them safe and healthy. He was an EMT and an ex-medic from our days as marines. Quiet, yeah, but honorable, someone who'd always have your back.

Then there was me.

I wasn't rich. Didn't have a job that satisfied me past paying the bills and the mortgage, and putting food on the table. There was no woman in my life that I could kiss when I needed to or hold in my arms when life got to be too much. But I barely had time to breathe, let alone date, so that was the last thing on my mind.

Bottom line? I did the best I could with what I was given. Anything else was just details.

CHAPTER 2

Addison

IF THERE WAS EVER A NIGHT IN MY LIFE WHEN I COULD'VE used a blindfold and earplugs, it was as I stood in O'Paddy's bar witnessing the hellish experience that was my first rugby after-party.

"What in the hell *is* this fuckery?" my best friend, McKenna, slurred, while her fourth rum and Coke in an hour spilled over the rim of her glass and onto the floor.

"How about *you* tell *me*?" I moved to sit on the stool I'd been leaning against, then propped my elbows back against the bar. "Since you're the one who chose this bar in the first place. Remember?" Scowling, I took a sip of my beer, ignoring her huff from my left. As the cool liquid slid down my throat, I scanned the massive display of male thighs on the dance floor just a few feet away.

One. Two. Three… At least fifteen pairs, by my count, all covered in matching black shorts that barely covered their goods. White numbers and the words *Carinthia Irish Rugby* were written across the backs of the guys' green-striped jerseys. Eyes narrowed, I watched them shifting and thrusting their hips to the rhythm of their strange chant while each of them took a turn speaking a line. Some appeared to be about my father's age, others fresh out of college—and every one of them looked as sexy and fierce as the next.

"That sure is a lot of man," I whispered, my throat going dry as I took in the sexpot in the center of it all. His hands were massive, clinging to the thighs of a tiny blond sitting squarely on his shoulders.

"That's a lot of cock, you mean."

I shrugged, not denying McKenna's observation as my gaze did a quick foot-to-neck perusal of the middle man I'd deemed Number Six—since that's what his jersey said.

Blondie swayed and giggled as he spun her around in a circle, and with both hands gripped tight in his crazy, black hair, she yanked hard, hollering out "Giddyap, cowboy." The team, along with Six, laughed and continued reciting their lines and shoving one another in their drunken stupors.

"Maybe I need one of *those* to get my mind off Paul." McKenna plopped down on the stool next to mine and laid her blond head on my shoulder.

"No. What you *need* is to go to Maine with your brother and sister-in-law and find some inner peace. Maybe avoid men altogether. Then when you come back, you'll have a fresh perspective and—"

A sandy-haired Duhamel-meets-Tatum hottie smacked into the side of her seat.

"Oh shit," Kenna squealed, tipping forward off the stool.

Sucked out of my therapist mode, I shoved the drunk

asshole back and reached for Kenna's hand to help her up. "You okay?"

With a glare pointed in my direction, Duhamel-Tatum pushed my hand away, playing the knight-in-black-rugby-shorts to Kenna. In a matter of seconds, she was on her feet, leaning against his large body like it was her newest lifeline. Her eyes widened as she took him in, black lashes batting against her cheeks in awe. I sighed. Her new plan to avoid men seemed null and void already. Not that I could blame her; Rude Man was gorgeous.

I turned away to give her a moment to recover—and flirt. Another half hour was all she had left on my watch. She was already three-quarters of the way past plastered and one-quarter of the way from full-on shit-faced and puking on her favorite Jimmy Choos. And for me to let her puke on her nine-hundred-dollar shoes would be a friendship fail.

Brokenhearted or not, McKenna needed an intervention when it came to the opposite sex…and quite possibly with rum too.

With curiosity being my biggest downfall, I took another second to search for Number Six out on the dance floor. When I found him, his back was still to me, and I sighed, regretting that I couldn't see his face.

At well over six feet, the guy was massively built—with a firm backside and nice calves to boot. Whether he was ex-military, a professional athlete, or just lucky to be blessed with muscular perfection, I didn't know. In any case, I'd have bet my left boob his face was gorgeous with a capital *G*.

The rugby team's weird chanting continued around us,

but Kenna's giggle was capturing my attention. Turning, I found her petting Mr. Hottie's chest. But for the first time in all the years we'd been running around together, the guy she had her sights set on wasn't taking the bait.

Interesting.

After the blond on Number Six's shoulders was dropped to the floor, despite the numerous groans from nearly every man in the room, he disappeared into the crowd like a ghost—unreal, untouchable even. Kind of like any man I found attractive nowadays. Bumping into my shoulder, Kenna—sans man and with frown on her face—turned her attention to the rugby crew like I'd done. "You ready? I'm not going to find what I need here tonight, sadly. I mean, where's a good lay when you need it, huh?" She frowned, eyes squinted into drunken slits.

I rolled my eyes. "I don't think what you need is here anyway. Trust me." I patted the back of her hand, pulling her toward the door.

"Don't coddle me, Addie. I'm not a child," she mumbled, tilting, tilting, tilting some more...

"Whoa." I grabbed her around the waist, yanking her to my side. "I'm not coddling you. I'm protecting you." My voice cracked. "You asked me not to let you do anything stupid tonight, remember? Taking home some random drunk in a bar qualifies as stupid."

"Fine." She sniffled, wiping at the wet mascara now dripping down her cheeks. "We'll go." Side-by-side, we fumbled our way forward, Kenna's eyelids drooping with every step we took. The girl was breaking my heart. Her stupid ex-boyfriend... If I had it in me to murder someone, he'd be my first victim.

"I'll make us hot fudge sundaes and put something funny on for us to watch at your house, okay?"

She nodded, wiping at her damp cheeks some more. "No chick flicks, right?"

My chest tightened. "Of course no chick flicks. I promise."

"Wait." She froze, eyes widening. "Gotta pee, first." Her mood shifted as she spun around.

"Do you need any help?" I asked.

Swaying to the left, she propped herself against the wall, red dress rising high on her thighs. "Gotta be strong. Paul said I'm weak. Weak girls go to the bathroom with their friends. I'm not weak."

She wouldn't let this go, not with the mention of *him*, so I nodded and curled my toes inside my boots so I wouldn't follow. "Fine. But if you're not back in five, I'm coming in after you," I called after her over the now-blaring music.

Rubbing my hand over my forehead, I sighed. If only I'd had enough guts to keep her home tonight in the first place. I loved her to pieces—wanted her to be happy more than anything else—but this wasn't the way to go about it.

Not that I was an expert in dealing with issues myself. I had a crap ton of them that I'd been avoiding like the plague lately. For one, I only had three weeks to go until my rent was due, yet I was also two days into being jobless. The preschool where I'd been working had shut its doors with no explanation, leaving me and twenty other women SOL. I would never ask McKenna for a loan. And my parents? They'd all but forgotten I existed, so that option was out.

Still…I was twenty-six years young. A strong, savvy woman with a four-year college degree under my belt. There was no doubt in my mind that I could find another job…eventually. And so what if I had to use what was left of my meager savings to pay next month's rent? That's what it was there for. Emergencies. I'd get through this. I had no other choice.

Needing to keep myself busy as I waited for Kenna, I jerked on my coat and planted myself in an empty chair just around the corner from the bathrooms. Setting my wallet and elbows on the table, I longed for a genie to grant me a wish—an IV drip of coffee so I could somehow manage to stay up late tonight to update my résumé and send it to places that bordered my hometown of Carinthia. With the school year already in session, I was screwed when it came to finding a job in any of the neighboring school systems, but I was a planner in need of a plan.

What I needed right this moment, though, was to find something that would bring in a steady stream of cash to pay for my rent, my living expenses, and the last of my student loans.

After standing in line at the unemployment office all day and scouring the internet for hours the night before, I'd almost given up. Until the moment I clicked on an ad for a hostess at a local waffle house. Part-time hours, decent pay… It was promising and could, hopefully, get me through a few more months. It was also the first local job that appealed to me. Sure, I had a degree in early childhood education, but when you lived in a small town like Carinthia, with one elementary school and now only one daycare, the options were limited.

Just when I was ready to go looking for Kenna, a voice interrupted my musings—all deep and hoarse—sending a bout of goose bumps up and down my arms.

Voice porn. That's exactly what it sounded like.

"You do realize its eighty-some degrees in here, right?"

I grabbed my wallet and set it on my lap. But when I attempted to swivel around in my chair to face him, he—whoever *he* was—placed his hands on the table along either side of my waist, keeping me from moving.

I stiffened, readying my elbow to drive back into his gut. "What are you doing?"

"Saying hello." Warm breath caressed my cheek as he lowered his chin to my shoulder. Not touching, but just enough to crowd me. The scent of beer and after-shave invaded my senses, and I couldn't help but inhale, latching on to the scent with all sorts of shame. A still-faceless creeper should not make my tummy tumble like an overloaded dryer.

God, I needed to get some even more than Kenna did.

"Well, you said your hello. Now say your goodbye. I'm not interested."

I dragged my gaze down his arms, eyes widening at the sight of his hands.

Strong fingers. Fingers with nails as clean as my own. The same set of fingers I'd seen wrapped around the thighs of the girl on the dance floor.

Oh God. Of all the guys to approach me, it had to be this one?

"Can't help myself," he whispered. "How about I help you out of this coat?" I tightened my hold on my wallet as his hand grazed the lapel of my jacket.

"Do you happen to know what personal space is?" I gritted my teeth, warm, yummy smell be damned.

"Hmm..." Tugging a section of my hair away from my shoulder, he trailed one of his fingers down my arm until his fingers were back on the table. "Not when there are pretty ladies like you—"

"Save it." I shivered, warning bells dinging inside my head. "I don't do strangers at the bar."

"Neither do I. Lucky for you I'm just looking for some conversation."

I highly doubted that. "I don't have time for a chat. Now if you'll excuse me"—I stood and nudged one of his arms out of my way, ignoring the rattle of laughter against my shoulder—"I need to go find my friend." I glanced around him toward the bathroom, avoiding his gaze.

"What does your friend look like?" He cleared his throat, sexy voice gone and all business as he moved to sit on the other chair at the table. Was it my imagination, or did he sound nervous?

Still, it wasn't any of his business, but... "She's blond, real tall, skinny, red dress. Drunk off her ass."

"Ah. One of those, huh?" He sighed, the sound all high and mighty—knowing too. I hated self-righteous men more than any other kind. "Need help looking for her?"

"If that's some kind of skeezy pickup line to try to get me alone, then..." I blinked, hating myself for failing in my attempt to stay composed when I finally met his dark gaze.

Holy. Hell. This man took gorgeousness to another level—to orgasmic at first sight. Blue eyes, dark hair, dark brows, pink lips, and...dimples?

Damn, damn, double damn. Why'd there have to be dimples involved?

"Not that desperate, sweetheart. Trust me." He scowled.

Ah, so it would seem Number Six was easily offended.

"Sorry. That came out wrong." I shrugged one shoulder, not really sorry at all.

His lips twitched. "That so?"

I nodded, needing to avoid looking into his eyes. But the alternative was his mouth, which was gorgeous too. Or his chest, which was big and bulky and...

Who was I kidding? This man was straight-up eye candy all over.

"You're forgiven." He winked before grabbing my hand. "Now, follow me."

"What are you doing?" I dug my heels into the floor as he tried to pull me along behind him.

"Finding your friend."

"I'm perfectly capable of finding her on my own, thank you."

He pursed his lips. "No denying that." He glanced back at the bar. "But it looks to me like your *friend* needs more help than you can give her."

ACKNOWLEDGMENTS

They say writing a book is a lot like raising kids, that it takes a village, and I have to agree. Because without the support of so many people, this book—this series— never would have happened.

To my husband, Chris. God, where do I even start when it comes to you? You're my rock. My number one fan. My world, even when things don't always look the clearest. The day you were diagnosed with cancer was basically the scariest day of my life. Not sure if I ever told you how much I cried after I left that doctor's office. Not sure if you want to know either. But I did cry. So much so that I had to pull over in the Target parking lot just to clear my eyes. I knew you weren't going anywhere, that you'd fight the ugly disease and beat it 'til it was bloody. But just the thought nearly killed me, then watching you suffer? Hardest four months of my life. Now, all these months later, cancer-free and feistier than ever, there is nobody else who makes me prouder, who makes me laugh as much as you do. Though I'm not always the most cheerful woman, especially when bookish life gets me down, you still manage to pull me out of my funks. You're not just my husband, Christopher Wayne, but my best friend too. I can't imagine what would have happened had you not put that ring under that piece of paper in the passenger's seat of our car at that gas station in Platteville, Wisconsin.

Kelsey, Kelsey, Kelsey… As my oldest daughter, I had the pleasure of loving you long before your sisters, obviously. And every day that's passed since is another day where I can't get enough of you, regardless of the fact that we butt heads over almost everything. You're the sweetest of the sweet, KK. The most amazing teenager I know. Continue to be who you are; continue to love all things PLL and TWD. And just know that loving you is the easiest thing I've ever done.

Emma Grace… As my middle daughter, I couldn't have asked for a better gift in life. You take after your dad when it comes to humor, but everything else is me. Your quirks and love of bad boys and all things Hamilton make me believe that life doesn't have to be normal to be amazing. That normal is also totally overrated. May you forever sing in the car, curse at the TV, and never care who or what stands in your way in life. Loving you makes me whole.

Bella Boo… As my youngest daughter, you've gifted me with more smiles and hugs and happiness than I ever could have imagined. You are so smart, B. So sweet, and kind, and everything a mother could hope for in a seven-year-old little girl. The whine that comes out of your little lips may put wrinkles by my eyes, but I wear those wrinkles with pride. Everything you are is everything I've hoped to have. Loving you, Bella, completes me.

As far as agents go, Stacey Donaghy, you are the best of the best. You're not only whip smart and know your way around all things publishing, but you're my friend. And sometimes that means more to me than anything else.

To the Sourcebooks team. You've made my dreams come true and continue to show me what a publishing house should truly be about. You've given my characters homes, and I will forever be thankful for you all.

Katrina Emmel, Jennifer Griswel, and Jessica Calla... My CPs, my rocks, my three best friends. You ladies are my life and I'm beyond thankful to know you all. And though our worlds are virtual for now, I undoubtedly can say that there are no three greater women alive than you all.

My Happily Ever Always ladies, Kelly Siskind and Jamie Howard. You two rock my world. God, how I love the way you make me laugh, the way you brighten my Mondays and Fridays. To be paired with you all is the biggest blessing ever.

JoDeen Anderson... How you deal with my insanity is beyond me, but as far as assistants go, you're the best of the best. Thank you for all you do. xoxo

Jazmin from Three Filthy Bookers... You were my first Colly fan, and you have *no* idea what that meant to me...*means* to me, more so. I will forever write my boys with you in mind now, praying and hoping that you'll continue loving them for years to come. You're the sweetest person, and I am so glad to know you.

To Christina June. You beta read an early version of this book for me and led me down the right path as far as his idiocy went. I'm so thankful to know you and call you a friend.

To my fans. The ones who've emailed, messaged, or posted on my pages... I sure as heck hope that Max and

Lee-Lee gave you the same rush and love as they did for me. Thank you for reading. Without you, I couldn't do this.

ABOUT THE AUTHOR

Heather Van Fleet is a stay-at-home mom turned book boyfriend connoisseur. She's a wife to her high school sweetheart and a mom to three girls, and in her spare time, you can find her with her head buried in her Kindle, while guzzling copious amounts of coffee.

Heather graduated from Black Hawk College in 2003 with an associate's degree and has worked in the publishing industry for more than five years. She's represented by Stacey Donaghy of Donaghy Literary Group.

Find her at HeatherVanFleet.com.

RECKLESS HEARTS

It's three alpha men and a baby in this steamy
contemporary romance series

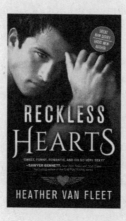

Addison Booker needs a job desperately. She shows up to
interview for a nanny position only to find the sexy, cocky
man she can't get out of her head. Collin Montgomery
knows hiring her is a bad idea—she's the hottest, smartest
woman he's ever met and they disagree about almost
everything—but Addison is so good with little Chloe. And
there's no substitute for chemistry, right?

"An emotional, heartfelt, and absolutely beautiful
story. I wanted each character to be my best friend."

—Jennifer Blackwood, *USA Today*
bestselling author

BLANK CANVAS

A dark contemporary romance series from
award-winning author Adriana Anders

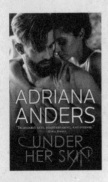

Under Her Skin

This gentle giant's scarred hands may
be the warmest touch she'll ever
know. If only life were a fairy tale
where the world gives you second
chances…

By Her Touch

He thought he was beyond saving. A
cop turned undercover gang member
turned…whatever he is now. He
thought no one would ever see him as
anything but a beast. Until he found
her. Until she changed everything.

In His Hands

The rules are simple: Never speak to outsiders. Never yearn for something more. And never, ever seek the pleasure of a stolen kiss…or a whispered promise that with him, she can finally be free.

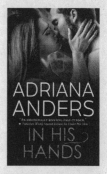

"Incredibly sexy, heartbreaking, and intense."

—*Kirkus Reviews* for *Under Her Skin*

"Gripping and emotionally satisfying."

**—*Publishers Weekly* Starred Review
for *By His Touch***